Falling for Autumn

A Novel by Heather Topham Wood

D1005162

FALLING FOR AUTUMN
Copyright: Heather Topham Wood
Published: April 15, 2014

Dedication

To the strong women of the world who refuse to let their scars define them.

"Come to the edge.' 'We can't. We're afraid.' 'Come to the edge.' 'We can't. We will fall!' 'Come to the edge.' And they came. And he pushed them. And they flew."

—Guillaume Apollinaire

Chapter One

I hated college parties. As a freshman, I understood it was part of the college experience. An escape from curfews and prying parents while learning to be my own person. I didn't mind the social aspect of it. It was the men I minded—the college boys with their assessing eyes and lecherous grins. I knew what they wanted and I'd die first before I gave it to them.

My roommate, Lexi, shot me a sympathetic look as I shook my head at another drunken boy who tried to grind against my ass. It took him a minute to pick up on my disinterest, but when he found me unmoving against him, he decided to move on to more receptive game.

Classes for the spring semester were starting the next day and our floormate Casey insisted we kick off the semester right by going to a party. The Football House had earned its name from the half dozen or so players living at the off-campus residence. Looking at its rundown exterior, I thought it could be called a few other off-color names, but Casey claimed it would be the best place for us to venture out.

Casey, Lexi, and I made an awkward trio, but our friendship somehow worked. Lexi was quiet and likely spent almost as many hours studying as she did breathing. Her boyfriend, Finn, had a single room two floors above us and she slept there often. Lexi had no idea what a relief it had been when we first met; I needed a kind and understanding roommate and she fit the bill. Her scarcity at night was also a plus—she was rarely around when I yelled out in bed, my adrenaline spiking from the panic attacks that had started two years ago.

Last semester, Casey decided I'd make the ideal friend for her to coax out to assorted campus events. Since I wasn't interested in hooking up and she was attempting to stay faithful to her boyfriend back home, I'd act as a buffer when she found herself tempted to stray. I usually begged off, but she was particularly insistent that night.

Lexi refilled her blue plastic cup and scrunched up her face in distaste as she took a sip of the keg beer. I refilled mine and I was certain my expression mirrored hers. The beer was flat and warm and I questioned for the hundredth time why I was at the party.

Casey came up from behind and draped her arms across our shoulders. "Lexi and Autumn, can't you at least try to be social for one night?" Her blue eyes were unfocused, but her voice was laced with disdain. "You're both sitting in the corner looking like someone died."

Lexi shot me a look and it silently passed between us that we'd be escorting Casey into her dorm room later. She was underage and it wouldn't be good at all if our floor's resident advisor spotted her. We'd have to stealthily sneak her past security and hope she didn't make a scene in the process.

Checking my watch again, I wondered if Casey would let us leave before midnight. The number of students had thinned out slightly since we arrived a couple of hours ago, but it would probably be at least another hour until Casey would be ready to go.

Most of the crowd was packed into the finished basement of the three-story house. The appeal was the open space and it was where the kegs were kept during the party. One of the guys who lived at the house was also a deejay and had his setup in the far corner. He wasn't half bad and I liked the sensation of the bass pumping through my blood.

"Holy shit, Autumn! Why is Blake Preston staring at you?" Casey stage whispered. To be heard over the deafening music, the question came out more as a shout.

"Who?" I looked around uncertainly and didn't notice anyone staring in my direction. "Who's Blake Preston?"

Lexi laughed while Casey's jaw dropped. "Do you go to the same college as us? How do you not know *Blake Preston*?" When I didn't answer, Casey continued, "He's a junior and incredibly fucking hot. He's like the star of our football team. The entire female population gives a collective sigh when he goes out on the field."

By Casey's rundown, I immediately knew it wasn't likely he'd be staring at me. Although I was pretty enough, I purposely downplayed my appearance. My dark blond hair was pulled back into a ponytail and I had skipped the eye makeup required to make my honey brown eyes pop. I wore jeans and a plain black T-shirt. Before we left the dorm, Casey tried to march me back to my room to change, but I told her to take me as I was or leave me behind.

I looked around again and found myself drawn in by a pair of gorgeous green eyes. They were spectacular—the color of gemstones—and it took me a while to tear my gaze away and survey the eyes' owner. He was tall with broad shoulders and I would've guessed he was on the team even without Casey revealing his status. His hair was light brown, styled longer in the front and shorter on the sides. My eyes were drawn past his high-sculpted cheekbones to his strong jaw with just the right amount of stubble on his chin. Casey was right—he was *fucking hot*.

He didn't appear flirtatious as he watched me from across the room. In fact, he looked at me with disdain, a muscle ticking in his jaw. I narrowed my eyes to let him know that despite his ability to crush me with a single blow, I wasn't intimidated. He didn't look away.

I turned back to my friends while the skin on the back of my neck prickled. "You made it sound like he's checking me out. He's giving me a pissed off look. I have no idea why, I don't even know him."

"That's not a pissed off look. That's an 'I'm hot and I think you're hot, so let's get naked together' look. Autumn, you have to go talk to him," Casey insisted.

I looked to Lexi for help. "You're with me, right? He looks like he hates me on sight."

Lexi shrugged. "I'm not sure. I hear he's with a lot of girls, so maybe that's his pick-up technique. He sends them smoldering looks from across the room at parties and they end up putty in his hands."

"Then I definitely wouldn't be interested. I'm not responding to some man whorish jock's smoldering looks." I shuddered at the possibility. It had been a mistake coming to the party and expecting the men to be different. I was sure there must be a good guy or two in the bunch, but I had too hard of a shell around me to consider finding him.

I hoped more than ever Lexi would decide to call it a night and give Finn a call to pick us up. Since we were freshmen, we weren't permitted to park our cars on campus. Luckily, Finn had an older brother on campus and they shared his car. Finn had begged off on going to the party, but would chauffeur us back to the dorms when we were ready to leave.

Casey sulked over my refusal to approach Blake and I shifted awkwardly. Not only was the conversation making me uneasy, but it was also the fact I could feel Blake's eyes boring into my back. I made my escape by claiming I was off to the bathroom and promised to return in five minutes. Instead I made a beeline for the back door and shivered once the frigid January air greeted me.

Cook University, which I attended, was a mid-sized college

in central Pennsylvania. It was about an hour and a half from my hometown of Newpine, Pennsylvania. I had wanted to escape the suffocation of living in a small town with people who seemed to have small minds. However, I was super close with my parents and didn't want to move far enough away where regular visits would be difficult.

The backyard of the Football House was relatively quiet. Only people like me, those desperate for isolation, would venture out in the chilly weather. There were a half dozen students gathered in a semicircle toward the back of the yard, most likely sharing a joint, while my presence remained unnoticed. I blew out my breath in front of me, mesmerized by the crystallization in the air.

The back door opened and slammed shut loudly behind me. Startled, I spun around. My beer sloshed over the side of my cup and wet the brown boots of the guy standing before me. The motion lights switched on and I was faced with a now familiar pair of green eyes.

I clutched at my heart. "Damn! You scared me!" Actually, I'd been primed to kick him in the nuts. I didn't take well to being startled, especially by hulking men.

"I could see that. I have a pair of drenched feet to prove your point," he said.

I almost rolled my eyes when I heard him speak. Of course, his voice would be as sexy as the rest of him. His tone was husky and there was underlying sensuality in the way his mouth moved as he talked. He pronounced each syllable slowly, giving me plenty of time to watch his full lips move seductively.

I pushed down any lusty stirrings and allowed my annoyance to take its place. "Maybe that will serve as a reminder to not creep up on someone."

"I'll keep that in mind," he said softly.

I expected him to leave, but he stood in place next to me. I cast him a sidelong glance, trying to go unnoticed as I checked him out further. He was much taller than my five foot six and I guessed he weighed almost twice as much as I did. He wasn't husky; instead, he was broad and muscular. He wore a long-sleeved white T-shirt and his biceps were drool-worthy as they strained against the fabric. The T-shirt was fitted and I could make out the rigid planes of his chest and abs. It was the off-season and I wondered how he could get any more cut during the regular football season.

Something about Blake was making me anxious and I gave in to my urge to flee. Without another word, I turned to go. His voice stopped me. "Why are you here?"

It was such an odd question. I laughed nervously. "What do you mean? In the physical or metaphysical sense? Like why I'm at this party or why was I ever born?"

He chuckled, but when I caught his eye, I didn't see humor there. His eyes were too bright, too probing. "Why are you at this party? I've never seen you at the house before." He spoke like it was an accusation.

What was he, the party police? His questions rankled me. It was borderline offensive and I couldn't get a read on his motives. It didn't feel like he was hitting on me. Instead, he genuinely wanted me to justify what brought me to the party and into his presence.

"I'm going. Nice meeting you, I guess," I said, taking another step toward the door. "I know you didn't bother asking me my name, but it's Autumn, by the way."

His fingers slipped around my wrist to stop me from going. I expected to hate the sensation, to despise the feel of a man's hand on my skin. I inwardly cringed because I enjoyed it. His palm was soft and warm and his grip wasn't rough. It was a gentle caress I missed once his hand pulled away. "Sorry…I'm being an ass. I'm Blake."

He watched me after revealing his name and I almost doubled over with laughter. He was awaiting a reaction, like I'd swoon once I found out one of the school's most talented football players was talking to little old me. After I said nothing, he continued, "I only meant I would've seen you before if you had come by. You're hard not to notice."

Evidently, he had changed his tactic, picking up on my irritation. I wasn't flattered by his attention; I was confused by it. Although his words sounded like a compliment, the delivery didn't sell it.

"I really should get back to my friends. I'll see you around," I said, belatedly wishing for the nerve to say more. I wanted to ask him why he had followed me outside. I wanted to know what about my presence offended him so. It was the strangest and most unsettling meeting and I had no idea what to make of him.

He didn't protest as I made my way to the door. "See you around," he replied, his voice flat.

What in the world? I hoped my path would never cross Blake Preston's again. He wasn't at all like Casey described. He was intense and didn't come across like the hotshot playboy jock trying to charm his way into my panties. There was torment he was trying to hide and I saw a brief glimpse of the emotion in his eyes as I walked away. I recognized it because I saw it each morning when I looked at my own reflection.

Chapter Two

Arms were roughly grabbing at me. They locked my body in place. I tried to scream, but my throat closed up, resulting in only a whooshing sound. Panic rose up and the need to have my body freed from its prison was more than I could take. I wanted to fight, it was the only way I could escape, but my limbs wouldn't cooperate. The force holding me down was too powerful and I despised the helplessness of the situation. I needed to break free. It was the only way I'd survive—

An insistent ringing sounded in my ears, forcing me out of the nightmare. My heart pumped wildly as I blindly reached for my cell phone on my nightstand. "Hello," I croaked.

"Autumn, honey, are you okay?"

My mom's reassuring voice had an instant soothing effect. I'd seen her a couple of days earlier when my parents helped me move back to campus, but I already missed them terribly. They'd been my calm during so many of my storms the past couple of years.

"I'm fine. Just another nightmare," I confessed.

"Have you been taking the Xanax Dr. Fabian prescribed?"

"I'm trying to deal with the anxiety without it," I said.

"Honey, don't try to be a martyr. If the pills help you, don't be afraid to use them."

My mom was right, but I'd become hesitant about using the anti-anxiety medication. I didn't want to become reliant on pills. I had to learn how to cope with the feelings on my own.

My therapist, Dr. Fabian, told me to redirect my emotions into something positive when faced with anxiety. But sometimes the panic hit me like a tidal wave and pulled me out to sea. Those were the times I struggled the most.

I glanced at the time, and a groan escaped. It was after nine and I had a nine-thirty class on the opposite side of campus. I looked over at the twin bed on the other side of the room and found it empty. Lexi must've cut out early this morning. It would take a couple of weeks until we became accustomed to one another's spring class schedules.

"Mom, I have to go. It's my first art history class and I don't want to be late." My mother clicked off only after I made promises to call her and to take the medication if I needed it.

Jumping out of bed, I grabbed a gray sweater and a pair of leggings from my closet and slipped on a pair of gray boots. The dorm room I shared with Lexi was utilitarian with doubles of each piece of furniture: two twin beds, two desks, two chairs, and two dressers. We shared a single closet, each taking one side to store our clothing.

We had moved the furniture around when we first arrived to maximize the space. Both of our beds were set on opposite sides of the room next to the double windows. Lexi's desk sat between the beds while my desk was to the left of the room at the foot of my bed. Our dressers were placed side by side against the right wall with a small television angled on top to allow both of us to watch while lying in bed.

Lexi was a fan of vibrant reds and I coordinated my sheet set to match hers. Her side of the room was filled with all of her great loves: a poster of Paris at nighttime, a photo collage of her with her best friends from back home, and a Cook University school flag. The walls on my designated side of the room were empty, reflecting how I saw my insides. I was waiting to find something inspiring enough that I'd want to stare at it for the next five months.

While brushing my teeth in front of the mirror, I noticed

the exhaustion ever present in my features. I used a coat of mascara to bring out the golden brown shade of my eyes and applied scarlet lipstick to put color back into my pale full lips. After running a brush through my unruly dark blond hair and securing it with a clip, I hustled out of my room. My hair fell in waves down to my mid-back and it took me at least an hour to get it to cooperate and not look as if I'd been stuck outside during a hurricane.

On my way across campus, I rechecked my schedule for the building and room number of my class. Cook University's academic buildings were arranged in a circular pattern on one side of the campus with the dormitories set on the other side. It was about a fifteen-minute walk to get from the dorms to most classes and I increased my pace to get to the arts building on time.

Art history was a required general ed class. Since I was torn over my major, I decided to take the general education courses I needed during my freshman and sophomore years, hoping a few electives would help me find my niche.

Breezing into class with a few minutes to spare, I stopped just inside the doorway, scanning the room to see if I recognized anyone. A few students started to gather behind me and I hurried forward while trying to find the nearest empty desk.

"Autumn, over here," a voice called to my left. Following the direction of the voice, I groaned inwardly as I saw Blake gesturing at me. He set a pencil on the desk next to him as I took slow and measured steps to the back of the classroom. Typically, I sat at the front, but an invisible force pulled me to him. Based on our awkward first meeting, I was surprised by my willingness to go anywhere near him.

A petite girl with dark curly hair reached the chair before I did. As she moved to sit next to Blake, he gave her a sheepish grin. "Sorry, Laura, I promised Autumn I'd save her a seat."

Laura spun around and I saw heat flare in her dark eyes as she appraised me from head to toe. She was beautiful, with full red lips and round eyes with midnight black lashes. If Blake was passing her over for me, he was a fool. Before I could offer up the chair to her, she darted to the other side of the room. I barely knew Blake and it was already the second awkward situation I found myself in with him.

"Thanks," I mumbled. Placing my backpack next to my chair, I felt Blake watching me as I pulled out a notebook and opened it. I shifted in my seat. "So, art history, huh?"

"Yeah, it was either this or intro to art and I suck at drawing. Once I finish this and my philosophy class, I'll have all the general ed classes I need for graduation." He leaned back into his chair, forcing me to turn around to address him. His long legs stretched in front of him, and an air of confidence surrounded him.

"What's your major?"

"Economics," he answered. "Once I'm done playing football, I'll probably go for my MBA."

"Are you any good?"

"What? At football?" he asked with surprise evident in his expression. While he seemed to mull over my question, I studied his features once again. The dim lighting at the party hadn't done him justice. His eyes were an even more vibrant green than I'd realized, with darker flecks swirling in their depths. His light-brown hair was absurdly messy, but looked perfectly styled at the same time.

"Yeah," I replied.

"I'm guessing you never went to a game then because you wouldn't be asking that question otherwise."

I bit down on my lower lip. Why was I bothering to talk to him? I hated guys like him. I'd gone to high school with his carbon copies. They thought because they could throw a damn ball, they were entitled. Blake was treading a fine line between coming off as self-assured and acting like a condescending dick.

He seemed to read my expression. "I'm not trying to sound arrogant, but I'm a running back and I've scored the most touchdowns for the season. I was featured in the campus newspaper a bunch of times. I was also the MVP of the team. Ringing a bell yet?" I shook my head. He laughed and I relaxed my shoulders at the sound. His laugh was unrestrained and made his chest vibrate. "I guess I built myself up in my head. It's refreshing to be brought down a notch."

The professor walked in, saving me from replying. Art history was a newfound interest of mine and I had the urge to drool as we went over the syllabus. We were concentrating on a broad spectrum of art works and I looked forward to studying the Renaissance, Baroque, and Rococo periods since they featured many of my favorite artists.

After the professor discussed several slides we'd be studying more in depth later in the semester, she flicked the lights on and announced the end of class. I looked over at Blake and saw him stretch lazily before climbing out of his chair.

I gave him a short wave after I gathered my books and began walking out of the classroom. "All right, I'll see you on Thursday then."

Instead of replying, Blake fell into step next to me, flashing a charismatic smile as he caught my eye. "Where are you headed?"

"Umm…" I trailed off. After pulling the straps of my backpack tighter, I said, "I don't have class for another couple of hours, so I'll probably get something to eat before going to the library."

"Good, I'm starved. I'll come with you," he said and pushed open the building doors. Once outside on the walkway, I stopped in my tracks. Noticing I was no longer walking with him, he double backed and faced me. "What are you doing?"

"Blake, I wasn't inviting you to eat with me."

"Okay," he said, stretching out the syllables slowly. "We're both hungry, why wouldn't we just grab something to eat together?"

My face flushed and I suddenly felt exposed. The way he

said it made me feel foolish. Like going to eat with him was no big deal. He had no clue it was the closest I'd been to a date since I was seventeen years old. At nineteen, I couldn't even have breakfast with someone of the opposite sex without having an internal freak-out.

"I'm a little confused about your reasons for hanging out with me." I swallowed roughly and looked past him at the other students walking around the campus. "I'm not interested in sleeping with you. I may be a freshman girl and maybe you think that means I'll be an easy lay or something…"

His laugh was sudden and his expression open. He was a different Blake from the one I met at the party two nights earlier. He was handsome and charming and his reputation as a lady-killer seemed more believable. It was such a dramatic shift, it made me curious if I only imagined the hostility I sensed at the party.

"You don't take much shit, do you? We've talked for a total of five minutes and you've already told me you have no clue who I am and accused me of thinking you were an easy lay."

I felt ridiculous. I had gone to college to start a new life, reinvent myself, and hope the past stayed back in Newpine. It was a lofty goal with my newfound realization of the impossibility of it happening. My past was always there, waiting in the shadows, readying for the opportunity to jump out and unravel me completely.

"I didn't mean to offend you, but look at it from my perspective. You were staring at me at the party in a not so nice way and a little rude when we spoke outside. Then you flip the switch, wanting to sit with me in class and have breakfast together." I pulled my coat tighter as the wind picked up.

"Sorry." He paused, the humor in his voice fading. "You reminded me of someone and it freaked me out," he said. The sincerity of his tone convinced me he was being truthful. His eyes filled with hurt for a flash before he suppressed it. I wondered who in his past warranted such a reaction. Blake added, "Since we're in the class together, I figure we could hang out. Study for the tests or go to the museum together." As part of our final paper, we had to visit either the Philadelphia Museum of Art or the Metropolitan Museum of Art and pick a piece to write an essay on. I'd never visited an art museum and was looking forward to the trip.

"Well, you do know Laura if you're looking for a study buddy," I supplied and immediately wished the words back. *A study buddy?* I hadn't always been this inept at conversation with the opposite sex.

His smile was boyish, displaying a dimple in his left cheek. My muscles clenched at the sight, my body fighting against the unwanted attraction. I felt far away from my surroundings and I couldn't stop watching him.

"I hooked up with Laura last semester. She'll want something from me if we're *study buddies*," he said wryly. With his grin widening, he let me know he was just teasing me. "Since you and I are obviously not into each other in that way, it won't end up being complicated."

My jaw went slack and I hoped I recovered quickly enough for him to miss my reaction. I didn't want to be involved with a guy, but it still stung to hear he wasn't interested in me. I should've been thankful, but my pride was hurt.

I rallied. I didn't want romance, so it was a good thing Blake didn't see me as dateable material. The Blake from the party wasn't someone I'd want to be friends with, but the Blake 2.0 standing in front of me had potential. "Okay then, where should we eat?"

Chapter Three

"Is all that food just for you?"

I looked at Blake's tray in surprise. His breakfast consisted of a plate of scrambled eggs with bacon, a bagel with peanut butter, a banana, an apple, and two containers of milk.

We had gone to the cafeteria in the center of campus. It served breakfast until noon and had more food choices than the smaller restaurants and cafés scattered around campus. After finding an unoccupied table by the door, Blake dug into his meal with enthusiasm.

"You should see what I eat when I'm training. I try to eat six thousand calories a day then," he remarked and took a bite of bacon. I shook my head in disbelief and took a tentative bite of my buttered bagel. My appetite had a tendency to come and go, causing an unexpected weight loss. Gradually, the weight was returning and I hoped my curves with it.

"Hey, Autumn." I looked up and smiled at my friend Josh approaching our table. He lived on the same floor as Lexi's boyfriend, Finn, and had been in my biology class last semester. We exchanged emails over winter break, but I hadn't run into him since moving back to campus last week.

"Hi, Josh. How was the rest of your break?"

"Boring, I couldn't wait to come back. I didn't see you in second section biology. Are you taking a different professor than

Greene?"

"I decided to wait until next year to take it. I'm actually in art history at that time with Blake. Josh, this is Blake Preston." I gestured with my fork between the two guys. I turned away from Josh to address Blake. "Blake, this is Josh Matthews."

Blake stopped eating and gave Josh an assessing look before smiling. "Hey."

Josh ran a hand through his thick black hair nervously. "I'm actually a big fan. I went to every home game in the fall. That last catch you made in the fourth quarter against SUNY was incredible."

I smiled privately. It was adorable to see Josh all excited over meeting Blake. Maybe I'd see if some of the games were on YouTube and find out what all the fuss was about.

"Good to see you have friends with good taste," Blake said pointedly to me. Addressing Josh, he continued, "You should've brought Autumn to a game last semester."

"Autumn hates football and said the players were probably a bunch of dickheads anyway. She would stay at the dorm and study while the rest of us went to the games."

Blake's smile faded. I gave Josh an annoyed look. "I never said that. I *said* I was too busy to go and that I went to high school with a few jackass football players."

"Sorry," Josh said but his tone was unapologetic. He adjusted his dark-rimmed glasses and shifted his weight. "I have to run before I'm late to my next class. You'll have to stop by my room to say hi when you and Lexi come over to Finn's. See you, Blake."

Blake nodded in his direction.

"Okay, bye," I said distractedly. Chewing on my thumbnail, I peered at his back while he walked toward the exit.

Blake broke into my thoughts. "He likes you. That's why he made that comment about football players. He was marking you."

"Marking me?"

"Yeah, he was trying to tell me to keep my hands off of you, that he wants you." Blake peered at me curiously. "Do you like him?"

"No," I answered too quickly. I took a breath and then added, "We're just friends. He's never hit on me or anything."

"Another study buddy?" Blake laughed.

"Remind me again why I'm eating breakfast with you?"

"Relax, I'm messing with you." He stopped speaking momentarily to wave to a few of his teammates seated on the other side of the cafeteria. He met my gaze again. "I'm trying to figure you out. I'm not your type, makes me curious if your friend Clark Kent is more your speed."

I rolled my eyes at his description before saying, "No one is my type. I don't want to date right now."

His dimpled smile made me almost regret the words. His eyes sparkled as they took their time regarding me. As he leaned back into his chair and the fabric of his shirt pulled against the hard planes of his chest, I became tongue-tied. He was too hot for words and I had a horrible feeling he could see inside of my head and knew what I was thinking.

I wiggled in my seat and started, "So, we should talk about the trip to the museum for class."

He smiled humorlessly as I changed the subject. "I'll get you to talk one day, Autumn, and find out what you're really like."

***

After finishing classes for the day, I returned to an empty dorm room. Lexi had texted me earlier to say she'd be in Finn's room if I wanted to stop by. I decided to stay put and replay the things Blake said in a constant loop in my head. An apprehensive feeling had taken form after his comment about finding out what I was really like.

The appealing thing about college for me was anonymity. I

grew up in the same town with the same people my entire childhood. It gave me a false sense of security. As if knowing people for my whole life would keep them from turning on me. Like they owed me their loyalty.

When I came to Cook, there were no expectations, no rumors to contend with. I could be the quiet and studious girl, not the slut I was considered in my hometown. My best friends were the first ones to turn on me, the ones to come up with the nickname Whorey Dorey, using my last name for inspiration.

The football and basketball players were the worst offenders. The boys I had cheered for used the rumors and lies as their permission slips to treat my body like they owned it. Their greedy hands reached for me as I walked numbly through the hallways, grabbing at my ass and breasts. It got to the point where I couldn't finish my senior year of high school and had to be homeschooled.

Yes, everyone in Newpine thought they knew the real Autumn Dorey, the seventeen-year-old Lolita who wore tight sweaters and short skirts. None of them knew me. And the people I met at Cook would probably never know the real me either. I was forced to become a hybrid—piecing together whatever parts of myself I needed to survive.

I turned on my laptop with every intention of studying. After a lengthy sigh, I allowed my curiosity to get the better of me and logged onto YouTube. In the search engine, I typed *Blake Preston Cook University*. I clicked on the first video, taken last year at the season opener.

Watching Blake play affected me more than I would've liked. He filled out his uniform fantastically, a football god in our school's blue and gold colors. But what got to me the most was the way he moved across the field. He was six feet of pure muscle, but he glided around his opponents with the grace of a dancer. His speed and agility were unmatched by the players on the other teams and each time he made a catch, my breath hitched.

Watching Blake play football made me pensive. I used to love going to games and cheering on the players. I missed the noise of the crowd and the rush after our team won. There were things I would come to despise about cheering, but the game itself wasn't one of them. My father was a football fanatic and I attended Eagles games with him before I could walk. The boys of Newpine High had taken enough away from me; I wouldn't allow them to ruin my love of football, too.

I was so caught up in a video of our school's game against Fordham University, I didn't hear Lexi come into our room. She whistled behind me. "That boy can catch a ball."

I minimized the video and turned around to face Lexi. "Blake's in my art history class. I wanted to see why everyone acts like he's the shit."

"Because he kind of is," Lexi replied. She sat down on her bed, pushing a strand of her short dark hair behind her left ear. "I already heard about him being in your class. Josh came by Finn's room tonight and said he ran into you and Blake."

I groaned. "Josh was acting really strange. He told Blake I said the football players were dickheads." I drummed my nails on my desk. "Blake said he thought Josh liked me."

"Duh," Lexi said, her lips twisting into a smirk. "He's had a huge crush on you since last semester. He's asked me to set the two of you up like a dozen times, but I keep telling him you'd probably say no." Lexi blew out a breath, blowing her bangs out of her eyes. "Why don't you date? Does it have something to do with your panic attacks?"

"Part of the reason," I admitted softly. There was so much Lexi didn't know about me because I couldn't peel back the layers and show her the vulnerable and broken Autumn. Lexi had seen glimpses when my panic would build like a crescendo, ending with broken pleas to make it stop.

It was impossible to keep everything from Lexi; we lived within a twenty-by-twenty-foot room together. I never had peace at night as everything I tried to lock away escaped from the confines of my brain. But to tell her everything would be too risky. I didn't want to pollute my new friendships by telling them about the mistakes I could never fix.

"I get that we've only known each other for six months, but you've been a freaking awesome roommate and friend. If you ever want to talk about *anything,* and I mean anything, I'm here."

The offer was out there. She was giving me the opportunity to confess all of my secrets. She wanted more from me, so much more than I could give her in return.

"Thanks, Lexi."

An unwavering resolve shone in Lexi's brown eyes, making me nervous. She wasn't going to let the conversation drop. "Did something bad happen to you? Did a guy hurt you?"

I trusted Lexi, I honestly did, but I had made the mistake before of trusting the wrong people. What she wanted was something I wasn't sure I could give. I learned the hard way what could happen when you let your guard down.

I made the split-second decision to open up a bit to Lexi. I wouldn't divulge everything, but maybe it wouldn't hurt to offer up *something* to her. Friendships couldn't blossom if they were built on lies.

"I had to be homeschooled for my final year of high school. There were these guys…" I trailed off and clenched and unclenched my hands as the memories resurfaced. "They wouldn't leave me alone. They were mostly athletes from our football and basketball teams. They spread rumors, saying I was a slut and a nympho, a bunch of other stupid shit, too, like how I snuck into the boys' locker room after games and would give a blow job to the guy who made the winning basket."

"That's awful. What a bunch of assholes."

"Yes, they were. I probably could've dealt with it if they had just spread rumors. But then they started to get handsy and I was terrified each morning to go to school."

"Did you report them?"

I nodded. "My parents did, but I decided not to come forward with the names of who was harassing me."

Lexi's eyes were shocked. "Why not?"

"Because they were the stars of the school and it was my word against theirs. They also sent anonymous threats online. I was scared of how they would retaliate if I pursued it." I had regrets about not trying to get the boys in trouble, but I was already psychologically beaten down at that point. There were other battles still ahead of me and I couldn't imagine fighting anyone else. And the boys had gotten what they wanted—they had driven me off.

"I knew something must've happened to make you so skittish about guys, but I had no idea what it was. I thought maybe you had a bad sexual experience, but I was also confused because you had told me you were…"

"A virgin," I finished for her. "I am."

Lexi blew out a long breath. "Autumn, those guys sound like sick freaks, but that doesn't mean all men are like that." She looked at me meaningfully and added gently, "It doesn't mean all jocks are like that either."

"I know," I said quickly. It was a habit to assume all football and basketball players were out to get me. The truth was there had been a select few who tormented me. The rest had simply turned the other way, pretending they no longer saw me. Maybe they hadn't since I went to great lengths to hide under oversized sweatshirts, hoping for invisibility.

"Blake may have a rep as a womanizer, but it could be like the same thing that happened to you. Maybe they're only rumors."

"I don't like Blake," I sputtered out. Lexi smiled knowingly, prompting me to continue, "Besides, he told me he's not interested in me like that."

"Hmm," Lexi said, thoughtfully tapping her lips. "I find that hard to believe. And I think you're protesting too much about being hot for our school's sexiest football player. I think you have it *bad* for him."

I grinned, glad for the touch of levity. "I don't have it bad for him. I just find him intriguing for some reason."

"Sure you don't like him, that's why you're cyberstalking him," Lexi teased.

"If we're going to study together, I figured I should get to know him better."

"Panting at videos of him in his football uniform won't help you research his academic aptitude," Lexi laughed. "Wait until Casey hears you're hanging out with him, she's going to murder you in a jealous rage."

"Well, if things don't work out with her boyfriend back home, I'll play matchmaker between the two of them."

As I conjured up a picture of Casey and Blake together in my head, my stomach revolted. I didn't want to be attracted to him, but it was hard not to be. His face and body were perfectly sculpted, all chiseled lines and hard in all the right places. With a pair of gorgeous eyes and a sensual mouth to boot, it was perfectly understandable how I could find myself fantasizing over what it'd be like to kiss him.

Blake wasn't good for my mental health. If I wanted to venture out into the dating pool again, a guy like Josh would be a much better choice. Maybe it was time to work toward being free of my demons. I came to Cook to escape and free myself of the opinions of the people in my hometown. Most importantly, I came to take back control of my life.

Chapter Four

Blake's pencil was again resting upon the desk next to him. I hid a smile as I climbed into the chair. He was sporting a pair of aviator sunglasses and groaned a greeting when I said hello.

"You okay?"

"No, rough night. I was going to skip, but figured I'd come off as a douche if I asked to steal your notes already." He pulled off the glasses, placing them on top of his desk. "I was going to see if you and your roommate wanted to stop by the Football House, but you never gave me your number."

"What, do you have a party at your house every night?"

I sounded a little judgmental and acknowledged I was resentful at times. A small part of me missed going out, partying with careless abandon. There was a girl named Faye on the high school cheerleading squad who had free rein over her family's guesthouse. I had a lot of my firsts at Faye's and the reckless moments of partying would eventually come back to haunt me. When everything went to hell, she was one of the first to dig up photos of me at her house. Shameful pictures painting me as a different person than I actually was. The pictures of the drinking games were bad enough, but the overtly sexualized photos were what destroyed me. It was humiliating to know my parents would likely see photos of me flashing my bra and panties. I was fifteen and sixteen years old in most of the images, immature and thoughtless. Never realizing every action had consequences.

Blake was answering me. "I don't live there. I have an apartment off campus with my friend Darien." He added with an exaggerated shudder, "Besides, that house is a shithole from all the parties there. When I go to bed at night, I don't want to worry about catching crabs."

"Thanks for the visual," I replied dryly.

Once the professor arrived, I tried to focus on the lecture. My nerves were fried, partly to do with the guy sitting five feet away from me. He put me on edge and I wished for the tedium of last semester, when I had dressed and acted without any thought to attracting the opposite sex. Before art history class that morning, I'd woken up early to shower and style my hair, taking extra time to run my fingers through the long locks to create a sexy tousled look. I'd put on mascara and pink lip gloss, not overdoing my makeup, but hoping to accentuate my best features.

I couldn't explain what was behind my efforts. Blake had told me he wasn't into me in that way. I reasoned my motivation was to chase what I couldn't have. Blake was *safe* and it was the reason my crush was growing. Because honestly if Blake liked me, I wouldn't know what to do with him. I hadn't been physical with a guy in two years and had trouble mentally prepping myself to take that step. One of my biggest fears was I'd never be able to be intimate again with a man.

"Are we going to breakfast again?" Blake asked me at the end of class. I nodded and followed him out of the arts building. He put back on his sunglasses and matched my stride. I tried not to become hyperaware of how he was close enough that I could feel his body heat.

Once we were seated with our trays of food and the table put distance between our bodies, I relaxed. I hadn't felt unnerved by him the last time we ate together and I was trying to pinpoint the change in my attitude. It most likely had to do with my regular schedule of watching him play football on my computer.

There was a raw masculinity about him on the football field that I found sexy as hell. He was all fluid motion as the ball glided into his arms and he ran with determination down the field. When he took off his helmet at the conclusion of the game, his hair plastered with sweat and his tanned skin glistening, my pulse began to race and my mouth dried up. He was utterly beautiful.

I laughed as I looked at his plate of food. "Is that your hangover cure?" He had two fried eggs smothered with salsa and shredded cheese on top of two flour tortillas.

"Yes, I didn't have time to get an Egg McMuffin this morning, that's my usual go-to cure." After a minute of chewing thoughtfully, he said, "So, you don't go out a lot? I was serious when I said I never saw you at parties before."

I shrugged. "I'm trying to keep my priorities straight. My grades were just okay in high school, but my GPA last semester was three point eight."

"So, what do you do for fun?"

"I don't know. Read, go to the movies, normal stuff."

"Were you different in high school?"

The question annoyed me and I deflected. "Isn't everyone?"

"Not really, I don't think I changed that much. What were you into before you came to college?"

"What's with all the questions?" I asked, my hold on the orange juice container tightening. I shook off my irritation and said, "I was into being the most popular girl and leaving high school as the homecoming queen. I was into bullshit stuff that shouldn't have mattered to me."

He frowned. "Why doesn't that matter? Doesn't everyone want to be popular?"

"Do you ever get tired of being the person everyone expects you to be? Like what if you got injured tomorrow and lost the ability to play? What would happen then?" I demanded, feeling myself getting worked up over the topic. "Would your friends still be around? Would every girl on campus still fawn over you?"

He brought his hands up and laced his fingers behind his head. "You're being a little insulting. I'm wounded you think the campus only worships me because I can play football. You forgot how I look fucking amazing and my reputation for being an animal in bed."

Startled, I looked up. *Oh god, not the dimples,* I thought. I let go of the death grip I had on the orange juice. Blake should run, run fast. I had too many issues and somehow he was bringing them to the surface. I relaxed once it dawned on me he was teasing. "Cocky as fuck too."

He laughed, most likely relieved that the intensity of the conversation had dissipated. "Never would've thought you had a dirty mouth, Autumn. You're definitely a contradiction."

"What do you mean?"

"It's like you want to be a nerd girl because it's safer that way. You seem afraid of people seeing what you're really like and believe hiding behind this fake front is going to protect you."

We locked eyes and I found myself tongue-tied. How could he analyze me so well after hanging out only a few short times together? I was wrong about Blake. He wouldn't lose anything if he couldn't play football. He was too smart, too charismatic to not have anything but a charmed life.

I didn't want to be bitter and I hated Blake seeing glimpses of that side of my personality. But it was hard not to feel betrayed. If things had been different and everything went to shit for one of my friends, I would've stood by them. I wouldn't have sided with the majority and cast them out friendless and humiliated.

***

In the days following, I had an English literature paper due and spent most of my spare time working on it. Twice a week, after our art history class, Blake and I settled into a routine of going to eat together. We got along well enough, but his probing questions about high school bothered me. It made me suspicious, and I wondered if his questions were more than mere curiosity. My first thought was he hailed from somewhere near Newpine and maybe he'd heard the stories and was trying to confirm if they were true. It eased my mind when I discovered he was from Clark, a city about forty minutes from where I grew up.

As we spent time together, I became accustomed to the envious looks of other girls. He was tall, athletic, and handsome and I could empathize with the girls who looked thunderstruck as he walked past them. Sometimes I wanted to ask Blake how many women he had actually been with. But I was afraid the answer would shatter my crush and confirm he was way out of my league.

My literature text was in my lap as I sat cross-legged on my bed. I was attempting to find a quote to work into my paper. Lexi had been studying as well until she hopped off of her bed to answer a knock at our door.

"Hi, Josh," Lexi said with casual indifference. I set my book down and raised my eyebrows in her direction. She shot a wink my way behind Josh and I quelled the urge to bolt. It was safe to assume his arrival was her attempt at setting us up. I had thought it was something I wanted, but Blake was confusing my feelings. I couldn't understand him. He was making it a point to get to know me, but would come off as cold at times, keeping me at arm's length.

Lexi made a show of looking at her watch. "You know what? I told Finn we would meet up and head to the gym. I'll have to catch you both later."

Before a protest could escape my lips, Lexi grabbed her purse and shot out of the room. I took note of the boots she was wearing—not exactly something she'd have on for working out. I planned to pay her back later for the impromptu setup. I didn't like the feeling of being bulldozed into dating Josh.

Josh sat down on my desk chair while I remained on my bed. He smiled in my direction and I relaxed. Josh was safe; I'd been alone with him before without my panic rearing its ugly head. However, I was pleased to note Lexi left the door ajar before bailing on me.

"How are your classes going?" Josh asked.

"I can't complain. It may be a different story once we get closer to midterms," I said.

"Are you going home anytime soon?"

"Not until spring break. My parents insist on picking me up. They won't let me take the train. I hate to make them do the drive unless I'm going to be home for more than a weekend."

My parents had closed ranks after my junior year in high school. They put me on a short leash and in all honesty I didn't mind it. I no longer had any friends back home, so it wasn't like I had anywhere to go. In my parents' minds, they'd given me too much freedom. They reasoned if I'd been better supervised, my downfall would've never happened. A two-hour train ride was something they decided was too dangerous for me to do on my own.

"I'm going to wait until spring break too. You know, since we'll both be around on the weekends, we should plan to get together some time." Josh was trying hard to sound casual, but the sheen on his brow clued me in on his anxiousness. He was sweet and cute, but I never thought of him as anything more than a friend. I never felt butterflies long after seeing him. Going out with Josh wouldn't be fair to him. Josh deserved a girl whose toes curled each time she thought about kissing him.

"We should do that, but just so you know, I'm not looking to date. I like you, but…"

He interrupted. "We don't have to label it. We could go out to dinner and just take it from there."

"Dinner sounds date-like."

"Why? We've gotten food together before. Besides, you eat with Blake all the time and you're not dating." He persisted, "I saw him dropping off Kaylee—remember her, the blond cheerleader we took biology with last semester?—at her dorm yesterday morning. She was wearing a short red dress so I'm assuming it wasn't for a breakfast date."

Josh was testing my reaction. He had no idea how well I could hide inside of myself, showing a calm exterior when a storm was raging. It had been key to my survival when the floor dropped out from under me and I was left alone. I was harassed mercilessly with no one to stand by me. Showing a reaction would've only made things worse.

Concentrating on leaving my face expressionless, I shrugged. I wasn't surprised about Blake having a one-night stand; I wasn't immune to hearing the rumors about his reputation. Since we met, my ears perked up whenever his name was mentioned in conversation. I never asked him about the rumors and we instead spoke of what I considered our safety net: art history, football, and college. Blake had a tendency to work the conversation around to high school time and time again, but he was picking up on my discomfort about the topic. It disappointed me to think he was the type to peak in high school and always looking back on his so-called glory days.

"I didn't want to tell you at first, but I figured you were too smart to have feelings for him." Josh leaned in closer and said in a conspiratorial whisper, "He's not exactly the right kind of guy for a nice girl like you."

Oh Josh, I thought. He was trying hard and I should've been flattered by his compliment, but it rubbed me the wrong way. It was unfair of him to assume anything about Blake. He was a twenty-one-year-old football player who looked as though he belonged on a billboard for an underwear campaign. He wasn't in a committed relationship as far as I could tell. If he wanted to sleep around, it was his business.

"Blake's a friend and that's all," I murmured.

"Will you consider it then? Going to dinner with me?"

My head bobbed up and down automatically. "Yes, dinner sounds great." I had already checked out of the conversation, my mind continuously wandering to Blake. Would I have more enthusiasm if he was the one asking?

The guilt was immediate once I saw Josh's eagerness. Although he said it wasn't a date, I could see the expectations there. His objective was clear: take me to dinner and win me over with his charms.

I liked Josh and he was attractive; Blake's Clark Kent nickname wasn't far off. The longer strands of his dark hair fell into his eyes from time to time. His dark glasses concealed his eyes, but when he removed them, I could see the crystal blue color. If I hadn't slammed the mental walls down on the possibility of dating, I'd probably be thrilled to have a guy like him interested in me.

Hastily, he finalized plans, arranging for us to have dinner Friday night. He was going to ask Finn to borrow his car to take me off campus. Despite my qualms over the non-date, a meal not coming from takeout containers or the cafeteria did sound appealing. He rushed off with promises to call me with the details, his hurried exit indicating his fear I'd change my mind.

There were dozens of reasons I didn't date, but one of the big ones was my last relationship was a disaster. What I believed was the start of an epic love story ended with me humiliated and picking up the pieces of my shattered heart. Out of everyone in my life, Hunter's disloyalty cut the deepest. But it would've been a lie to say he blindsided me with his personality switch. Months before we broke up I started to see hints of what lay beneath his charming smiles.

Chapter Five

"How can you tease me by wearing that fucking skirt, Autumn? Ever hear of blue balls?" Hunter mumbled into my neck as his fingers crept up my thighs.

We were in his basement and I had found my way onto his lap twenty minutes ago when his mother left for coffee with a friend. Hunter confessed she was really going to get drunk with a high likelihood of stumbling back into the house after midnight. Her drinking was getting progressively worse and I saw the effect it was having on Hunter. Since his dad left them both two months earlier, Hunter had changed. An anger at the injustices of his life caused him to fall into dark moods during which I often ended up the target of his vileness.

Because of how much I cared for Hunter, I managed to take his personality switch in stride. He was feeling abandoned and I wouldn't walk away when he was going through something so devastating. But I wasn't a doormat and warned him about the way he treated me. I would leave him if things didn't change soon. It had seemed to work for a while, but a new Hunter emerged. One who clung to me desperately when we were alone, demanding I give him everything—including my virginity.

Hunter hauled me closer, his large hands covering my ass completely. He was center for our high school's basketball team and we had known each other since grade school. Before we became a couple, we were friendly. But besides saying hello in the hallways, we never had a conversation lasting more than five seconds. After one of his basketball games during our sophomore year, I'd been shocked when I found him outside of the girls' locker room waiting for me. He had showered after the game and his blond hair had darkened from the moisture. His blue eyes were earnest as he called out my name. I pulled my cheerleading gear bag close to my body as I awkwardly followed him into a quiet corner of the hallway. I had just been yelling cheers for him: Ya gotta dribble, pass, shoot to score, Ya gotta pivot, two-three-four! But being alone with him left me speechless. When he asked me out I blurted out yes before stammering out excuses about my parents waiting for me.

A year later, there was nary a trace of that sweet and earnest boy in sight. I wanted that boy back, the one who picked flowers for me before our first date and who left notes in my locker. Not the sexually aggressive man he was growing to be, the one who was possessive and domineering.

Hunter's fingers looped around the string of my underwear and he yanked down. I put my hands over his, struggling with him to put my panties back in place. Instead he swatted my hands away and reached under the material to stick three fingers inside of me. I reared back, landing awkwardly on the couch next to him. Heat flooded my face and I glared at him. His smug smile made me violent.

"I knew you wanted me. I don't know why you're trying to play innocent when your pussy is begging for it," he said, holding up his glistening fingers for emphasis.

"I don't care what my body says, my mouth says no," I hissed and added, "asshole."

My blood ran cold at his harsh laughter. I fled from the house with his mockery stinging my ears. I should've branded the memory into my brain and held onto it. Instead, I forgave him when he called later that night. He stumbled over his apology and promised to wait forever if that's what I needed.

His contrition caused me to wonder why I clung to my virginity like it was a life raft. I loved Hunter. Maybe I could help get back the light he had lost since his dad left.

The irony was the week my world fell apart was the same week I planned to have sex with Hunter. Our junior prom was scheduled for the weekend and instead of seeing the loss of my virginity on prom night as a cliché, I convinced myself of its romanticism. In the days after, when I was so crushed by sadness I couldn't get out of bed, I imagined divine intervention in play. Rationalizing that perhaps the timing of my world's implosion was meant to keep me from giving up my virginity to Hunter. By then, I vowed that not only would Hunter never touch me again, neither would any other man.

***

Josh was the perfect dinner date; he did and said all the right things. He opened doors for me, pulled out my chair at the restaurant, and insisted I order first. I dug deep inside, willing myself to feel something for the charming boy before me. Josh's entire demeanor radiated with goodness. I should've been attracted to that quality. I needed safe. Because falling for Blake Preston was a million miles away from safe. Not only did my crush guarantee a broken heart because of Blake's disinterest, but, at least on the surface, Blake seemed to possess the quality I hated most in men: the sense of arrogant entitlement.

The Italian restaurant Josh chose was nice and expensive. I was flattered—college students didn't normally have the luxury of dropping a hundred dollars on a meal. I tried to be a good date, smile when appropriate, laugh at his self-deprecating jokes, but I wasn't sure if he could see my carefully crafted mask disintegrating.

"How's the chicken?" Josh asked, using his fork to point to my barely touched chicken cacciatore. My nerves were too frayed to eat as much as I would've liked.

"Good. Chicken probably seems boring with all of the menu choices."

"I could never think of you as boring," he said sincerely before turning back to his tortellini with Italian sausage.

I hoped he didn't see my blush. I didn't know how to accept a compliment anymore. In high school, praise became like a drug to me. I blossomed under false compliments and feigned adoration. Hunter used to joke he dragged me out of oblivion, but in some ways it was true. Before, I was well liked with a lot of friends, but being Hunter's girlfriend put me at the top of the high school food chain. I was embarrassed by the person I used to be. I was superficial and a taker, never a giver. Blake seemed desperate to know the girl I was in high school, but what he didn't understand was I wanted that girl to have never existed.

At the end of the meal, Josh asked for dessert, but I declined. I had looked longingly at a piece of decadent chocolate cake earlier in the meal, but couldn't quiet my anxiety enough to stomach any more food. When I returned from a trip to the restroom, I found the check paid and a piece of cake wrapped up for me to go. I was touched by the gesture and he wouldn't hear of my attempts to pay for half of the meal. When he took my hand and led me out of the restaurant, Josh officially turned the non-date into a date.

It was early, a little after eight, and Josh wanted to take advantage of having a car to use. Freshmen were confined to the campus unless they had an upperclassman as a friend. A part of me wanted to go back to the dorm and process my feelings alone. Maybe I would find a spark between us if I tried harder. Josh looked so good on paper: cute, sweet, and smart, and I reasoned it wouldn't be long before the fireworks arrived.

After some gentle convincing, I found myself agreeing to coffee.

Once we arrived at the coffee house, Josh helped remove my coat. His fingers brushed over my shoulders and down my arms as he moved behind me. I had dressed up for the occasion after Lexi reamed me out for considering wearing black pants and a bulky black sweater. Although she frowned at my large selection of black clothing, she did suggest the black dress I eventually settled on. It had a full crochet overlay with sheer arms and a rounded neckline. The hem was above the knee, but not very short. Josh was average height so I selected low heels to avoid towering over him. His eyes bulged when he picked me up, prompting Lexi to shoot me a small knowing smile.

Josh relented when I insisted on paying for coffee. Every second I continued to play the charade with him the likelihood of him getting hurt increased. I liked Josh as a friend and I shouldn't have agreed to go out with him. He was blurring the lines and I was submitting, going along for the ride when I should've never said yes to dinner in the first place.

"So, how's biology coming? I'm going to take it sometime next year, so you'll have to share your notes," I said as I blew away steam from my latte.

Josh smiled. "It's not bad, only an extension on everything we studied last semester," he said. "But I do miss you as my lab partner. We had lab for the first time on Thursday and I partnered with Kaylee."

"I didn't know you were friends," I said while staring at the wall behind him.

"We're not. But she said I looked smart, so I'd help her get a good grade." He rolled his eyes. "She didn't do much during the lab period, only text Blake."

Ah, I thought, *now I understand what's going on*. He saw Blake as a rival and figured he'd dig up dirt through Kaylee. Josh put too much power into my relationship with Blake. Blake was a casual acquaintance who I saw twice a week for class and breakfast. Blake told me from the beginning he wasn't interested in me. I was still trying to figure out why he wanted to be friends, but after spending time with Blake I believed wholeheartedly he didn't feel anything romantic for me. He flirted with me, but his words didn't hold any weight. I could almost sense a wall between us he had constructed. It hadn't gotten past me that although Blake spent a lot of time dredging up my past, he told me very little about himself.

I waved my hand. "That's nice. Although I don't think symbiosis actually works between lab partners." I tried to derail the conversation by taking a long sip of my coffee. It was burning hot, scalding my throat as I forced it down.

Josh's penetrating stare as I set the coffee down made me uneasy. Finally, he cleared his throat and changed the subject. Our conversation over coffee was much less awkward. I think without the romantic trappings, I felt like more myself. I pretended our outing was merely two friends having coffee together. When Josh wasn't hung up on Blake, he was actually easy to get along with. With two older sisters who adored him, Josh had plenty of anecdotes about the ways they embarrassed their baby brother growing up.

I always envied people with siblings. Being an only child gave me an inflated sense of responsibility. I was my parents' legacy and if I failed at life, they wouldn't have another chance. Siblings are also built-in friends and something I desperately needed two years earlier.

It was relatively early when we finished coffee, but Josh didn't put up a fight when I suggested we return to the dorm. I wanted to end things on a good note and decide where I wanted to take the relationship with him. My feelings were still platonic, but I questioned whether I should give it another try and see if something more developed. I didn't want a relationship, but as disastrous as things turned out with Hunter, there were some aspects I still missed. I missed the face-splitting grin I had when he called. Also, I longed to have someone look at me like he did, as if I was the only person in the world who mattered. When things were good, Hunter made me feel like the sun and he'd bend down to worship before me.

After parking Finn's Ford Focus in the student lot, Josh

walked me to my room. When he lingered at the door, I didn't know how to end the night. Should I shake his hand? Pull him in for a hug? Before I could overanalyze, I saw him press his lips together and angle his body toward mine. As he leaned in for a kiss, I stepped back and blushed.

I was a fraud—pretending to be able to date. I hadn't kissed anyone in close to two years and my feelings hadn't changed. *Just fucking kiss him*, I chided myself. But it would be cosmically wrong to go along with it. I was in constant battle against my submissive side and I wasn't about to embrace it to spare hurt feelings.

"I'm sorry, but I told you I wasn't ready to date," I said, staring at his dress shoes. Josh had made an effort with his appearance for dinner as well. His khaki pants were pressed and he'd replaced his typical worn T-shirt with a button-down oxford.

Josh sighed. "I'm sorry. I understand this wasn't supposed to be a date. But I really like you. I know you have stuff going on in your life…"

I cut him off. "What are you talking about? What stuff?"

His voice became soothing. "I've heard about your panic attacks. My older sister suffers from them and she's always told me how horrible they feel—like you're trying to breathe underwater."

I was on the verge of tears, embarrassed my weakness had become gossip fodder for the only friends I made at college. "I have to go," I said softly and didn't wait for his reply. He opened his mouth to protest, but I unlocked my door and slipped inside my room. I pressed my ear against the door and after he gave a heavy sigh, I heard him retreat.

Ugly emotions were swirling around me and I hated how vulnerable Josh had left me. The panic attacks were my private pain, but unfortunately many of the symptoms couldn't be concealed. At night they would come, sneaking their way into my sleep, wrecking my dreams and forcing me awake. I screamed and thrashed at times when I was stuck between sleep and consciousness. Lexi was an understanding roommate, but she must've told Finn and Josh about the inconvenience of having a head case for a roommate.

I couldn't stay and wait for Lexi. If she was with Finn, Josh might stop by and tell them both what had happened. Leaving my coat on, I hurried out of my dorm room. I took the stairs two at a time as I made my way to the first floor and outside of the dorm.

Freezing wind whipped against my skin and I pulled my wool coat closer to my body. The campus was quiet as I walked toward the student center. It was barely ten o'clock and most students had better plans than heading to the convenience store on campus and gorging on junk food. I had brought along a paperback with the plan to find a little corner inside of the student center to get cozy until I built up the nerve to face Lexi.

The convenience store was the perfect spot to load up on anything overladen with fat and calories. As I maneuvered through the aisles, I picked up enough junk food to induce an immediate coronary. With my arms overloaded, I chided myself for my overreaction. It was a kiss for god's sake, I wasn't agreeing to marry Josh by pressing our lips together. So what if I hadn't felt my insides turn to mush when he tried to kiss me? I had to get accustomed to the idea this could be my new reality. I was damaged with most of my reactions beyond my control. I may never again feel my heart in my throat when a guy decided to kiss me.

"Hey, you wiped out all of the cookies, are you planning to share?"

I swung around, caught by surprise. The jerking motion caused me to lose my grip on my snack pile and several of the snack cakes and candy bars fell to the ground. My comfort food scattered across a pair of dark blue running sneakers attached to a pair of muscular legs. My eyes lingered as they scanned from the bottom to the top, leaving me breathless by the time I settled on Blake's face. I fantasized about touching him, running my fingertips over each muscle in his abs. He was devastatingly handsome and if Blake's bemused expression was any indication, I hadn't done a good job of concealing my sudden attraction to him.

Instead of answering, I fell to the ground and gathered up the snacks I pilfered from the shelves. "Excuse me," I mumbled and sidestepped around him to head to the cashier. Once my food was deposited on the counter, I whirled to face Blake. "How's it going?"

"Fine, just making a food run for me and my roommate. We're in the middle of a Madden Xbox war."

"And you came here?" I asked, remembering he didn't live on campus. I could hear the accusation in my voice but didn't care. My attraction to him bothered me and I didn't like the feeling that he was poking at my vulnerabilities with a stick. Blake witnessing a moment of weakness didn't sit well with me. I fought against the labels placed upon me—weak, damaged, pathetic—and I refused to feel that way. The only way I survived was by being a fighter and I wouldn't go backwards.

"The store accepts our meal plan cards. I thought I'd save some cash instead of heading to 7-Eleven," Blake elaborated. He checked me out in the same leisurely manner as I had done to him moments earlier. There was a detached look in his eyes as he stared at my bare legs. My appearance seemed to not affect him until I noted how roughly he swallowed before speaking again. "Going somewhere?"

"Actually getting back from a date." I didn't want him to see the disappointment in my face about my date with Josh. Swiftly, I turned to the cashier and handed over my card. He handed me the weighed down plastic bag and I made room for Blake to put down his own purchases.

"Oh yeah? With who?" Blake tried and failed to keep his tone as unaffected as his facial expression.

Sometimes I felt a pull toward him and other times my

inner voice kept telling me to *run, run far*. Blake didn't want to like me and I couldn't get romantically involved. I never could get a read on his motivation for being friends. On the surface, we didn't seem to have a lot in common.

"Josh," I answered shortly. I didn't want to badmouth Josh and I felt embarrassed for him all of a sudden. Blake would be able to tell the date was an obvious failure by the early hour and my attempts at seeking solace through copious amounts of junk food.

Blake opened his mouth to reply, but quickly shut it. He scrutinized me for a long moment before asking, "What are you doing right now?"

"Eating," I answered and held up my shopping bag for emphasis.

"Want to come over? You can eat at my place and watch me kick Darien's ass in video games."

"As fun as that sounds, I'm going to pass," I said and added, "I'll see you Tuesday in class."

Blake was close on my heels as I made my way out of the store. He said to my back, "Autumn, you should come over, it'll be fun. If you don't feel like staying for long, it's not a big deal. I'll drive you back to campus in a couple of hours."

I turned to face him. Even with the subdued lighting outdoors, I could still make out the way his green eyes gleamed as he watched me. It was one of the few times in our acquaintance I felt Blake was sincere. He honestly seemed to want to spend some time together without an ulterior motive.

"I probably won't be the best company." I inhaled deeply and then said in a rush, "The date with Josh was terrible. It was awkward and when he tried to kiss me I couldn't go through with it. I'm upset about it and I thought eating chocolate while reading my book in the lounge would make me feel better."

Leaning back on his heels, Blake considered me for a long minute. He was perceptive and I could see the questions running through his head. Kisses were given away as freely as sticks of gum by most people at our college and were meaningless to most. Even if I was only mildly attracted to Josh, I shouldn't be so worked up over a kiss.

It all boiled down to my unwillingness to make amends with my past. I couldn't get over what happened and I could never move forward in my life until I learned to accept it. Beneath the bitterness and pain, I was a romantic at heart. I wanted to be swept away by a kiss and not terrified over what would follow after the kiss.

"You can eat your chocolate and read your book at my place. Maybe Darien and I could give you advice to help you out."

"I guess it's better than moping on my own." I squinted at him. "Plus it will give me a chance to own you at *Call of Duty*."

Blake laughed and I followed him out of the convenience store. Conversation was stilted as I trailed behind him through the parking lot. I wanted to spend time with Blake, but he made me uneasy. As much as I stressed over my date with Josh, I knew my heart was safe with him. With Blake, I could make no such guarantees.

Chapter Six

Blake's car was unexpected. His confidence and faint air of privilege gave me the impression he was wealthy and would drive a car flaunting his luxurious lifestyle. In fact, his car was a Chevy sedan at least ten years old with several large dings on the doors. It didn't bother me that Blake had an old beater; in a sense it made him more appealing. It brought him down from the stratosphere back to earth.

While Blake got rid of the clutter on the passenger seat, I took an inventory of the items. Involuntarily my eyebrows raised as I noted the pink sweatshirt draped over the seat. Blake cleared his throat and said, "Sorry about the mess. I was with my sister yesterday and she left all of her crap in my car."

I relaxed into the seat next to him. "Younger sister?"

"Yes, she's sixteen and horrible. She thinks because I live an hour away I'm still at her beck and call. I didn't have classes yesterday afternoon and she connived me into driving her and her friends around shopping." He stopped at a red light and turned to me. "Do you have any sisters or brothers?"

"No, only child." I shrugged. "Is it just you and your sister? That's nice you're there for her."

"Yeah, it's just the two of us. I spend a lot of time at home with her or she comes to stay with me some weekends. This car has seen some miles."

I was impressed with his devotion to his little sister. Although he was complaining about her, his fond smile told me he cared deeply for her. "At least she'll be driving soon," I offered.

"Doubtful since she'd need to work in order to afford a car and she has an aversion to manual labor," he laughed.

"Would your parents help her out with a car?"

His spine straightened and by the tense set of his jaw I realized I'd unexpectedly walked into a mine field. Before I could analyze what I said wrong, Blake spoke. "My mom's a receptionist at a doctor's office and her pay barely covers the bills. My father is...dead."

"I had no idea," I muttered. Not that I expected Blake to go around advertising his deceased father, but the conversation was making me realize how little I knew about him. During our time together, the spotlight was always on me. It was the first time I was able to get more background on him.

Blake's features smoothed out. "I don't really talk about it, but it's not a big deal. He died when I was little. I don't even remember him."

I was put in the awkward position of deciding whether or not to ask him what happened to his father. Thankfully, Blake picked up on my inner turmoil. "He was in a car accident on his way home from work. A woman ran a red light and it was all over for them both."

I swallowed hard before turning away to look out the window. Knowing about his father made me think about how much I appreciated my own parents. They never blamed me for what had happened junior year, even when I blamed myself. My mom and dad were the only people I felt hadn't put me under a microscope, looking for ways to exploit every blemish. My parents lost friends over the past couple of years because of their devotion, but I was certain they didn't hold me accountable for their losses.

Blake broke the crushing silence. "No need to get all

weirded out about my dad. My mom was okay and she tried to make up for the no dad thing. I was kind of a prick kid and she never put up with it. I was angry a lot—picking fights in school and not doing my homework. She had a boyfriend that got me into football and it helped me a lot. Healthier outlet to channel my temper or some Psych 101 shit like that."

I turned back to face him. "And now you're in college and the school's star running back."

"I'm surprised you remember my position since you haven't been to any of our games."

"I guess I'll have to go next year then and see if I'm impressed."

Blake smiled and it was contagious. It gave me hope we'd get out of our respective funks and salvage the rest of the night. Minutes later, he pulled into a sprawling apartment complex and stopped the car in front of one of the brick buildings. I followed him to his apartment, where he unlocked the door. As soon as it opened, I could hear the sound of referee whistles and cheering crowds coming from the video game. Walking into the living room, I saw a video game controller get launched across the room and a string of expletives released from the form sitting on the couch. The figure turned in my direction and straightened up.

"We have a new challenger. She doesn't play Madden, but she's thrown down the gauntlet for *Call of Duty*." Blake gestured to me with a tilt of his head before going further into the apartment. He set the bags of food on the kitchen counter and began stocking their refrigerator and cabinets with his purchases.

The apartment was open, with the living room, dining room and kitchen connected. The space wasn't large, but plenty of room for Blake and his roommate. To the right of the living room was a hallway leading to two bedrooms and a bathroom.

"Hi, I'm Darien." Blake's roommate stood up, holding out his hand. I did a quick inventory as his large hand dwarfed my own. Darien was tall, a couple of inches above Blake, but had a leaner frame. His hair was shaved with only a slight amount of peach fuzz on his scalp. I immediately took to him, possibly because of his warm brown eyes and bright smile as he shook my hand.

"I'm Autumn," I replied. Darien's eyes quickly cut over to Blake in the kitchen before returning back to me. His look hinted that Blake had mentioned me at some point. What concerned me was how taken aback he appeared. It made me feel like he was questioning why Blake had invited trouble into their apartment.

Darien's smile returned easily, making me second-guess what I was reading into the look. Being the target of bullies in high school left me with a heightened sense of paranoia and I always questioned people's motives. I had thought Faye, Hunter, and my other friends would always have my back. When they betrayed me, I became mistrustful of everyone around me. Going away to college was a new beginning, but I was still constantly reminding myself to not go looking for trouble.

Darien walked over to the video game console and switched the discs. "So, a hot girl who likes video games? Blake didn't tell me he was bringing my dream girl home."

Blake reentered the living room and rolled his eyes at Darien. He asked me, "Do you want something to drink? A beer or I think I have wine coolers?"

Darien snickered. "The wine coolers are for all Blake's 'dates' he brings over." Darien used air quotes to make his point. Blake leveled him with a deadly stare and I could still hear Darien chuckling as he resumed loading the video game disc.

"I heard you were dating Kaylee. I took biology with her last semester," I piped up before I could stop myself. I should be trying to steer the conversation away from Blake's dating life, not acting like I was keeping tabs on who he was dating.

"We went out a couple of times. I didn't know you were friends."

I almost guffawed at his last statement. In another lifetime, I would've been attracted to a friendship with Kaylee like a moth to a flame. Sometimes I would watch her in class, easily imagining being just like her if my life hadn't gone down the path it had. I probably would've continued cheerleading through college, surrounding myself with other members of the squad, and been a mainstay at the football and basketball games. I fancied myself still in love with Hunter, but if our relationship fizzled, I'd find myself on the arm of another star athlete. I bit my lip as I snuck a glance at Blake. Was the future I thought I was escaping inevitable? Instead of falling for a nice bookish guy like Josh, was my traitorous heart leading me to fall for a Hunter clone?

I realized Blake was waiting for me to elaborate on how I knew about him and Kaylee. "We're not friends. Someone just mentioned you were…" I paused and then supplied, "dating." I sat down on the black leather couch to avoid looking Blake in the face. I bounced as Darien fell back into the cushions next to me. Blake sat to my left on the matching loveseat.

Blake smirked. "Let me guess…does this somebody look like Superman's alter ego and have fantasies starring you as his Lois Lane?"

I picked up one of the throw pillows and launched it in his direction. I'd been friends with Blake for several weeks and teasing me about Josh had become one of his favorite pastimes. It was the reason I purposely kept my date plans from him. "Even if that was the case, it isn't anymore. He'll probably avoid me from now on after tonight."

"What's up with that? Why torture the poor guy with a date if you didn't like him?"

"I like Josh." At Blake's infuriating smile, I insisted, "*I do like Josh.* He's good-looking, smart, and a genuinely nice guy." Blake mimed a yawn and Darien burst out with a short laugh. "What's so funny?" I demanded, swinging my head between the two of them.

Blake shook his head. "You sound like a robot—repeating the things you've told yourself you should like about him. Just because he fits into this category of your perfect guy doesn't mean you're going to fall for him."

I fell back further into the couch and sighed. "Maybe you're right," I conceded. "We had a nice time tonight, but everything felt forced."

The reason I couldn't kiss Josh was undeniably clear at that moment. I was afraid I would feel one of two things: absolutely nothing or abject terror. Honestly, it was the reason I hadn't kissed anyone in more than two years. My expectations were outrageous. I wanted the boy I kissed again to wipe away all of the repulsion associated with the last time my lips were pressed against another.

"Of course I'm right. I'm an expert on two subjects: sex and football." Blake shrugged and picked up one of the game controllers.

"We were talking about kissing, not sex. Even if I kissed Josh that was as far as things were going," I said and picked up one of the other controllers. Maybe kicking Blake's ass in video games would relieve some of my frustrations.

"A good girl? I like it. I might have to make it my mission to corrupt you," Darien teased.

"Impossible, I'm incorruptible. Trying to corrupt me is only setting yourself up for failure."

"I'm up for the challenge. Too many girls give it up way too easily. I wouldn't mind a little chase."

"You'd be running in place. I'm the wallflower, the one in the corner of the party sipping her beer and wishing she was home reading a book." I kept my tone light, but the summary wasn't far from the truth.

"Just because you're in college doesn't mean you have to change who you are." Blake's gruff voice interrupted Darien's response. Glancing at Blake, I noticed he had turned brooding while I'd been verbally sparring with Darien. I hadn't been offended by Darien; I could tell the flirting was harmless. But something about Blake's words stung.

"What do you know about me in high school? I've told you a few things, but that doesn't mean you know anything about who I was. I may have been different in high school, but I hope you're not suggesting..." I couldn't get the rest of the sentence out because the word felt so wrong. I was going to say *I hope you're not suggesting I was a slut*. But it didn't matter if I was a slut or not. I hated how men and women felt the need to label a person's sexuality. I was a virgin, but if I wasn't, it shouldn't matter. I despised the idea that if I slept around, it gave men and women the opportunity to judge me and permit the transgressions of others.

"I just don't get you. People go to college to rebel, go crazy a little bit. You're going in the opposite direction."

Darien stood up abruptly. "I'll be back in a few. I have to call Matt back and I'm going to make something to eat." Darien bolted out of the room and I didn't blame him. Blake's moodiness had made me uncomfortable as well. I was embarrassed by his behavior, especially since we had a witness to his hot and cold act.

As I looked at him, I tried to get him as well. Against my better judgment, I liked him, but I couldn't deny there was another side to him. A caustic side I had no tolerance in dealing with when I could've stuck to my original plan of junk food and reading. "Do you mind taking me home?" I stood up and grabbed the jacket I had laid across the back of the couch. I was pulling on my coat before he had an opportunity to respond.

"Autumn, why are you getting mad?"

"Because you're making snap judgments about me and I don't appreciate it. Why do you care if I changed who I was between high school and college? You're always bringing up high school and it's annoying. High school is over and the Autumn from back then no longer exists." I exhaled shakily and pushed down the desire to cry. "And the presumption that you know what I was like back then is *wrong*."

"Then tell me," he said softly.

Blake's defenses were down, making me more confused than ever. Was he having the same feelings? Was it the reason he wanted me to open up to him? But why wasn't he picking up on the obvious—that I didn't want to return to the past?

"When someone meets you for the first time, what assumptions do they make about you because of football? Maybe that you're a stupid jock? You could be going for your PhD, but because you're amazing at football, you get slapped with an unfair label."

"And what about you?"

"I was Whorey Dorey in high school and everyone believed the rumors about me because they felt I perpetuated them by wearing short skirts and being a flirt. I didn't come to college to be Whorey Dorey, I came here to find out who I am outside of the labels."

Blake's face scrunched up in distaste. "That's a lame nickname. I'm betting your high school didn't graduate too many future brain surgeons."

I managed to smile. "It is a lame nickname." I sat back down and edged closer to him. I leaned forward with my elbows on my thighs. Our knees were inches apart and I stared at the closeness of our legs. "I can't go backwards and keep talking about the assholes I went to school with. If we're going to be friends, I need you to leave it alone."

"Okay," he said. His eyebrows pulled together as he regarded me. "I'm stubborn, but I'm not a total dick. If you don't want to talk about high school, I won't bring it up again. But remember, you can tell me anything and I'm not going to judge."

I had the strangest sense of déjà vu at the moment, recalling a similar conversation with Hunter. He had begged me for the truth again and again, pleas that fell on deaf ears. When he confronted me with the rumors, my denials no longer mattered. It was my fault and I'd have to pay for my sins. He nominated himself as juror, judge, and executioner.

I focused back on the here and now. "Thanks for the offer. Now, can you do what you promised and get my mind off of my crap date by giving me a chance to blast you in *Call of Duty*?"

"Bring it, Autumn."

Chapter Seven

"You bitch! I waited for you, put up with your teasing act for months. And you were fucking someone else." Hunter spat the words in my face and I spun my head to escape his vitriol.

"It's not true, what they're saying. You know me." I tried to keep my voice small while wishing I could shrink away more and more until I disappeared completely.

"Dan said you blew him a month before we started dating. Why the fuck would he make something like that up?"

"Because he's a piece of shit that always hated us together. This gives him the perfect chance to turn you against me. Hunter, please, I need you. Faye and the rest of my friends aren't calling me back. I've been on Facebook, I know what they're saying, but maybe if they see us together, it will go away."

"Fine, then give me something in return. Fuck me right now. Take off your clothes and spread those legs you've been spreading for everyone but me." Hunter reached forward and his fingers encircled my wrist. He yanked me roughly to him and I collided with his chest. Before I could protest, his hands were pulling at my pants.

***

Cowering beneath my blanket, I resolved to stop thinking about

Hunter. He'd been on my mind way too much and somehow found a way to penetrate my dreams. I hadn't seen Hunter since I stopped going to Newpine High School and finished out my senior year at home. At times, the temptation came to look him up online, but I refrained. Nothing good would come out of reading about Hunter's charmed life after our breakup.

"Autumn?" Lexi whispered and turned on the light. She'd been asleep when I returned from Blake's and I silently crept into the room to avoid having the awkward conversation about my date with Josh.

"Sorry, bad dream," I muttered, peeking my head out from under the blanket. I looked at the clock, noting it was after seven, and decided I might as well stay awake. I'd returned after one in the morning but could fit in a nap later if I needed the extra sleep. With my heart pounding and my head spinning, sleep would be fleeting.

"How was your night? I passed out at midnight and you weren't home yet," Lexi said cheerfully. I assumed Josh hadn't been in touch with her by the hopeful tone of her voice.

"It was fun," I answered honestly. Once the awkwardness between Blake and me disappeared, I had a good time with him and Darien. Darien continued to flirt and at times it seemed to annoy Blake. But Blake never protested. He was sending out a clear signal: we were friends and nothing more.

"Really? Where did he take you to dinner?"

"The date with Josh was fine, we went to Piazza's and then coffee, but we ended the night early." I sat up in bed. "I ran into Blake and hung out at his apartment with him and his roommate."

"If you went to Blake's place that doesn't sound like Josh is going to get a second date."

I aimed to keep my voice neutral. "Did you tell Josh about my panic attacks? He brought it up and I wasn't prepared for it. I ran inside our room and shut the door in his face."

"No, of course I didn't tell him," Lexi breathed out. "Oh

no, I'm going to kill Finn. I mentioned last semester I was worried about you and he must've said something to Josh. I'm really sorry."

"It's okay." It was fine because I had to give Lexi credit. She could've put in a room change request the week after I moved in and had my first panic attack. If her worst transgression was telling her boyfriend her roommate was one small step away from psychiatric commitment status, I could hardly blame her.

"I'm sorry I pushed Josh on you too. I knew you didn't see him that way, but he's a good guy and I thought maybe he could help you get out there and start dating again." Lexi wrung out her hands. "I think I was being selfish and imagining how much fun it would be if you were dating Finn's best friend."

"I like Josh, but I can't see him as more than a friend. Even if we tried to casually date, I don't think it would be fair to either of us."

"But you like Blake as more than a friend."

My physical attraction to Blake started as soon as we met, but an unrequited crush was something I could handle. When he drove me back to campus the night before, I recognized how my feelings had changed. Kissing Blake had been an unreachable fantasy, but while we were alone in the quiet intimacy of his car, I wanted the real thing. "I do, but nothing is going to happen."

"Why not?"

"I have my…*stuff* and Blake has his own." I didn't want to tell Lexi about Blake's father. It seemed like something he didn't advertise and I didn't want to blab something he told me in confidence. I wasn't sure if Blake was keeping me at a distance because of his father or some other reason. He was stingy about sharing too many personal details about his life so I was left playing a never-ending guessing game.

"Well, I'm done pushing you. I'm not going to be labeled a horrible friend because I'm coercing you to date when you have no desire to," Lexi said resolutely before lying back down in her bed.

Smiling softly, I wondered how long her promise would last. She was deliriously happy with Finn and I found people in love liked to set their friends up to share in the bliss. I was happy for her and it was uplifting to see a healthy relationship. I'd been in the most toxic relationship possible and I was grateful to Hunter for one single thing only—breaking up with me. If he had stood by me, then I would've ended up putting up with his cruelty for who knows how long before I finally wised up.

***

On Tuesday, Josh finally called. I considered calling him first, but I was embarrassed over our date and wasn't sure what to say. I didn't know if I needed to apologize or if it would be better to pretend none of the awkwardness happened.

"Hello."

"Hi, Autumn. I'm glad I caught you, I thought maybe you went out with Lexi and Finn."

An hour earlier, Lexi and Finn left for an off-campus party. Blake mentioned during class he would be there as well, but I decided to pass. I liked the quiet in the dorms on Tuesdays and found it the best time to catch up on my class work for the week. Most of the students didn't have early classes on Wednesday, which had turned Tuesday nights into a major campus party night. Dorm parties were rare because of security roaming the halls after hours, so most of the gatherings took place off campus.

"No, staying in tonight. What about you?"

"I'm getting over a stomach bug that started yesterday. I was finally able to get out of bed today, but I'm still feeling like crap."

"That's too bad. Hope you feel better," I chirped. I chewed on my thumb as I was greeted by awkward silence. Finally, I started, "Listen, Josh—"

"Autumn, I'm sorry—" he broke in.

"You don't need to apologize. I had a great time at dinner and I know you were trying to help by bringing up the panic attacks. Maybe I do need to talk to someone on a regular basis about them."

"I don't think less of you and I don't want you to think we were badmouthing you behind your back. Lexi had said something to Finn and we were trying to figure out how to help you."

"I understand. You're a good friend, Josh, and I don't want to mess it up," I said gently.

"I get it. I wish it wasn't the case, but you made it clear you weren't looking for a boyfriend. But I hope I didn't make things weird between us."

"No, we're totally fine. We should get together for lunch later in the week and test things out. I bet there won't be a trace of weirdness."

Josh sounded relieved and we made plans to get together on Friday for lunch. It would be easy to shy away, but I had only a handful of friends. I didn't want to lose Josh because our attempts at a romance fizzled out.

Later, I stared up at the ceiling while trying unsuccessfully to fall asleep. Lexi texted me before midnight to let me know she was sleeping up in Finn's room. She never invited Finn to our room, although I told her I wouldn't mind. I was a little uncomfortable with the idea of Finn witnessing one of my panic attacks, but the offer was my attempt at being a good roommate. There was no handbook on how to appease a normal roommate who had to deal with my emotional breakdowns.

It felt like my eyes were barely closed when I awoke to the sound of persistent knocking. I lifted up onto my elbows and groaned at the clock when I saw it was after three in the morning. I thought I heard once people went crazy from lack of sleep. If that was true, I was halfway there. I clambered over to the door and looked through the keyhole. Blake was shuffling side to side with his hands in his pockets. Before I could process him at my door, he lifted his right hand and knocked again.

"Autumn," he called through the doorway.

"What the hell?" I whispered before swinging open the door.

"Hey, you are awake," Blake said brightly. He looked me up and down and smiled as his eyes raked over my zebra-printed pajama pants and black tank top.

"No, I wasn't awake. What are you doing here?" I demanded and looked him over as well. He was wearing a black sweater and a pair of dark jeans that hung low on his hips. With his bleary gaze and goofy expression, I guessed he had way too much to drink at the party.

"You don't sound glad to see me. I bet most girls on your floor would be thrilled to find me knocking at their doors." He raised his voice and yelled, "Hey, can I crash in someone's room? It's Blake Preston, you may have heard of me."

The deserted hallway amplified his voice and I fought the desire to throttle him. A minute later, Casey stuck her head outside of her door down the hall. She was dressed in a long T-shirt and cute high-cut shorts that accentuated her toned legs. "You can come in my room." She fluttered her eyelashes and grinned at Blake.

"See, I told you." Blake smiled back in Casey's direction.

I rolled my eyes while grabbing him by the arms. As I pulled him inside, I ground out, "You're going to get me in trouble with the RA." I closed the door behind him and whirled around. "How did you get in the dorm anyway? You need a key card after two because the outside doors lock."

He waved me off. "You underestimate me. I have a face people love to trust. It wasn't hard to convince someone to let me inside."

I crossed my arms over my chest. "Why are you breaking into my dorm? And how did you get on campus? Please tell me you didn't drive drunk."

"Are you always so negative? I thought after Saturday, we bonded and you'd be happy to see me."

"Not at three in the morning when I'm trying to sleep."

He walked further into the room and scanned it with a shrewd expression. His eyes rested on my bed for long enough I assumed he'd guessed my side of the room. He spared a glance at Lexi's bed. "Where's your roommate?"

"She stays with her boyfriend sometimes." Before walking over to him, I turned the overhead light on. The quiet dim of my desk lamp made the room feel too intimate. Blake had become a friend, but I wasn't comfortable with him in my space. "You didn't answer my question, did you drive here?"

"No, I caught a ride back to campus with a friend. And before you ask, no, he wasn't drinking. Is this your bed?" After I nodded, he sank into the mattress with his feet planted on the floor in front of him. "It's pretty grim on your side of the room, Autumn. Where are all of your pictures? Compared to your roommate's side, I feel like I'm in a prison cell."

I smacked his shoulder. "I didn't know you were into interior decorating. Maybe I should pay you by the hour to spruce up my dorm room."

"You're on. I'll hang up pictures of me and draw hearts around my face," he teased.

"Maybe put your pictures on a dartboard instead," I retorted. "Blake, seriously, what are you doing here?"

"I don't know, honestly. I was hoping you'd come out and when you weren't there, I figured I'd stop by here and see what you were up to. I had fun the other night."

He fell back onto my bed and I watched the mattress bounce with his weight. The sight of Blake in my bed was almost comical. He was huge and his limbs hung awkwardly over the side. Instead of feeling panic at the idea of a boy in my bed, I was starting to wonder what it would feel like to crawl next to him. I gave my head a powerful shake to clear out the distracting thoughts.

"How did you plan to get home? Is your friend driving you back?"

He sat up and gave me an impish smile. "I didn't catch his number, so I'm not sure that's an option. Darien left the party a couple of hours ago, so I could call him to get me. Unless you decide to take pity on me and let me sleep here."

"Here?" I squeaked. "With me?"

"Not sleeping together," he chuckled. "Just sleeping at the same time. I could just take your bed while you sleep in your roommate's bed."

"Or you could take the floor," I huffed.

"Or we could share your bed," he countered. At my expression, he fell back onto the bed and laughed again. I couldn't decide if I should pummel him while he was drunk or wait until he sobered up. "Floor it is," he groaned.

I chewed my lip as I watched him bring his body upright. I tried to gauge how terrible it would be for Blake to sleep in my room. Did I feel safe enough with him? Despite him being an over-muscled giant of a man, he treated me gently. What if I had a panic attack while he was here? It was far from ideal, but it was a small worry compared to risking his safety. I wouldn't be able to live with the guilt if I kicked him out and something bad happened to him.

Going over to my closet, I pulled out extra bedding I had stored. "Here's a pillow and a blanket," I said and laid them on top of his lap.

He took hold of my hand and held onto my forearm as he rose off of the bed. "Thanks. I'm glad we're friends."

Blake was consistently putting the friend label on us. I didn't know if the constant reminder was for his benefit or mine. Maybe he picked up on my growing feelings and wanted to let me down gently, the same way I had with Josh earlier. If he was worried I'd act on my feelings, I could have told him the chances were very slim.

"Yeah, same here. Now go to bed, so I can get back to sleep."

Blake released my arm and settled on the throw rug with his blankets and pillows. It didn't look very comfortable, but no one invited him to crash in my room. I'm not sure what drunken thought brought him to me, but I had too many conflicting feelings over letting him into my bed with or without me in it. After turning off the lights, I crawled under my warm blankets.

Too wired to sleep, I instead concentrated on the sounds of Blake shifting positions on the floor. The room felt overly warm and I understood the temperature change had everything to do with the thought of a gorgeous guy I liked sprawled out inches away from where I slept.

I wondered what it would be like if things became sexual between the two of us. I had pictured sex with Hunter when we were dating, but I was also sixteen at the time. We had fooled around, but he was my first boyfriend and I had no other experience to compare to. Blake's partner number could be anywhere from one to one hundred for all I knew. It was safe to assume he was more experienced than my loser high school boyfriend and could make my first time incredible. Hunter's idea for ridding me of my virginity involved a six-pack and the backseat of his friend's car.

Blake seemed like the type of guy to take his time. I closed my eyes and saw him teasing me with his tongue while his fingers slowly traveled the length of my body. His kisses would deepen and I would want nothing more than to share my body with him. Instead of waiting for him to peel off my panties, I would do it for him. He would be eager to enter me, but instead of rushing things, he'd prolong every pleasurable sensation. Fingering me, sucking my nipples, kissing my navel, until our bodies came together.

Oh god, I thought, *I'm having dirty thoughts not about just anyone, but about the guy sleeping in my room.* Fantasizing about sex was a normal thing for most people, but in my case, it was unheard of. There were moments when I imagined ice forming around my nether regions and no man able to melt it. But a late-night visit from Blake left me panting and my panties wet.

I tried to think of inane things to banish my lust. I cringed over the idea Blake would be able to guess where my head had just been. I hoped I wasn't sending out sex pheromones, advertising that being friends was the furthest thing from my mind.

I started at the sound of his voice. "Autumn, are you still awake?"

"Yeah," I whispered.

"I never thought when I saw you at the party, I'd end up here. But I want you to know before you end up hating me that I do like you and you didn't deserve what those assholes did to you in school."

My throat constricted. "It was just high school bullies; it doesn't matter anymore."

"It does and I wish I could go back in time and kick all of their asses for you."

"Thanks." I paused and mulled over his words before asking, "Why will I end up hating you?"

"Because one day you're going to see what kind of man I really am and hate me for it."

"No one's perfect, Blake. I've done things I'm not proud of. What could be so bad I'd hate you for it?"

The silence was heady as I waited for his reply. His pronouncement felt like an extension of the insistence of our friendship—he was warning me away from him. But if he was so scared of me falling for him, why did he force himself into my life?

"Because I have so much rage and it's ripping apart everything good I have inside of me. I'm fucking toxic, Autumn, and you deserve better than to be mistreated by another dick."

"Blake, you're not like those guys in school—"

He didn't let me finish. "You only know the parts of me I let you see. I've done shit, fucked-up shit that's probably unforgivable."

I was rendered speechless because as strong as my feelings were for Blake, I wouldn't be blind to a person's faults. I made that mistake before and I didn't want to do it again. Blake had never hinted at a darker side of himself, but I'd come to know men who fooled the masses with their easy smiles, concealing their black hearts.

I rolled over on my side to face away from Blake and called out, "I'm tired, Blake. Goodnight."

Maybe I was a fool to turn my back on him after his warnings, but the bad guys didn't warn you first. No, the truly wicked ones lured you in with kindness and then blindsided you with their mercilessness.

Chapter Eight

It was the second week of my senior year and I was hiding out in the stairwell. I had taken for granted how good it felt to be surrounded by friends, not being on the outside looking in. Maybe I could've dealt with the no friends issue, but the hateful whispers and glances as I walked the hallways were more than I could bear. There were also the unseen hands, the quick pinches and grazes that happened while I tried to hold my head up high in the hallway. I never found the culprits, but the touches were unsubtle messages—the boys would do what they wanted to me and I was powerless against them. The summer had been hell, but going back to school was its own unique brand of torture.

It was my lunch hour and the time of day I dreaded the most. Walking into the cafeteria on the first day thinking everything would be fine was a mistake. The hatred for me was far reaching. The pretties, the girls I had considered my best friends, had thrown the first stone and everyone else had fallen in line like the good sheep they were. Hunter's rejection had only reinforced what my friends were saying. Autumn was a slut and a liar.

Sitting at a lunch table alone for an hour had made time slow down. Everything had seemed amplified—the whispers felt like screams and the sidelong glances were like slaps in the face. No one wanted to sit with me; it would be too much of an open invitation to become a new target of Faye and Hunter. Faye and

Hunter had no issue with openly mocking me from across the room. They would point and laugh, cajoling the others at their table. When my eyes clashed with Hunter's, I was the first to look away and it killed me a little inside. My hatred grew a thousand-fold; I was disgusted he had the ability to make me cower. I had to dig into my reserves and find the strength that had gotten me through the summer.

I was naïve to believe Hunter and Faye could be ignored. The breakup with Hunter was ugly, but Faye was deceptive and made me believe at first she would always be my friend. Later, I would come to find out she was using whatever I said to her as ammunition. To her, unpopularity was contagious and she would do whatever it took to show she was nothing like me. I never found out whether Faye believed what was said or what made her hate me so. Was it because she felt I lied to her? Or was it because I no longer could play the role of her innocent virginal best friend?

Until I found the strength to face the bullies, hiding out seemed like my only option. Faye and Hunter weren't going to let up any time soon and my sense of self-preservation drove me to avoid them at all costs. The stairwell was usually deserted between periods and seemed like the only place on campus I could be alone. I drew my knees to my chest and wished I could curl up into a little ball, close my eyes, and blink myself out of existence.

Sometimes I hated myself and wished I'd never opened my big fat mouth. I could've handled Mr. Bridges for another year—it wasn't like I'd still have him as my teacher. I could've walked by his door every day and kept a grin on my face in the process. I was a cheerleader, for god's sakes; if anyone had mastered the art of false smiles, it was me. Not that cheerleading was an option anymore. Even if members of the squad didn't ostracize me, Mr. Bridges—Coach Bridges—was an integral part of our school's football legacy.

Newpine was a football town; I, along with most everyone else in the town, lived and breathed the sport. Newpine High School had a winning streak of championship titles and it was attributed to the coaching staff. The football program was a joke before Coach Bridges came to the high school and whooped our sorry-ass team into shape. Walking into the stadium again would be inviting back the memory of a monster I wished to forget.

Voices at the bottom of the stairwell jolted me out of my daze. I scrambled to my feet, but I wasn't quick enough. I panicked as I heard stomping feet moving closer and saw two sets of broad shoulders enter my view. I cursed my luck as I identified the voices as seniors Talon and Carter, football players and friends of Hunter's. I turned toward the landing above and clumsily hurried toward the exit.

Fingers wrapping around my waist stopped me. The feeling of someone touching me again led to an instantaneous fight or flight response. In my rush, I lost my balance and would've tumbled down the stairs if rough hands didn't break my fall. I righted myself on the landing and twirled to face the boys. Carter sidestepped around me and moved between the stairwell exit and me. Talon remained planted in front of me and crossed his arms in front of his chest. His lip curled as he examined me.

I was trapped and it was a feeling I loathed. The loss of control, the idea of someone else controlling my fate—those sensations bred my nightmares. The panic couldn't be suppressed by the pills prescribed by the psychiatrist and I was left gasping for air as my heart threatened to leap out of my chest.

"What a sad day. Autumn Dorey…" Talon stopped and cleared his throat. "Excuse me, Whorey Dorey is such a freak she can't even go into the cafeteria." He noticed my untouched paper bag lunch on the step and launched it down the stairwell with a swift kick. The bag slammed into the wall and the diet soda exploded. The can swirled around on the ground as the liquid seeped out of it to drench the floor.

If I weren't so terrified, I would have probably rolled my eyes at the cliché he was being. Sometimes I wondered whether I had blinders on the entire time I was in high school. How else could I've been friends with boys like Talon and Carter? Was my vanity the reason for my great fall from grace? Maybe going through hell had its perks, including my twenty/twenty vision in regards to my former friends.

"Leave me alone, Talon." I kept my voice even and my tone low. Showing Talon fear would be a mistake. He was like bacteria and my panic would provide him a moist environment to thrive in.

"And if I don't?" He took a step forward and I instinctively moved backwards. I had forgotten Carter momentarily, a mistake I realized as he grabbed me roughly from behind. He pinned my arms to my sides while pushing me forward. Serving me up to Talon without a second thought. Talon moved in and I squirmed as his palm caressed my cheek. "Hunter told us about all the sick shit you were into, wanting him to stick his dick in your ass and asking him to come on your face."

"Hunter's a fucking liar," I spat out. I should've let them all say what they wanted, but Hunter's stupid slut-shaming campaign against me was reaching a feverish pitch. I imagined the lies were his way of healing his wounded pride while also proving I was promiscuous and had asked for those things done to me. Even if Hunter's lies were true, it was bullshit that the Neanderthals before me believed I somehow deserved their sexual aggression. "Let me go or I'll scream…"

Carter cut me off. "What are you going to scream…rape? We all know how good you are at crying rape when things don't go your way."

"Fuck you," I sobbed. Talon's hands moved away from my face and he reached for my breasts. He cupped them roughly before his thumb grazed over my right nipple. He gave it a twist, making me gasp. I cried out, "Stop it! Help me…" I was calling out between sobs, praying for salvation.

Carter pulled me to him with his right arm while covering my mouth with his free hand. I fought against him, trying to loosen his grip. Finally, he stilled as I heard the door at the bottom of the stairs open.

"Hello, is someone in here?"

I didn't recognize the voice, but it sounded authoritative enough that my relief was palpable. Talon exchanged a panicked look with Carter over my head. Tossing me like a rag doll, they both sprinted toward the doors behind me. The commotion caused the teacher's steps to become hurried and my body sagged against the railing. I was safe...for now, I thought. But I wondered how long until it happened again. And what if next time there was no one to scare the boys off?

Chapter Nine

"Autumn, I'm going to head out." I forced my eyes opened and my heart momentarily stopped. Seeing a large male figure standing over my bed was unexpected. I gasped and sat up straight. After a few calming breaths, I was able to shake off the remnants of sleep and remember Blake had spent the night in my room.

"Okay, see you in class."

He rocked back and forth on his heels and shoved his hands into his pockets. "Thanks for letting me stay here."

"It's fine." I shrugged as if it wasn't a big deal. He had no idea how much trust it took to spend the night with him alone.

"Do you have classes this morning?"

"No, just a night class."

"I was thinking we could go to the museum, maybe work on our project." Blake looked sheepish and it didn't fit in with his usual arrogance. I suspected he was struggling with his feelings toward me. He seemed torn in two—one part of him resisting us growing closer while the other part was drawn to me. I'd been entirely focused on my issues, my reasons for keeping everyone at a distance, and I had missed how off Blake's behavior had been. I wondered if it was some type of game to him—the back and forth between drawing me in and then pushing me away.

"Okay," I agreed. We had to go to the museum for class and it would be easier to go together since Blake had the car. I was rationalizing because the real reason I wanted to spend more time with him was hard to digest. I wanted to spend more time with Blake because I wanted to disprove what he said the night before. I didn't want to believe he was toxic, but he was hiding things. Blake had said he had so much rage inside and I was certain that rage had to be born out of something from his past.

"Darien is going to pick me up and then after I go home to shower and change I'll come back to get you. If it works for you, I'll pick you up in a couple of hours and we'll drive to the Philly museum."

Before I could reply, the sound of the door opening startled me. Blake turned at the noise as Lexi walked into the room. She took a step back as Blake came into her view, most likely never expecting to see a man in our room at such an early hour.

Her mouth dropped and I saw her struggling to recover from Blake's presence. "I'm sorry, I thought you were alone," she stuttered. My lips parted and I found myself speechless while Blake looked nonplussed. He smiled widely, putting his mask firmly back in place.

"I'm Blake, you must be the roommate."

"Lexi," she replied with her mouth opening and closing. She looked past Blake to me and I gave her a shrug.

"Well, Darien will kick my ass if I'm not outside waiting for him. So I better go." He turned to face me. "I'll text you when I'm on my way." With a wave to both Lexi and me, he was gone. The room felt emptier without his overpowering presence.

Lexi stayed rooted to the spot next to our door. Her eyes narrowed with suspicion wrapping around her words. "Did Blake sleep here?"

I pointed to the makeshift bed on the floor. "He knocked on the door drunk at three a.m. and asked to crash here."

Lexi's eyes widened and she moved further into the room.

She set her overnight bag on her bed and then sat down. She smoothed her comforter before meeting my eyes. "Are you and him a thing?"

"No," I answered shortly. "He told me last night I would end up hating him one day."

Lexi's nose twitched. "Why would you hate him?"

"Apparently he's a dick with anger issues." I tossed the comforter off of me and turned to face her. "What he said should freak me out, but it doesn't."

"Why?"

"Because he's never shown that side to me and I felt like he was just saying those things to scare me. Like if he's such an asshole why would he bother giving me a heads-up?"

"Maybe it was just drunken babbling. Finn told me one time after he was drinking he was responsible for inventing the cronut."

I smiled. "It's weird, Lexi. There's no logical reason why I should be drawn to him, but I can't help it. I like him."

"Autumn, he's a smoking hot football player—you don't need to sell it to me." She smiled and said, "Have you kissed?"

"No, but I've thought about it…*a lot*." Lexi laughed at my admission. "But he's putting me in the friend zone for some reason."

"His actions are sending a completely different message. Most guys don't come to a girl's dorm room in the middle of the night because she's such a good friend."

"We'll see what happens. I don't want to overthink it and end up hurt. I know he's been seeing other girls, so I'm going to keep my expectations low. It's not like I'm going to fall in love with the guy." Lexi's eyebrows lifted. I tilted forward. "*I'm not*. I may want to kiss him, but I have some sense of self-preservation. I'm not going to pretend he's suddenly going to change for me and want to have an exclusive relationship."

"So you only want to kiss him? Without any feelings and without anything else happening…"

"Would it be crazy to have my first time be with Blake? Probably. But maybe it would be incredible…" I groaned and rubbed my palms across my cheeks. "Look at me, I sound crazy. We haven't even kissed and I'm talking about sleeping with him."

"You're not crazy. It sounds like he's the first guy in forever you really like. That's a big deal. Be smart and take your time getting to know him first, but don't close yourself off because of rumors about him."

Lexi had a point. I should've never given any clout to the rumors about Blake, considering my history with hateful gossip. I wanted to get to know him better and decide what kind of person he truly was for myself.

"This is boring," Blake complained while faking a yawn.

"You suggested coming here," I said and moved to stand in front of the next painting.

Blake followed at my heels. "I thought we could just buy the tickets, show the professor, and then look up the pictures online. Let's blow this off and go get cheesesteaks for lunch."

I held up my notebook. "I still have to pick out a painting and take notes. We need to do an overview of one of the pieces and then discuss the imagery, symbolism, brushwork, and use of color."

Blake pulled a face. "I was in class, I heard the assignment."

"Sure you did," I said and patted his arm. "Maybe if you stopped binge drinking, you wouldn't have to rely on me to tutor you."

"All right, let's do this. Can we find some better pictures to look at? I hate the blurry nature ones…"

"Impressionist paintings. And you say you pay attention in class." I pointed down the hall to our left. "I'll continue here and you can go search for a few nude paintings to occupy yourself."

"Sure, that will get me an A in the class; hand in a porn

paper. Anyway I prefer the real thing to the pictures."

Instead of answering, I continued to travel slowly from painting to painting, searching for one that grabbed me and I could write a stellar paper on. I liked being inside the forced quiet of the Philadelphia Museum of Art. Conversations were whispers in between reverent stares as the visitors got to glimpse objects of beauty created through the centuries. I preferred the older works, so we had started our tour in the European Art Gallery. The museum was three floors and I doubted we would be able to view all of the collections in a single visit. I wouldn't have minded spending the entire day wandering the museum, but Blake's interest had been waning for the past hour and a half since we arrived.

"Do you want to check out the American wing? Maybe we could find a football drawing you can wax poetic on."

"A change of scenery sounds good." Blake nodded. "And I'm going to ignore your sarcasm."

The American wing was nearby on the same floor. The area was mostly empty and our steps echoed through the wing. The interior design was minimalist, allowing the artwork to shine. I sat down on one of the benches in the center of the room and surveyed the area.

My skin prickled as I felt Blake's arm brush up against my own as he took a seat next to me on the bench. My breath had caught when he picked me up outside of the dorms. He had worn a dark green sweater and the color was perfect on him. He was freshly showered with a few stray droplets running down the side of his face. When I took a seat in his car, I had wanted to reach over and remove them with my fingertips. I had kept my hands down at my sides and instead looked out the window for most of the ride. Blake was beautiful in a dangerous way and it was part of my self-preservation to have a look-but-don't-touch policy in place.

Focusing back on the paintings, I saw flashes of pink and white on canvas that caught my eye. I stood back up to get a closer look at the floral painting. It was easy to identify the work as Georgia O'Keefe—I considered her one of my favorite American artists.

"*Two Calla Lilies on Pink*." Blake joined me, reading aloud the accompanying label. "You like this one?"

"I do. I love how the yellow of the pistils pops against the pink and white. I also love the detail of the petals, how it creates movement in the work."

He lowered his lashes and scrutinized me. "You are really into this, aren't you?"

I ignored his question and continued, "I read that a lot of critics described O'Keefe's paintings as representations of female sexuality, but that was never her intention. She wanted to bring attention to something beautiful that may otherwise go unnoticed."

"Shit, Autumn, why did you tell me that? Now guess what I keep seeing when I look at the painting?"

I giggled, probably a bad move since I didn't want to encourage him. It was funny to experience an art museum with Blake; he was completely a fish out of water. He lacked the confidence I had seen around campus and in the football videos. I was comfortable in the museum setting; I liked the quiet and how the paintings were able to evoke such strong emotions with a single glance. Since I mastered the ability of emotional suppression, it was a relief to allow myself to feel for once.

"I think this is going to be my pick for the paper," I said. "Do you want to search around for your choice?"

"Sure, can I borrow a pen and paper?"

I ripped out a piece of notebook paper and dug into my purse for a pencil. Handing it over, I said, "No pens allowed. Meet me back here when you're done or call me."

Fifteen minutes later, Blake hadn't returned. I stuffed my notes into my bag and took the time to wander around the exhibits. I liked Blake's company, but I didn't feel inclined to rush along with him by my side. Alone, I could stare at each piece and get lost in the world created by the artist. When Blake had been next to me, I found myself preoccupied. I would catch his scent and my body would tighten in anticipation. Or I would hear his steady breathing and get lost in the sound. Blake was enchanting me and I was doing nothing to stop it.

After half an hour with no sign of him, I sent him a text to find out where he had wandered off. He replied back to meet him in the lobby. With his stomach most likely driving him toward the exit, I wasn't surprised he had finished in record time. Entering the lobby, I found him within seconds, my gaze drawn to him. I smiled as I saw him casually leaning against the wall across the room. He was a good head above most people there and the shirt he had worn for the day could barely contain his well-developed arms and chest. He was a completely different species than any other boy I had known. He was strong and masculine, and his presence demanded everyone's attention. As the grin refused to leave my face, I became certain I wasn't the first girl enthralled by Blake Preston.

He moved away from the wall at my approach and returned my smile. "Are you ready to go?"

"Yes. Did you find something to write your paper on?"

He nodded. "There was a sailboat painting I liked. Figured I could pull some stuff out of my ass and say despite the struggles faced by the crew because of the storm, the artist included sunlight in the distance as a symbol of hope."

"Very profound," I said. "Cheesesteak time?"

"I actually bought you something," Blake said and picked up a shopping bag set on the floor beside him.

I removed it from his hands when he held it out for me. My eyebrows lifted as I noticed the cylinder shape of the package. I looked at the tag on the packaging before giving him a questioning look.

He explained, "They had a poster version of the flower painting you liked. I thought you could hang it up. Maybe get rid of those bare walls you're so fond of." I watched his Adam's apple bob as he tried to bring a little levity to the mood. "You can't hold me accountable for any dirty thoughts I may have when I come over though."

He rendered me speechless and I was desperately trying to put a lid on the emotions wanting to bubble over. My only companion for two years had been fear and anxiety. But Blake was eliciting feelings I had forgotten about. He made me feel like there was a world of possibility open. Blake Preston had managed to get under my skin.

"Thank you," I managed, my eyes dropping to his sneakers. I had so many questions and I wasn't ready for him to see them yet. Were we only friends? Or was every day we spent together leading up to more? For someone who insisted on keeping things platonic, he was becoming the master of changing the rules.

"The museum wasn't as bad as I expected. And now we get to do the *Rocky* movie thing and run up and down the steps outside."

"That's such a touristy thing to do. And it's February. I'd rather just get into your car and crank up the heat."

"You're making me lazy. March is going to be the start of my training. I have to get rid of the beer gut." He tapped his flat stomach for emphasis. "Want to start running with me when it warms up?"

"Sure, I'll go, as long as you aren't opposed to a slow jog. I haven't been running in forever." My lips twisted into a smirk. "You know what I always wanted to do?"

"What?"

"Try pushing one of those pads that look like mannequins. I would always hear the guys grunting during football practice and it looked so easy to me."

"Do you mean the sleds? They're harder than you think."

"I thought it was a defense thing. Do you use them for training?"

"Yup, running backs do drills with them all the time. They

help me practice hitting and running through the line. You'd be surprised how much you learn to hate those things after hours of hitting them over and over again."

"So, can I try it?"

"I'll see what I can arrange," he said. "But before we get back in training mode, let's splurge on those cheesesteaks."

Chapter Ten

I imagined the Philadelphia trip to be a turning point in my relationship with Blake. I mapped out an imaginary progression in my head, culminating in Blake confessing he'd come to care for me, and admitting he wanted to be more than friends. And I *wanted* that to happen. I knew it was risky letting my guard down, but he was the first guy to convince me the benefits outweighed the risks.

But nothing changed. We remained stagnant and despite the signals I tried to send that I wouldn't totally be averse to the idea of kissing, he didn't try to take things further. I questioned if I misread things. Maybe the gift and the late-night visit to my room didn't mean anything. Lexi insisted things weren't all in my head, but she wasn't completely objective. She saw how much I cared for Blake and would try to spare me from hurt feelings.

Lexi told me to take a leap of faith and make the first move. Yet I was terrified he would try to let me down easy. At least in limbo I could pretend the possibility was there. If I told him how I felt and he rejected me, I'd still be forced to see him at least twice a week until the semester ended in May.

Two weeks after the museum trip, the weather began to warm. As soon as the temperature hit sixty degrees, I'd wear sandals until the first snowfall. Instead of going out, I was spending my Friday night working on my pedicure. I had just finished painting my toenails when the phone rang. While screwing the cap back on the white nail polish, I balanced the phone between my shoulder and ear.

"Hi, Mom."

"Hi, hon, I wasn't sure if I'd catch you. No plans tonight?"

I could tell there was something off by her tone but didn't question it right away. My mom would tell me whatever was on her mind as soon as she was ready. Long ago, we had promised each other full disclosure. It hadn't been easy telling her some of the racier things I'd been involved in when partying with Faye and Hunter, but it was necessary for her to fully understand what we'd be up against.

"Not really. I had an early dinner with Lexi and Casey and then came back to the dorm to do my nails. What are you up to?"

"Cleaned the house from top to bottom while trying to gather up the nerve to call you." I heard her take a steadying breath. "I have some bad news."

"What is it?"

"It's about…Thomas Bridges."

I closed my eyes, hating how a single person could cause my blood to run cold by simply hearing his name. My parents and I rarely said his name, even after the arrest. We would refer to Mr. Bridges as *him*, as if he was a non-person and not the man who took everything from me.

"What about him?" I whispered.

"I mean I can't really believe how quickly the time has passed, but since the maximum sentence was only five years, I guess it should be expected…"

"Mom," I interrupted gently. "What are you talking about?"

"He's up for parole. Our lawyer called after his interview with the parole board. They took your victim impact statement into consideration, but since this was his first offense…"

"He's getting out?"

"His release is set for May. I'm so sorry, but I don't want you to think this changes anything. You're still safe. He's not allowed to contact you and he still has to abide by the conditions of his parole or he goes right back to jail."

My mom was still speaking, but my mind was elsewhere. I could feel the old wounds reopening, threatening to bleed me dry. I wanted to weep a river of tears and drown in them. I should've prepared better, but there was no way to get used to the idea that the devil would no longer be in his cage.

"Did you know about the hearing?"

"Yes, but our lawyer said it wasn't likely he would be granted parole. He thought it would be another year or so before it could happen. There are overcrowding issues at the prison he's been serving his sentence, so maybe that had something to do with it."

Or maybe because Mr. Bridges was skilled at making people see what he wanted them to see. I'd been a victim of his deception. Trusting Mr. Bridges had been easy. Appearing nonthreatening was what he did best.

"Hon, you're away at college and the last thing I want is for you to worry. But I'm not sure if the papers are going to pick up on his release and start running stories about the case again. No one knows where you went away to school, just your father and I. You won't be bothered on campus, only the local gossips will be chomping at the bit."

"I'll avoid the local news websites. Last time I went digging online, I didn't see too many flattering articles about me." After a beat, I started, "Mom, I'm sorry for all of this. I ran away and you're still in Newpine dealing with it. Maybe I should've never…"

"Don't you dare, Autumn Dorey. Never say you regret coming forward. If you hadn't spoken up about the things going on in that school, you and every other female student in Newpine would've been at risk." My mother's harsh tone softened when she added, "You did the right thing and I'm proud of you for it. Things were hard for us at first but in all honesty it helped weed out the people who weren't our true friends to begin with. But I know this town doesn't hold the greatest memories for you. That's why I thought we could spend the summer at the shore."

"What about work?"

"I've earned enough days off to spend the summer at the beach with my beautiful and incredible daughter. Your dad may not be able to take off for the entire time, but he'll come down on the weekends and for at least two weeks."

My father worked as an electrical engineer and my mother was a customer service representative for an insurance agency. My dad's schedule could be hectic depending on the size of the project he was working on.

"Isn't that a lot of money to rent a shore house?"

"Not as bad as you think. A lot of the owners are willing to discount the prices if you agree to rent for the entire summer. It saves them the hassle of having to deal with different renters. Besides, when was the last time we've taken an extravagant vacation? I think our last trip was Disney World when you were thirteen. You're in college now and we likely won't have this chance again."

I smiled against the churning feeling in my belly. What would I ever have done without her? I remember thinking of her as an annoyance, an overbearing mother who wanted to constantly know where I was going and who I was with. I owed her and it was the reason I would hold back my tears until I hung up the phone.

"It sounds amazing, Mom."

"Great! I'll email you some houses I've been looking at and you can let me know what you think." Some of the false cheer diminished from her voice as she said, "I understand how hard this is for you. If it were up to me, they would've locked him away forever. But he's out of our lives and you never have to see his worthless hide again."

My heart began to thump erratically and I needed to get off the phone. It became hard for me to speak as a choking sensation locked down on me.

"Thanks, Mom. I'll call you when I get the email of the houses."

Reluctantly, my mom let me off the line. My eyes rested on my dresser. The anti-anxiety medicine was close by, but I hadn't touched it in weeks. It wasn't a mystery why I was beginning to rely on it less. Gradually, I'd been letting go, believing I could be normal again. I had become the director of a romantic screenplay starring Blake and myself. It had been playing on a loop in my head, but I should've known my past was inescapable.

"Fuck," I cursed and slammed my hand against the wall. My palm burned and I shook it out to relieve the pain. I told my mother Lexi would be home soon, but the truth was she had left for the weekend after dinner. She was visiting Finn's family for the first time. It was unfortunate timing, because in all honesty, I could've used a friend at that moment. I was ready to tell her everything. I hated the burden of keeping all of my emotions bottled up.

I liked Casey, but we weren't close enough to exchange confidences. We talked about the ups and downs with her boyfriend and how hard it was to be in a long-distance relationship. We also had a few laughs when we dissected episodes of *The Bachelor* or exchanged celebrity gossip. But that was as deep as it got.

I dialed Blake and hung up once his voicemail picked up. I wasn't going to tell him about Mr. Bridges, but I wanted to see what his plans were for the night. I'd be willing to spend hours getting lost in video games with him and Darien as long as it provided a distraction.

I tried not to think about it, but I began to wonder what it would be like for Mr. Bridges to be free and live a normal life again. Would his family welcome him back? Teaching was out of the question, but would he find another job and start over? Maybe there would be another girl like me. Another girl who would think she was the one in control, the one who held all the power over him. Then he would rip the floor out from under her and she'd be left broken in irreparable ways.

I cried for hours, sobbing until my head ached and my tear ducts were emptied out. I was mourning the loss of the Autumn who would never be. The one who didn't always have to run and could stand her ground. Because as nice as it was for my mom to offer up a shore house for the summer, it was just another exit strategy for me.

After plunging the room into absolute darkness, I curled up in my bed. Although I could hear the sounds of everyone in the dorm through the walls, I felt alone. I had fooled myself into believing college would heal the scars. No one could truly completely start over. Even if I moved across the world, hearing the name Thomas Bridges would still revert me to a sobbing heap on the floor.

I called the stronger part of my personality forward—the part of me that took control when the weight of my pain was more than I could take. Could I do anything to change the parole board's mind? Maybe I should've been an active part of getting Mr. Bridges to pay for his crimes, but I'd been shielded for most of the process. Neither my parents nor I had wanted to go through a messy trial and a plea bargain deal had been reached. Five years had sounded like enough at the time. But did a couple of years erase the horror I felt every time I closed my eyes and saw his sharp features looming above me?

I drifted in and out of sleep until a sharp knock at the door made me sit up in bed. I debated whether or not to answer, knowing who it was without having to look through the peephole. I thought about ignoring Blake, but I had been the one to call him. However, it was after two in the morning and Blake wasn't at my room to cheer me up. He was here to crash after another night of debauchery. By Blake's regular schedule of heavy drinking, I was thinking how wrong I'd been to assume I was the one with serious issues.

Swinging open the door, I kept my scowl firmly in place. Blake stumbled back from the sudden movement and set his hand on the doorframe to steady him. Before he could say anything, I demanded, "What the hell are you doing here? I'm not your sponsor."

"I have to talk to you. I need to tell you something and there's no way I'll spit it out if I'm sober."

He was worse off than I anticipated. His eyes were glazed and I was afraid he would face-plant if he let go of the doorframe. "How much did you drink tonight?"

Holding up his thumb and his forefinger for emphasis, he said, "Just a bit. Don made his own moonshine and I may have gotten a little carried away."

"What do you want?"

"Can I come in? I don't want to have this conversation in the middle of the hallway."

"No," I said firmly and held my hands out in front of me when he lifted a foot to take a step forward. "It's not a good night. Find whoever dropped you off and get a ride home. Call me when you're not about to puke on my floor."

"Autumn..." he sighed. As he trailed off, his eyes sharpened and he stared at me until I grew self-conscious and shifted side to side. "Were you crying?"

I turned my head away from him. "Yes, and my tolerance for your bullshit is at an all-time low tonight. I don't know how you got the idea you have an open invitation to come to my dorm room whenever you like. It's rude to me and would be annoying as hell to my roommate if she was here."

"Do you want to talk about why you were crying?"

"No."

"Do you really want me to leave?"

I opened my mouth to send him away, but the words became stuck. Inexplicably, I didn't want him to leave. Being alone would force me back under the covers to wallow about Mr. Bridges. But what could Blake offer me? I wanted to use Blake to forget, but that would be a dangerous game to play. How far would I be willing to go to wipe Mr. Bridges completely from my brain?

An errant hiccup escaped against my will and before I knew it, my tears had returned. I hadn't wanted to cry in front of Blake. But I was so tired of being alone. I never wanted this life. I never wanted to be on guard all of the time and overly cautious about who I chose to let in. Maybe Blake wasn't perfect, but he was *there*.

"Come in," I managed and stepped aside. I closed the door once he passed me. Instead of turning, I pressed my forehead against the door and tried to rein in the tears. I had been doing so well for weeks, not feeling the suffocation of my despair. I was certain Mr. Bridges would revel in my state, triumphant I'd given him so much control over my life.

Blake's arms slipped around my waist and I stumbled backwards. Crashing into his hard chest, I straightened up. I wiped at my tears and whispered, "I'm sorry. I'm fine, really…"

"Come here," he said into my ear. The lights were still off and he gently pulled on my waist to lead me away from the door and closer to the bed.

"Where?"

"To bed." I stiffened and he added, "I'm not going to try anything, I promise."

Could I believe Blake's promises? Although I had categorized him as cut from the same cloth as Hunter, it wasn't true. Blake wasn't perfect, but he also wasn't another monster I had to be scared of. If he told me he wouldn't try anything, I trusted him to stand by his words.

He climbed into my bed, a shadowy figure illuminated only by the building's exterior lighting shining through the curtains.

He pulled me down with him while he pressed his back against the wall to make room on the small bed. The mattress was an extra-long twin and Blake's size made it impossible for us not to be pressed against one another. He removed his shoes and the only sound in the room was the plop as they fell against the linoleum floor.

His right hand stayed on my waist and I leaned my head against his chest. His body heat was comforting and his close proximity eased my sorrow. I thought it would be awkward to lie in bed with Blake, but at the moment it felt perfectly normal. I felt selfish to not push him away. I was a mess and my heart couldn't take much more. Having unreciprocated feelings for Blake was only adding to my already fragile state.

But I needed him more than I would ever admit to anyone. I breathed in his rich masculine scent and tried to draw comfort from it. I wouldn't have minded remaining silent, next to Blake's reassuring presence. My anxiety was easing and I could picture falling into a dreamless slumber. But Blake's voice was anxious as he asked, "What's wrong? Why were you crying?"

His tone sounded guilty and a hysterical giggle almost passed my lips. I wanted to laugh at his conceit, tell him his ego was truly inflated if he believed he was the cause of my heartache. Not being the object of Blake's affection paled in comparison to what it felt like to know my tormentor was going to be released from prison.

"I don't want to talk about it." My tone was firm and if he pushed it, he'd have to go. "What did you come to tell me?"

"It's not important now." The shame was still heavy in his voice and I didn't know what he felt so bad about telling me. Maybe he was dating someone? He hadn't mentioned anyone since Kaylee, but I avoided talking about his love life. I had been dropping hints about how I liked him more than a friend, so maybe he was feeling guilty and had come to let me down gently. "Autumn, you can tell me anything. I swear I'm not going to judge you…"

"Judge me? What are you talking about?"

"I mean that whatever you say to me won't change anything between us. We're friends and I want to know everything about you. Whatever has you upset, you can talk to me about…"

I didn't let him finish. "I can't, Blake. I just want to turn my brain off for a few hours and not even think about it."

Blake took a long minute to reply. His face softened and his eyes searched mine. "Okay. Just try to relax and I'll be here when you wake up. I honestly only want to be your friend."

He pulled me closer to him and I burrowed into the softness of his sweater. He sounded so sincere and I wanted to reassure him I did understand what he was saying. But the problem was I didn't want only to be his friend.

Chapter Eleven

Lazily, I stretched my arms out and hit my elbow into the wall. I winced as I forced one eye open at a time. It wasn't a wall I knocked into, but Blake's abs as he slumbered next to me. His arm was draped across my body and I shifted, trying to move without waking him. The only thing I accomplished by my squirming was being greeted by a part of Blake I had yet to meet.

"Oh god," I squeaked as Blake mumbled in his sleep and pulled me in closer. At some point during the night, he had removed his pants and the only thing standing between me and his seven-inch (eight-inch?) erect penis was a thin layer of cotton.

Although I was a virgin, I had gone far enough with Hunter to know the basics of the male anatomy. And I was bursting with curiosity over what Blake looked like down below. I stealthily lifted up the blanket and tried to see beneath the covers to make out the shape of him straining against the seam in his boxers. If I were bold, I'd reach underneath the blanket and give him an extra good morning. I tilted my head lower and squinted to see if I could have a better look.

"What are you doing?"

"Oh crap! You startled me!" I slammed the blanket back down and climbed into a sitting position with my back pressed against the headboard. I was certain my face was the color of an eggplant as I avoided looking at Blake. I could feel his eyes watching me.

I finally looked over at him as he sat up in bed and ran his fingers through his hair. He had a cowlick in the back and it was adorable how his hair stuck up at odd angles despite his best efforts. I watched him swallow roughly before appraising me with apprehension clear in his eyes. "I have the worst hangover in the world and honestly things are a little blurry for me about last night. Did we…"

"No, of course not," I broke in. It hadn't been awkward last night, but now it felt mortifying to be alone in bed together. What if something had happened? By the stricken look on his face when he asked, I guessed it would've been something he regretted.

And what the hell was wrong with my brain? How did the boy next to me have the capacity to make me forget my hellish night and wake up full of desire and need?

"My pants…"

I looked around the room and saw his jeans lying at the base of the bed next to his shoes. "Over there," I pointed. "I guess you took them off while I was asleep."

"I'm sorry, I don't remember." He must've picked up on my discomfort because he attempted to lighten his tone. "At least I didn't strip down completely in the middle of the night. That has happened before."

I turned away as he dressed and tried to think of something witty to say, but I was at a loss. After the news I received the night before, the last thing I should've been distracted by was the half-naked man who had slept in my bed. But Blake had found a way to pull me out of my cold and despondent state and make me feel warm again.

After he dressed, he sank back down on the bed. His thigh brushed against my own and I felt heat everywhere. My mind kept drifting back to how minutes ago I'd been lusting over

Blake's body—picturing the ways I'd touch him. When I was with him, I felt like I would be able to live again. Maybe it was time to silence the inner voice telling me not to risk my heart with Blake and see what it would be like to kiss him.

I felt Blake's burning stare and I leveled my gaze on him. His eyes were gorgeous and I always felt caught off guard when I took him in fully. His lashes were thick with the tiniest traces of gold in them and the shade matched his sun-kissed skin. My eyes followed a line down from his eyes, past the day-old stubble on his cheeks to his lips. His mouth was full and sexy and his lips looked soft and inviting. I leaned in and waited for him to make the move. As the seconds ticked by, I realized my mistake. There wasn't burning attraction in his expression but a deep wariness.

Swinging my head away, I tried to temper the blush igniting my cheeks. How could I read things so completely wrong? I knew Blake had said we were only friends over and over again, but it hadn't explained the reason he pursued spending so much time with me. We ate together after class and he invited me to go places with him outside of school. Maybe wishing for our arrangement to be more than it was had been my fault. History was always repeating and I was fated to misread signals again and again.

"Autumn, I think I messed up. I shouldn't have come over here last night. I was drinking and I saw you called as I was leaving. It won't happen again."

He hung his head down low and my heart hurt over the dejected look on his face. My fingertips reached over and brushed the rough skin of his cheek. "Do you not like me? Is it an attraction thing?"

He shook his head and seemed annoyed by my question. "Don't do that. Don't look for ways to get me to say how beautiful you are."

"I'm not," I snapped, my temper flaring up. "It's just I know you see a lot of girls and I'm wondering why you're so against the idea of kissing me. Figured I would check to see why I don't meet your *standards*."

Blake jumped off the bed and glared down at me. "Autumn, you're acting like the same people you claim to hate. You're making assumptions about me based on what people at school say. I'm not the type of guy to run around hooking up with girls and bragging about it."

He shamed me and I bit down on my lip hard. He was right. Who was I to judge him or the girls he dated? I was embarrassed by his rejection and lashed out because of it. Besides a few vague references to Laura and Kaylee, Blake didn't tell me much about his love life. "You're right, I thought I was above the rumor mill. Obviously I'm not."

"I'm not trying to be an ass here. I may have given you shit about Josh, but if you're looking to get involved with someone, he's the right kind of guy for you. We're not good for each other."

"Why? Is it because I look like your ex?"

I felt the air whoosh out of the room and he stumbled back in surprise over my question. "What? Where would you get that idea?"

"You were staring me down at that party and said later I reminded you of someone. It didn't sound like a favorable comparison so I assumed it was an ex-girlfriend."

"You're nothing like her," he said and I saw him glancing at the wall behind me. I turned and we both sat in silence staring at the poster he had bought from the museum. "I'm a goddamn mess and if you got involved with me, it would be a fucking disaster. I can't give you half of what you deserve."

"So, it's you then?"

"If you knew everything about me, you'd be running as far away from me as humanly possible."

"Tell me and let me decide for myself."

My past was checkered with mistakes and maybe he would feel differently about me when he found out. If he opened up, maybe I could reciprocate and let him in. Personal histories could be messy, but maybe sharing our secrets could bring us closer. I didn't want him to walk out, because he gave me hope—hope I could be normal one day. It felt good to be curled into his side and to feel safe once again.

Judging by the look on Blake's face, he likened opening up to me to undergoing open-heart surgery without anesthesia. I was disappointed in him and angry for putting myself in this situation. I was latching onto the first man who had made me feel like I wasn't a freak incapable of affection. Where could a relationship with Blake possibly lead? We didn't even have a solid foundation of friendship to build on.

"You should leave," I announced at his silent refusal to tell me anything about himself. How did things take a drastic turn in the past fifteen minutes? I had imagined a morning full of passionate kisses and desperate embraces and instead somehow ended up throwing Blake out after his unexpected rejection.

"I'm a coward," he said, "and as much as you deserve to know the truth about me, I can't tell you. I like you and I can't stand the idea of you thinking I'm a piece of garbage."

My headache from the night before had returned in full force. For once, I was going to listen to him and believe our relationship would end up being destructive. "Just leave then. If you think I need to stay away from you, then go and don't come back here again. Don't call me either."

"This sucks. I've never…"

"Please, Blake. Don't make me sit here and listen to you fumble through another apology while telling me I'd be better off without you because you're such an asshole. Fine, you win. You can leave here knowing what a complete douche I think you are. You sent me mixed signals and I refuse to believe everything I'd been feeling was all in my head." Blake tapped his foot as I spoke. When he didn't move or respond, I added, "You need to go now."

Finally, he turned on his heel and stalked to the door. I

refused to cry as I watched him rush out of the room. I flinched as the door closed behind him and I fought the urge to call him back and smooth things over. But I decided to say to hell with that idea. I didn't get his endgame and why the sudden change of heart. He had been the one to seek me out and invite me to spend more and more time with him. If he had been so worried about me hating him, why did he allow us to get so close? His behavior was inexplicable and I felt like I was missing a huge piece of the Blake puzzle. *But I was done*. I'd see Blake in class, but otherwise I would pretend like he didn't exist.

***

"Blake keeps looking over here. Should I give him the finger?" Casey joked and crunched into her apple.

"No, we're pretending he doesn't exist."

Casey studied me as she took another bite. "Did he try to talk to you in class?"

I shook my head. I now dreaded art history and it pissed me off because it was one of my favorite subjects. My stomach roiled every time I walked across campus to the arts building. I had found an empty seat across the room from Blake and taken up residence there since our falling out. By the third class in my new seat, Laura had laid claim on my old spot next to Blake.

Other than a text apology from Blake the day of our fight, we hadn't spoken. I replied back to leave me alone and lose my number. He had waved in class, but otherwise he didn't attempt to break down the invisible barriers I surrounded myself with since he told me he would ruin me. Maybe I did need to protect myself against Blake and after my experience with self-important men, I'd be a fool to not take his warnings seriously.

But there was no denying Blake was different. For all of the noise he made about being bad for me, I never saw anything to give me pause and cause me to feel afraid of him. He definitely had issues with drinking and apparently some horrible past he kept alluding to, but he'd treated me with respect and I usually had a lot of fun with him.

"Are you sure you're telling me everything? I did see him go into your room in the middle of the night. I would totally take advantage of the fact you have a single with Lexi practically living with Finn. She lucked out getting a boyfriend without a roommate." Casey's face lit up. "Now that I broke up with Jason, maybe I could borrow your room some nights?"

"No way, I don't want you to bring some dudes back to my room and soil my blankets."

"I could use Lexi's bed." Her eyebrows waggled up and down. "I swear Molly never leaves our room. She has a more dull social life than you."

"Thanks, Casey," I mumbled and bit into my sandwich. It was a struggle to not avert my gaze to Blake's. I didn't know what I was trying to prove by eating in the cafeteria when I knew he came here after our class. It was the same reason I resumed classes my senior year after the Mr. Bridges incident. I hadn't gone to classes for the remainder of my junior year, but held onto the conviction I'd return fearless. Like back then, I wanted it to be known that no one could break me.

Casey's schedule worked out where she could meet me to eat before she went to her afternoon classes. "We're single and smoking hot freshman. We should be going out every night and earning new notches on our bedposts."

"I think that's a guy thing."

She waved me off. "I'm a modern woman. I've been with the same guy since I was fourteen. I tried to make it work, but if we're meant to be together, it will happen. For now, I want to try someone new on for size." She smirked and added, "If you and Blake aren't a thing…"

"You just want me to get into a girl fight with you over him."

"Can we do it now? I'll accidentally rip your shirt off and get him all hot and bothered. He'll be crying into his Cheerios over how he was a bastard to you."

"Thanks, but I'm done with Blake's bullshit."

"Are you sure? I wouldn't normally put up with a guy who jerks me around, but for that ass I might reconsider my policy."

"His moods are all over the place. He could be the funniest and sweetest guy one minute and then suddenly become super intense and withdrawn."

Casey heaved a sigh. "All the hot ones in college are crazy. I haven't met one normal good-looking guy since we got here. They are either super-possessive creeps or narcissistic losers with zero personality."

"I'm not sure if Blake falls into those categories, but maybe things happen for a reason. I didn't think I wanted to date, but maybe if the right guy comes along, I'd be open to it."

Blake couldn't be the only one able to defrost my lustful cravings. Josh and I didn't have any sexual chemistry, but Blake at least showed me the interest was still there. At least Mr. Bridges hadn't obliterated everything in his wake.

"Let's go out this weekend. We'll party hop and see if anyone catches your eye."

"You just warned me about how awful college guys are."

"We won't pick super-hot guys to talk to. We'll choose the marginally good-looking ones. They may eventually get a paunch and lose their hair, but at least they won't be calling us for bail money in six months."

I chuckled and then snuck a glance toward Blake. He was sitting with a few other players from the team we had seen before when eating together. I still felt the pull when I looked at him, but as time passed I was sure it would lessen. I was too smart to fall back into old patterns, but it didn't mean I couldn't go out and have fun with my new college friends.

"Okay, when do you want to go out?"

"How about Friday? My friend Amy is a sophomore with a car and she was planning to drive. I think the Football House is having a party, but we can skip it and go somewhere else."

"It doesn't matter. If Amy is driving, I'm not going to dictate where we can and can't go."

"It's fine. I think Sig Chi is having a party too. We'll stop by there and if it's lame, we'll move on." Casey tugged on one of her blond curls and her face brightened as she planned our night. "We're going to have so much fun, Autumn, I promise. By the end of the night, you'll be like who the hell is Blake Preston?"

Chapter Twelve

"You're Blake Preston's girl, right?"

"What?" I asked, appalled. "No."

The guy shrugged and slunk away without another word. Since we arrived at the party, it felt like a line had been painted around me that no man dared to cross. I thought going to a party that wasn't at the Football House would help me step away from Blake. But apparently, the men of Sig Chi were good friends with him and several other guys on the team.

At some point during our acquaintance, I'd apparently been linked to Blake. Although I insisted we weren't together, no one wanted to be accused of stepping into Blake's territory. If I'd been a casual fling, I had a feeling it would be fine. Since Blake and I had been seen together for several weeks, it was assumed I meant more than a casual hookup. They couldn't be further from the truth.

Casey ran up to me breathless. She'd been dancing and drinking for hours and I'd been keeping an eye out for her. None of the guys at the party had held her interest and she floated around for most of the night. She was the one to give me a heads-up on the Blake brand after I noticed the strange behavior of the frat brothers.

The house was larger than the Football House, but with a similar three-floor layout. It was loud and crowded, but I still

felt apart from it all. I had to keep giving myself a mental shake
to try and make an effort.

"*Fucking Blake Preston,*" Casey sneered and collapsed
against me. "You look gorgeous and that prick has ruined my
efforts."

Casey had decided it was makeover time for both of us and
we spent hours dressing for the party. I had told her she was
smoking crack when she tried to put me in a skirt, so she settled
on a pair of jeans I owned and one of her tops. It was a red top
with a scoop neckline and a back plunging below my shoulders.
I wanted to keep my hair low-key, but Casey styled it in a low
ponytail while adding textured waves. The style looked simple,
but she had me sit like a statue forever as she added volumizing
spray, styling mousse, and super-hold hairspray to perfect the
look. She was also good at applying makeup and we shared the
same shade of bronze eye shadow and scarlet lipstick.

Casey's friend Amy danced over to us and grabbed the
water bottle out of my hand. Taking a long chug, she said, "This
party is lame. Let's blow it off and get some food at the diner."

Amy and I had hit it off and I caught us rolling our eyes in
sync with Casey's outlandish remarks. Casey's relationship
ending had changed her and she was ready to explore what she
felt she'd been missing. Although I teased her, her fearlessness
was enviable.

"Fine by me," I agreed.

"No way. There has to be someone here halfway decent."
Casey moved her head side to side. Finally, she stopped and
turned back to me with a sly smile. "What's that guy's name
who lives on the other side of the hall and orders Chinese food
like every night?"

"Will?"

"Yeah, don't you talk to him sometimes?"

"Not really. He sometimes asks me if I want to order with
him. Apparently the place he calls only delivers if you order a
twenty-dollar minimum."

"Well, maybe he wants to see your takeout menu tonight."

"That's the dumbest innuendo I ever heard."

"Whatever, Autumn. He's over by the staircase. At least say hi to him before we go." She pushed me off before I could protest further.

Somewhere along the way I'd become uncomfortable in my own skin and the idea of flirting was a completely foreign concept. I made my way over to Will and felt more at ease when I noticed his welcoming smile.

"Hey, Autumn, I thought that was you and Casey. What's going on?"

"Nothing really. How are you?"

"I'm all right. Been studying for midterms all week. I've been barely pulling a C in my chemistry class and I'm a bio major."

I made a sympathetic face. Will definitely fell in line with Casey's requirements for the men we should look for. He wasn't going to make me quiver with need after a single look, but he had a boyishly handsome face, with white blond hair and wide-set brown eyes. His smile was nice and he had a faint southern accent. As we began to commiserate about the difficulty of our classes, I realized how nice it was to turn down the intensity and have a normal conversation with a cute guy. We'd never exchanged more than a few words as I told him my Chinese food order and I was opening myself up to learning more about him. Within a few minutes of talking, I had found out he was the son of two schoolteachers who relocated from North Carolina to Maryland when he was in middle school. I began to give him my standard background information when I felt Casey knock against me.

"Autumn, we need to leave," she hissed in my ear.

"Hi, Casey," Will said.

Casey nodded a greeting, but kept her focus on me. "I'm serious, we have to go now."

"Why?" Leave it to Casey to interrupt me when I started

talking to the one guy who hadn't treated me like I had the plague.

"Blake just got here and…he's not alone."

It took an effort, but I thought I succeeded at keeping a neutral expression. "So?"

"The Football House party got broken up early and a few of the guys came over. I saw him in the kitchen with a girl. The way she was hanging on him made it clear she was staking her claim for the night."

"I don't care," I ground out. Will looked uncomfortable while I wished I had a gag to shove in Casey's mouth. I appreciated the heads-up, but subtlety was not her strong suit. "Honestly, Blake and I were only friends. I'm not upset he's here with someone." I shot a smile I hoped was encouraging to Will, but by his expression, it probably came out looking deranged.

"Great!" Casey backed away. "Well, I'll leave you two alone then. Come and find me if you want to take off." Before turning back toward the throng of people, Casey gave me a meaningful look, conveying her happiness over my ability to move on.

"Are you and Casey close?"

I noticed Will watching Casey long after she left us. She rejoined Amy and they had their heads together, talking closely. His smile was shy as he watched her throw her head back, her laughter carrying over to where we stood.

"Yes. She makes me laugh and although she can come off as tough, she has a really big heart. I've been kind of down lately and she and my roommate have really helped me take my mind off of things."

"She has a boyfriend, right?"

"No, they broke up." The longing look on his face was all the convincing it took to see I wouldn't be the one set up for the night.

I was about to motion Casey back over when the feeling of

being watched diverted my attention. Every hair on the back of my neck prickled and I sighed, knowing an inevitable stare-down was about to take place. I was reminded of how Blake and I first met and wondered if we had come full circle as he likely shot daggers at me across the room. Refusing to let him interrupt my night any further, I looked expectantly at Will. "If you're interested, I could talk to her for you."

His cheeks colored. "I don't think I'm Casey's type."

"You'd be surprised."

"Were you meeting up with Blake? It looks like he's trying to get your attention."

"No. What's the deal with this school and him anyway? We're in college, why does everyone give a shit about who Blake's involved with?"

Will's eyes doubled in size. "Because he's the only reason our football team isn't a bunch of scrubs. They lost more games than they won before he started playing. He's sort of a celebrity around here."

"It's a sad state of affairs in our culture when being good at football gives him a god-like status at this school."

"I thought you liked him."

I inched forward and asked in a conspiratorial whisper, "Have you ever been screwed over by a girl? And then forced to see her move on? That's how it feels right now for me."

Will nodded. "That sucks. But think about how it must feel for her." He looked discreetly over my shoulder before meeting my eyes. "She's trying everything to get his attention and he can't be bothered. I really doubt anyone could be clumsy enough to drop a purse so many times in the span of five minutes."

I laughed. "I think I'll probably take Casey up on that offer to leave early. But don't worry, I'll talk you up the entire ride home."

He reached over and took my hand in his. He gave a gentle squeeze. I looked down at our hands intertwined and shot him a questioning look. He shrugged. "I was just thinking how much better it would've felt to have someone with me when I ran into the one who screwed me over."

"You *really* want me to put in a good word."

"Well, I thought it was a lost cause, but if she's single now…"

"I'll give you an insider tip. If you ask her out, don't suggest Chinese food—she hates it. Offer to take her out for Mexican food and she'll love you forever."

"You're the best," he said. I was surprised when he abruptly dropped my hand. But I caught on quick when a familiar scent assaulted me from behind.

"Hi, do you mind if I steal Autumn for a minute?" The mixture of Blake's woodsy cologne and citrusy deodorant intoxicated me when he moved in closer. His natural musk also created a longing that started deep in my belly and spread the more I breathed him in. His interruption caused an unwanted reaction in my body I wished I could subdue.

"Sure," Will replied quickly.

My jaw went slack as I started at how quickly my savior deserted me. "Seriously?" I had thought we shared a moment and Will was handing me off without a backwards glance.

At least he had the decency to look contrite. "Sorry, but he asked nicely. Besides, I help run the school's sportsbook. Don't want to do anything to mess up the spread for next year."

"I swear I need to transfer to a new school." I swung to face Blake. "What do you want?"

"Can I talk to you alone?" When I didn't answer, he added, "It will only take a sec."

I nodded and steeled myself. He was dressed in layers with a T-shirt and a hooded gray sweatshirt over it. His black pants molded perfectly to his body and I had to admit he looked incredible in everything he wore. He could put on a Hawaiian shirt and plaid shorts and still find a way to make it work.

Blake tilted his chin toward the stairway. "I'm friends with one of the guys who lives here. He won't mind if we talk in his

\room."

I rolled my eyes because I already knew about his tight friendships with the men of Sig Chi. I followed him up the stairs into the quiet section of the house. A few of the rooms were occupied, but the bass from below was muffled on the top level. A guy wearing a Sig Chi T-shirt came out of one of the bedrooms. He nodded to Blake before heading downstairs. Blake came to a vacated bedroom to the left of the stairwell and switched on the lights before entering. The room was sparsely furnished with a twin bed, desk, and dresser.

"How have you been?" Blake asked and stayed on his feet in the center of the room. I remained by the door and didn't close it after passing through.

I mulled over my reply for a second before asking, "Is that what you needed to talk to me in private about?"

"No, but we haven't talked in weeks and I wanted to see how you were. You told me to leave you alone and I was trying to respect that."

"Then what are we doing up here?"

Blake stared at the ceiling. "I miss hanging out with you. I screwed up that morning and I want to fix things between us."

"But why?" I clarified, "You've been telling me over and over again how you're bad for me and I'll end up hating you eventually. Why should I waste any more time on you if I'm only going to be hurt at the end?"

Blake's eyes clouded over. "This probably doesn't make much sense, but I've always done what's expected of me. And hurting you just seemed to be the direction I was heading whether or not I wanted to."

"You're right, it doesn't make sense to me."

Blake had such a strange look on his face and I felt more than ever I wasn't the only one with baggage. It was likely part of his draw—finding another human being who was as damaged as I was.

"When we met for the first time, I thought it was inevitable for me to hurt you. I figured the more time we spent together, the more likely it was you'd uncover all the bad shit everyone else in my life refuses to see." His smile was weak. "But you called me on everything. When I was an asshole, you told me. You had no problem admitting you didn't give two shits about how good I was at catching a ball. No one else does that and I liked it."

"But what bad shit is there, Blake?"

"I feel like I'm ready to explode at any given moment. Like the pressure from my family and the team is going to make me crack. Sometimes, it takes so much effort to not give in. I went through a period where I was always picking fights and playing football was the only time I felt calm enough to function."

"But what are you so angry about?"

"About my dad mostly." I made a sympathetic noise in the back of my throat. Although he was a baby when his father died, it must've been hard never knowing his dad. "I love my mom and she's done her best, but she's a lot to deal with. She's always pushing me and thinks football is going to be our way out of financial hell. I don't think she realizes going pro is something that may never happen."

"You don't like playing football?"

"I do, but it was better when I could think of it as a game. Ever since we started running into these money problems, she's become like a warped version of a stage mom. I got a concussion last year and she rode me until I was back on the field."

Meeting his mother just jumped on the list of things I never wanted to do. My parents were the exact opposite and I sympathized with how hard it must be to be thrust into the role as a breadwinner at twenty-one years old.

"Just because you're pissed off about certain aspects of your life, it doesn't mean you're going to screw up all of your relationships. I think you're relying too much on the concept of manifest destiny."

"What's that?"

"It's the idea your future is certain. You're your own person, Blake. You've never shown me this darker side and if it's there, you have it under control. I get pissed off at the world sometimes and want to lash out, but I don't think it makes me a bad person." I hesitated, but then took a step to close the gap between us. "You're funny and nice and you have a lot of friends that would do anything for you. I'm your friend too."

The relationship drama aside, I did want to be his friend. Blake was showing his vulnerability and I understood he was doing it to mend what had been broken between us. I was starting to understand him a little better. I wasn't a stranger to feeling the pressures of the outside world. Blake didn't have the easy life everyone suspected and it stirred up so many emotions inside of me.

"About that morning…"

I laced my fingers in front of me and swayed from side to side. "We really don't have to talk about it. I misread things and overreacted because my feelings were hurt. We can pretend it never happened."

"Autumn, I was telling you the truth. You deserve much better than what I have to offer." I didn't reply and waited as he cleared his throat. "But what if you're right and I'm not fated to be this fuck-up? What if I could change and be the guy you deserve?"

My head shot up and I looked up at him in disbelief. "But you've been telling me over and over again we were just friends."

"I've tried so hard to stay away and I said things to make it seem like I didn't have feelings for you. But if I could tell you one absolute truth right now it would be I've thought about kissing you every single day we've spent together." He smiled wryly. "And maybe on the days I didn't see you too."

My lips parted but I was unable to form a response. My heart leapt into my throat and my body shook with relief. Blake had been holding back his feelings and everything I felt over the last couple of months hadn't been all one-sided. He had been careful with my heart and it was another point proving he wasn't the man he thought he was. I didn't agree with how he tried to stop me from falling for him, but I believed wholeheartedly his actions were his warped way of protecting me.

My chest felt tight as he stepped forward and completely closed the space between us. His fingers caressed my cheek before he ran his thumb across my lips. "Can I kiss you, Autumn Dorey?"

He didn't know how perfect he was making the moment for me. We were in a rundown frat house and he had turned our first kiss into something amazing I would remember forever. Because he was *asking*. Blake wasn't plundering my lips as if it was his right; he was giving the choice to me.

"Yes," I breathed and lifted up onto my toes. I closed my eyes and seconds later Blake's lips were on mine. I had been kissed before, but kissing Blake was incomparable. Although his lips remained on my mouth, I felt his kiss everywhere. He ignited my body and I never wanted him to pull away. His lips were soft and the kiss sweet. With Blake's reputation, I expected more tongue and more aggression. I had made so many wrong assumptions about this guy—because he knew exactly the way to kiss me that would leave me weak in the knees.

I didn't know who pulled away first. I leaned into him and set my ear against his chest. His arms wrapped around my back and he rested his chin on top of my forehead. He felt solid against my body and it felt like I finally found someone who would get me. I had been ostracized, and living on my own felt like the only way I could be safe. But the amazing thing was being in Blake's arms didn't steal away my security blanket. Being with him gave me the sense I'd been wrong to shut away my heart. It erased the last lingering doubts I had about Blake being good for me.

His right hand worked its way up and down my back in a steady rhythm. His hand stopped at my mid-back before moving its way up to the center of my shoulder blades. The way his fingers moved over my skin was gentle, like he had a sixth sense over exactly the way to touch me.

He pecked the top of my head. "You have goose bumps. Why don't you take my sweatshirt?"

I untangled myself from his arms as he pulled the sweatshirt over his head. His T-shirt lifted with the movement and I tried not to drool as I saw his abs peek out. The goose bumps weren't from the cold, but I took the sweatshirt from his hands. He watched me as I put it on, swimming in the fabric. I rolled up the sleeves. His expression was pleased as he appraised me. "It looks good on you."

I quirked an eyebrow and pursed my lips. "I think my shirt looked better."

"It did," he laughed. "Maybe I want to keep all of your hotness to myself."

I pressed a quick kiss on his lips. "Claiming me already? I was the one who had to hear you came to the party with someone."

He looked genuinely confused and I was pleased. I liked Blake, but I understood I wasn't the only one. "I didn't *come* to the party with Tori. She hopped in Darien's car when we left the Football House. She's been glued to my side, but I let her know I wasn't interested." He grabbed my elbows and pulled me in closer. "I'm interested in someone else."

"And your sudden interest didn't happen to come from seeing me talk to another guy?"

"No, although it did suck. Especially since I know Will and he's a good guy. Makes it hard to think about punching him in the face." His expression turned earnest. "I was scared, Autumn, and I wanted to do the right thing. I've been miserable these past couple of weeks. So much that Darien has nicknamed me SSS—sad sack of shit. But when I saw you here tonight, the only thought running through my head was I may be a disaster, but the real tragedy would be if I never gave us a chance at working out."

I kissed him and infused my kiss with every shared sentiment I felt. I wanted him like no other and I was grateful for the chance to rediscover dormant feelings. Because feeling nothing was a fate no one should be tortured with. Kissing Blake was adding Technicolor to my black-and-white existence. I had friends and school, but love was never a possibility. My heart wasn't ready for love yet; it had too many locks guarding it. But the feelings Blake was bringing to the surface made me wonder if he would be the one to uncage my heart for good.

Chapter Thirteen

"Want to hit the library to study today?" Lexi asked as she gathered up her books into her backpack.

I paused as I brushed my teeth. "Maybe later. I'm meeting Blake in an hour to run the track."

"Brr. I know spring break is next week, but it feels like Mother Nature has forgotten to catch up." Lexi started searching under her bed for her shoes. She frowned when she pulled out a mismatched pair and began searching again. "So how is Mr. Preston treating my lovely roommate?"

"Good," I said and smoothed my hair into a ponytail. "Almost too good."

"What do you mean? I thought things were great since the party."

"They were." I shook my head. "They are. We have so much fun together and he's been really focused on getting back in shape and eating healthy again. And thankfully the drinking episodes seem to be behind him."

"Then why do you not sound happy?"

"I just thought he'd be more interested in the…" I paused, grasping for the right word. "…physical part of our relationship."

"Like sex?"

"I'm not saying I want to have sex, I mean I haven't even

told him I'm a virgin yet. But he's very…restrained when we're alone together."

"How so?"

"We've been alone together a few nights this week and the furthest we've gone is he accidentally grazed my boob with his arm. I guess I expected…"

"That Blake's super-stud reputation would have you butt naked in ten seconds flat?" Lexi prompted.

"Not exactly, but I'm not opposed to exploring things more with him. I'm just wondering what's holding him back. I don't want to look for problems that aren't there…"

"Which you probably are. Don't self-sabotage. I might've had doubts about Blake, but he's good for you." Lexi slipped on a pair of boots and stood up. "Look, you told him about how the guys at your high school were assholes and harassed you. And he knows you haven't dated since coming to college. I'm positive Blake is driven mad with desire every time he looks at you, but he's trying to be considerate."

"I'm not trying to self-sabotage. Blake is starting to mean so much to me, I don't want to be blindsided if it doesn't work out." I put on a pair of gloves and added, "My ex Hunter seemed like such a good guy at first. But he was anything but."

"Blake's not like Hunter and if he was you wouldn't be complaining about his lack of grabby hands. Relationships progress differently and for you I think it would be smart to take it slow."

Lexi made sense, but it was hard to explain what it was like for me. After years of being sexually repressed, I wanted to explore my desires. It wasn't that I required a partner to satisfy my needs, but I had a feeling it would be a lot more enjoyable if Blake were the one with his hands on me.

"I'm so freaking neurotic about this boy. What is it about him that's making me so crazy?"

"Believe me, I felt the same way about Finn when we first met. He was all I thought about and I'm grateful I got my head together enough to not get academically dismissed our first semester. I didn't realize it at the time, but I should've known the way I felt was a sure sign I'd fall in love."

Lexi thought she bored me when she spoke about her relationship with Finn, but I loved it. She was a true romantic and Finn complemented her perfectly. They had been together six months and were probably madly in love since the moment he accidentally knocked into her at orientation.

It was funny how my perception of love had changed. I would've sworn up and down I was in love with Hunter when we were dating. But I think it was simply an infatuation diminishing as I got to know more about him. I could also look back and realize I was sixteen years old with raging hormones. What did I know about love back then?

***

As I ran behind Blake on the campus track, I decided nothing had changed. Raging hormones were ruling my emotions again—because Blake was stunning and I couldn't stop admiring his body. He ran with confidence and every move he made was carefully crafted. He had complete control over his body and knew exactly how far too push it. There was an elegance in the way he exercised and I never saw him look so at ease.

His body was almost ridiculous in its perfection. He was tall and lean with every muscle perfectly sculpted. He didn't have the bulk of a lineman, but the way he was carved demonstrated his obvious strength.

The track looped around the football field with two sets of spectator stands on each side of the stadium. The brick athletic building backed up to the field and included an equipment room, gym, offices, and a swimming pool.

I stopped after a lap around the track, trying to catch my breath. Blake noticed I wasn't following and jogged back to where I stood. My panting sounded more pronounced next to his regulated breathing.

"Are you done?"

"I think so," I managed. "How far was it? A couple miles?"

Blake's lips twisted. "A quarter mile."

"What? No, I can't be that out of shape."

"Hmm…you won't be hearing me complain about your shape. Especially with that outfit you have on." He moved in closer. "I was expecting you to show up wearing baggy sweats and a sweatshirt and you come here looking like a sexy cat burglar."

I laughed and looked down at my clothing. I was wearing black compression workout pants with a matching black top. I had ordered the outfit from Under Armour back when Blake mentioned we should start working out together. "You got me. That was definitely the look I was trying for."

"It's gonna be hard to get my heart rate back down." His eyes swept over me and I preened at his unwavering gaze. The fabric was like a second skin and there was no hiding the curve of my breasts and belly as his eyes dipped lower. I watched his throat bob before he shook his head as if to clear his wayward thoughts. He kissed my cheek. "Do you mind if I do another couple of laps?"

I nodded and he took off running down the track. I was unsurprised by his sudden departure. It had become the status quo for Blake to splash cold water on the two of us as soon as anything became heated. I wasn't averse to taking it slow, but it made me confused over how Blake felt. I needed a sign from him, some action telling me he shared my feelings.

I couldn't think straight when Blake kissed me and I marveled at his self-control. When we kissed, I disappeared inside of a bubble where it was just him and me and nothing on the outside could touch us. I felt a million things when he kissed me and I wanted more and more. I wanted so much and maybe too much and I didn't know how to let him know it without coming on too strong.

I was all need and desire and although Blake cared about me, there was still an aloofness about him. A coldness, which made him keep me at arm's length. It felt like an extension of Blake's warnings and although we kissed, I wondered if he was still trying to protect me—still afraid of the disaster that would happen if we were together.

But it had been a week and as far as I could tell there was no axis switch. Blake hadn't transformed into an unfeeling monster who seemed intent on using me and disposing of me. We had the same friendship as before with the added benefit of kissing. What was he afraid of? I was fragile, but he didn't know the extent. Was I sending out some unknown signal saying *please don't touch me, I will break*? Because it wasn't how I felt.

With Blake, I wanted to be pressed against the length of him and have his lips set my skin aflame. Maybe my expectations were too high. I had gotten into my head Blake would replace all the bad stuff inside of me and help me create new memories. I wanted memories where being desired didn't end up with my dignity ripped to shreds.

Blake did a handful of laps before loping over and sitting on the bench next to me. The track was mostly deserted with a trio of runners having left several minutes after we arrived. After spring break, the track would likely be swarming with athletes as the spring sports season kicked off.

"So, I have a surprise for you," he said and tapped his leg into mine.

"What's that?"

"I have a buddy in the equipment department…" Blake paused as I pulled a face. "What?"

"How many buddies can you possibly have? You have friends everywhere in this school."

"Don't worry, sweetheart, I'll let you sit at the cool kids' table at lunchtime."

I huffed at his smug grin. "Whatever. You were saying…"

"Anyway, he dragged out one of the sleds for us to use on the field."

I blinked in surprise. "But aren't they huge?"

"The sleds with more than one man are hard to cart out into the field, but he left me the single man sled." He stood up and held out a hand to me. "Come on, let's see what you've got."

I hadn't noticed it before when we were running, but there was a sled set next to the field post. What I had pictured in my head was the five-person version, which all the players lifted together. Instead, this sled had a single red pad in the shape of a jersey attached to a metal pole centered on a large base.

I poked a finger at his chest. "This looks too easy. I wanted to tackle one of the huge contraptions."

"You'll be sore tomorrow, I promise."

"Okay, how does it work?"

"Start off by crouching down…"

I bent down in a football stance and pushed my ponytail out of my face to look up at him. "All right, I'm ready."

Blake tried to stealthily check out the view of my ass in the air and I temporarily put away the worry he was going to shove me back in the friend zone. There was something holding him back from giving himself to me completely but by the look of desire on his face, it was not a lack of attraction.

He caught me watching him and winked. I smiled in return and said, "Are you going to stare at my ass all day or teach me how to tackle this thing?"

"If that's a real option…" I giggled and he added, "But I'll show you what to do so you can fulfill your lifelong dream."

"I said it looked fun. I didn't say it was a lifelong dream."

Blake ignored me. "What you have to do is drive at the sled like it's a real opponent. You want to use the power in your legs to jump out of the stance and hit it as hard as you can…"

I didn't wait for him to finish and instead launched my body at the red pad. I slammed it with the palms of my hands and didn't expect the pad to move on contact. I stumbled forward and would have fallen flat on my face if Blake's arm didn't shoot out in front of me. "Slow down there, champ." He walked behind me and settled his hands on my hips. "You're going to wait for my call and then keep your hips low before exploding upwards to hit the pad and execute the block. You're not stopping once you touch the pad, you're driving through it."

I turned around and mock saluted him. "Got it, coach."

"Next time I'll bring my whistle."

I smiled ruefully and dropped back into position. It was definitely a turn-on to be in such a compromising position with Blake inches away from me. My hope was I'd also have the pleasure of watching him perform drills up close and personal.

"And go!"

I shot out and hit the dummy, but the force drove me back again. I let out a groan of frustration. Blake was right; I was going to be hurting tomorrow. "Ugh, this isn't fun at all."

"You just started. You need to tap into your aggression and use it to help you hit it harder."

"By now, you should know enough about me to see I'm not a very aggressive person."

"I disagree with that statement on the grounds you've called me an arrogant fuck before."

I scoffed. "You're paraphrasing and I believe I was smiling when I said it."

"Remember how I told you I get pissed off sometimes?" I nodded, urging him to continue. "Well, this kind of stuff helps me get it out. Instead of getting into fights, I started hitting things that were okay to hit."

I took a second to contemplate Blake's words. I wondered if he had a point about having an outlet, because the way I'd been handling my emotions had failed. I had run away, cocooning myself alone with the pain. I never got pissed over what had happened to me. I looked back and thought about what crappy friends I had, but I never embraced the fury. And I wasn't pissed my friends had failed me. They were obviously disloyal to begin with. The real thing that got me was the violation of trust. Because I had believed in Mr. Bridges— believed in his general goodness and trusted him implicitly. It was hard being the target of so much hate, being labeled as a Lolita, but the thing that made me angry was my misplaced faith in a man whose solitary goal was to ruin me. Two years was not nearly enough of an appropriate punishment.

I got back down and at Blake's call I lunged forward, imagining Mr. Bridges' face on the post. I exploded against the pad and tapped into my core strength to shove it roughly away from my body. I embraced the anger instead of locking it away in my vault. Because I was tired of being disenchanted, floating through life without the capacity to form any real connections because of my emotional paralysis. My anxiety stemmed from not only the echoes of my past, but the constant pressure to never let anyone see how I truly felt.

When I finished, Blake hugged me and I paid close attention to how his muscle flexed under his shirt as his grip tightened. I was bleary-eyed as I burrowed into his body. He didn't notice my response and kept his tone playful. "You're a natural. Maybe instead of being a cheerleader, you should've been playing football."

Tension coiled in my chest and I moved out of his hold. The fire burning between us was instantly extinguished. Gawking at him, I folded my arms over my chest. "How do you know I was a cheerleader?"

He barked out a short laugh, his face showing his confusion over the switch in my mood. "You told me."

I shook my head. "I never mentioned cheering to you." I studied him and asked, "What was the name of your high school again?"

"Clark," he answered. "Why?"

My shoulders lowered, the crushing weight on my chest lightening. "We never played your school in football, right?"

He was puzzled and I could see his mind working overtime trying to see where my line of questioning was going. "No."

Clark was about forty minutes away from Newpine and although I had heard of the town, our schools resided in different counties. Blake's mention of cheerleading made me wonder if he had played games at our school when I cheered. He was two years older than me and would have been on the football team through my sophomore year. But I knew the districts we played and Clark was never one of them.

Blake knowing I was a cheerleader made me feel paranoid, especially since I had come to Cook to regain my anonymity. I believed it was achievable since most media outlets outside of Newpine kept my name out of print. The narrowed-minded citizens of Newpine had no such qualms about sullying the reputation of a seventeen-year-old girl.

"Why do you look so worried? If you didn't mention it, maybe I assumed it when you were talking about how you were into homecoming during high school." His expression was tense and I chided myself for the overreaction. It shouldn't matter he knew about my cheerleading, but for some reason it bothered me. It made me suspicious of him and his motives. I wanted to trust him, but it had become so damn hard for me to believe in anyone.

"It's fine. I guess I was wondering if we could've met before."

He gave me a playful pout. "And you think you would forget this face?"

"Okay, maybe not."

I decided not to dwell on it because I was raising too many red flags by getting freaked out over a meaningless assumption. I laughed it off, hoping the hollowness could only be heard by me.

Although it was liberating to hit the sled, I had no desire to return to it. "Is there a football around? Want to play catch?"

He brightened. "Hell yeah."

Blake disappeared for a few minutes to a storage area for the sports equipment and came back with a pair of footballs. The disquieting sensation was still there, but I decided to not read into things. His explanation made perfect sense and I wanted to accept his answer. But being paranoid was better than being ignorant.

As he lumbered back toward me, I silenced my misgivings. He positioned me down the field and jogged a few yards away and faced me. When my first throw landed dead center between our positions, he moved in closer. With each throw, I tried to make him work harder for the catch. I purposely sent the ball high and then low. I never launched it straight, trying to make him dive left or right to get it. Blake was a good sport and attempted to make every catch.

"So, spring break is coming up..." I started as I caught the football. I positioned my fingertips between the laces and tried to put more power behind the throw by taking a step first. I was pleased to see the ball sail far over Blake's head.

He ran over to the ball and called back, "Any plans?"

"I'm going home for the week. My dad is picking me up on Friday. What about you?"

He chucked the ball back in my direction. "Cancun with a few buddies." My face fell and the ball dropped through my fingers. He laughed and held up his hands in surrender. "I'm so sorry, I couldn't resist. I was joking. I'm not going away."

"Whatever, like it would matter to me if you went to Cancun." I took out my frustration by wildly throwing the ball.

Blake's eyes danced as he said dryly, "Sure it wouldn't."

"It wouldn't. You're a free agent. I'm not going to tell you what you can and can't do."

"It's almost insulting how often you talk to me using sports metaphors." He gripped the football tightly as he said, "I'm not seeing anyone else, Autumn."

"I'm not asking," I answered automatically before adding in a lower tone, "I'm not seeing anyone else."

"I'm not asking," he teased. "But I still like the answer."

"Well, I like your answer too."

I blushed at his grin and allowed myself a moment to revel in how happy I was with him. Blake was constantly surprising me and I liked how he challenged me. He pushed me out of my comfort zone and I needed that. I was trying to live in the moment with Blake and not make predictions about our future, but his declaration made me curious. As though our relationship could be more than casual.

It was daunting to think about opening myself up to the possibility of falling in love with Blake. When Hunter and I broke up, my pride had been hurt more than my heart. If things didn't work out with Blake, I had the strongest sensation something inside me would be permanently fractured and no glue would be strong enough to put me back together again.

Chapter Fourteen

There was a heavy quiet as I passed the threshold once again into Newpine. I closed my eyes as my dad drove into town, trying to make the familiar rush of disgust vanish. Every landmark was too memorable, forcing every horrible event to the forefront of my mind. The ghosts refused to be silenced and, against my will, I heard his voice in my head.

"You don't belong here, Autumn. I've taught for years and I've come to recognize the signs. You have such potential and you hide it away to fit in with your peers. Once you break free of Newpine, you'll be unstoppable."

"Do you really think so?" It was my voice, but not my voice—a tone too full of longing and naïveté.

"I can help you. We'll keep up with the tutoring and when the time comes I'll help with your recommendation letters. I know several board members at the top schools in New York…"

"New York, seriously? I never imagined I could get into anywhere out of state. My parents do okay, but I'm not sure they'd be able to afford the cost."

"Don't worry. There's a lot of scholarship money open to you. You're involved in the student council and an athlete. If you get your math grade up, you'll have no problem at all impressing the scholarship committees."

"Mr. Bridges, I can't thank you enough. You actually make

pre-calc interesting and I've been doing the worksheets you've been giving me every night. If I get my grades up, I would take any help you would give me. I mean living and studying in the city would be incredible…"

***

I cringed as I recalled the conversation. I'd been as gullible as they came. Mr. Bridges could've offered to gift me the stars and I would've believed him. He wasn't particularly handsome, with an average face and a husky build. But it wasn't his looks that drew me into his orbit—it was an unmatched charisma. He made me believe his lies because he seemed to believe in them. If Mr. Bridges told me I would be unstoppable outside of my confining community, then I accepted it as an absolute.

The memories of the time he spent tutoring me were torture—I had granted him the ability to reach inside of me, wrap his hands around my heart, and squeeze. Hindsight was hell to someone like me. If I'd been smarter, I would've seen every interaction was all building up to a predatory relationship.

"How's school, hon?" My father turned down the radio and smiled over at me. He had taken a half day off of work to pick me up and I'd been ecstatic to see him arrive at my dorm. My dad wasn't much for talking on the phone, so it had been nice to catch up. We hadn't spoken for more than five-minute intervals since he had driven me to school in January. Although my dad never complained that the drives were an inconvenience, I was looking forward to returning to school my sophomore year with my car in tow. I owned a seven-year-old Toyota Corolla and it ran perfectly. It pulled at my gut each time I thought of it sitting unused in my parents' driveway. I also wanted to look for a part-time job next year and having my car back would make it possible.

"It's good. I like my schedule and classes. I told you this before, but I really lucked out with a great roommate."

He didn't make an effort to conceal his relief. Although I constantly told my parents how indebted I was to them, telling him I was okay meant more to him than anything else. They loved me fiercely and it showed in their every action since the moment I arrived home sobbing with my shirt skewed and my lipstick smeared. My mother was a force of nature and I feared her judgment over my actions. Because when it came down to it, I'd played a careless game with a dangerous man. I hated myself for what I'd done and the harshest judge through it all was myself. My mom never lectured, instead loaning me her strength when I needed it. She fought for me when I disappeared into a void so deep I never thought I'd find my way out of it.

My father and I had a less intense relationship and I appreciated it. He saw me crumbling and used his good humor to try and snap me out of my coma. I was a mess the summer between my junior and senior year. I barely crawled out of bed most days and when I did, I was manic. In the middle of an uncontrollable frenzy, I destroyed every mirror in my room because I decided I hated my reflection. I left my hair tangled and unwashed while I stayed in the same pair of grimy pajamas for days. My dad would come home from work and pretend like nothing was amiss. He spoke to me as if I wasn't a shell of the girl I'd been, telling me stories about work and corny jokes he heard. I would hear whispered arguments at night sometimes between my parents. My mother would accuse him of being in denial over what happened. But my dad's counterargument was since ninety-five percent of the day I was reliving every horrible moment, would it really hurt to not focus on the atrocities for five percent of it?

"Have you thought about your major at all?" I heard a note of excitement as his good mood continued.

"I was thinking of the possibility of social work." I blurted out the sentence without fully registering my words. But I found the statement felt true. "I thought it would be feel good to do a job for the rest of my life that involved helping people."

I wanted to help the victimized, the ones who were silenced and needed someone else to be their voice. I was tired of feeling sorry for myself and wanted to do something to make a difference. More and more, I thought about others who were in the middle of their own personal hells. I wasn't an expert on surviving by any means, but I wanted to learn how to be. Because that was what I felt life should be about—thriving even when the odds were stacked against you.

"You would be great at it. Before you pick your classes for the next semester, give me a call and you can let me know what courses you're planning to take."

"I will."

When we arrived, Mom was waiting on the porch. I shook my head in disbelief as I walked up the stone pathway. "What are you doing? It can't be more than fifty degrees out."

Without a reply, she scooped me up in a massive hug. My mother and I looked similar—the same honey-colored eyes and matching dark blond hair. Her hair was lighter than mine and I guessed she had been to the salon recently to touch up her highlights. My mother always smelled like an exotic blend of tropical flowers and green tea and when I caught her scent, it felt good to be home. My parents were my sanctuary, calming the rage in my heart brewing since arriving back in town.

My mother shivered and took me by the elbow as she led us inside. "I was too excited to see you! I couldn't sit still."

I pointed to her bare arms and said, "You could've put on a coat first." My mom was dressed in a short-sleeved blouse and black dress pants. I noticed her bare feet. "Or your shoes." My mother loathed wearing shoes. As soon as she arrived home, her heels were removed and set next to the door. She was also a neat freak and didn't want anyone bringing in dirt from the outside, sullying her perfect wood floors.

"It feels positively warm to me. It makes me think summer is around the corner. I was imagining the two of us lounging in beach chairs all day and swapping paperbacks."

"I saw the beach house rentals you emailed me. They look amazing, but I'm still worried about the price."

My mom sent my dad a conspiratorial wink over my head. "Our daughter worrying about money? After begging us each year to buy her the latest iPhone and trendy designer purse? I think college is making her soft."

"I agree. She was talking about being a social work major. Maybe she chose too much of a liberal arts college. We should've forced her into business school."

"Fine, it's your money and if you want to spend it on a beach house with an inflated rental price, feel free." My parents both laughed as I slipped off my sneakers and placed my bag by the door.

Our house was an extended cape with four bedrooms on the second floor. My parents had redone the ground floor a couple of years earlier, removing the downstairs office to create an expansive living room. One of the extra bedrooms was converted into their office space and they kept the other bedroom as a guestroom. Our kitchen was spacious and the three of us usually ate dinner at the small round table instead of using the formal dining room. I peeked my head into the kitchen before turning back to give my mom a grin. "You're making chili?"

"Of course, I know it's your favorite." She gestured for me to follow her to the kitchen table. "You can unpack later. Why don't we eat and you can tell me all about school?"

Nodding, I fell into one of the kitchen chairs. Within minutes, my mom placed a steaming bowl of her turkey chili in front of me. She had perfected the recipe over the years and whenever I ordered the dish at a restaurant, it always paled in comparison. I reached for a piece of cornbread from the bowl centered on the table and sopped up the liquid before taking a large satisfying bite. "I've been craving a real meal for weeks. The food in the cafeteria isn't bad, but it's good to eat something that doesn't have an expiration date five years from now."

My mom served my father and herself before relaxing into the chair next to mine. She blew gently on her spoon before taking a bite. "How are you? We've played phone tag for the past couple of weeks."

"I'm sorry about that. My schedule was hectic with midterms and by the time I caught a free minute to call you back, it was after midnight."

"I was worried," she admitted. Her eyes lowered and my father's gaze shifted away from me too.

He ran a hand through his black hair. "We were worried you weren't taking the news of the release very well."

"Oh." I hadn't forgotten about Mr. Bridges' release, but I hadn't allowed it to dampen the newfound happiness I found with Blake. It was exciting to start a new relationship and I didn't want to ruin it. Counting the days until Mr. Bridges' release would only fill me with righteous anger. "I've been fine, honestly. I was telling Dad how great school has been."

"Oh good." My mom released a long and shaky breath and added, "I shouldn't have brought it up, but I wanted to let you know we're here if you need to talk."

"Thanks."

Mercifully, my dad steered the conversation away from unsettling topics. We had a normal dinner without the feeling Thomas Bridges was an invisible presence taking up residence in the unoccupied fourth chair at the table.

After dinner, my mom asked my father to give us some "girl talk time" and he disappeared upstairs to watch TV. I loaded the dishwasher as my mom wiped down the counters. After the area was cleaned, she stood next to me, carefully inspecting me from head to toe.

"What is it? Do I have chili on my shirt?" I had worn home a simple white V-neck T-shirt paired with low-rise jeans.

"No, you look great. I think going away to college was the best thing for you." She paused, sucking in her lower lip before continuing. "I was worried over winter break. You seemed a little down and didn't talk to anyone while you were home. But now you seem like you're settling in nicely. Your eyes are brighter and it looks like you put on the weight you had lost." I opened up my mouth to protest, but she pressed a finger to my lips. "And don't complain about me saying you put on weight. You were rail thin before and now you have these gorgeous curves I would kill for."

I appreciated the compliment and had noticed my jeans and bras fitting nicely. With my anxiety under control, my appetite had returned and I was getting back to a normal weight. "I'm good, Mom. You honestly don't have to worry. I like school and I like the people there."

I had friends, good friends, like Lexi, Casey, and Josh. Even Will had been coming by to say hello from time to time, though I suspected he was using me to catch a glimpse of Casey. And it was liberating to be away from the high school hierarchies. In college I became aware that time was relative. When I went to Newpine High School, time had dragged on. I was stuck in place, waiting for my chance to escape. At Cook, time sped up and it felt like the stolen moments when I was with Blake would soon pass me by.

"You've met a boy."

"Huh?" The dish almost slipped out of my hand.

"You must be dating someone. Autumn, why didn't you tell me? I want to hear all about him." My mother closed the dishwasher and her eyes grew large in anticipation.

"Well, I didn't mention it because it's very new. We've only been seeing each other for a couple of weeks."

"That's great. What's he like? What does he look like?"

I couldn't help but smile as I conjured up Blake's face in my head. "He's nice and funny and extraordinarily good-looking. He's so handsome—perfect green eyes and light brown hair. He has let it grow longer now, but I doubt he'll ever have a bad hair day. He's tall, I never asked his exact height, but he must be at least six feet tall. I'm not short, but I feel minuscule standing next to him."

"He's from the college?"

"Yes, he's a junior—a business major."

"How did you meet?"

"At a party. We've been spending time together as friends for a couple of months. He's in my art history class and we were study buddies." I smirked at the term. Honestly, we hadn't gotten much studying done since kissing entered the equation. I sent Blake off to study for our midterm on his own, so we both had a chance of getting a passing grade. I felt confident I had done well on the exam and Blake promised he pulled an all-nighter to study.

"Autumn, he sounds wonderful. I like that you started out as friends first. That's the way your father and I got together. I was actually seeing someone else at the time, but the more time I spent with your dad the more I realized I was with the wrong man." My mother's eyes clouded over and she sighed. "What's his name?"

"Blake." I chewed on my lower lip before finally exhaling one long breath. My mom wasn't going to be pleased, but if my relationship with Blake became serious, she'd find out eventually. "He's also a football player for the college."

My mother's eyes narrowed and I wished she wouldn't be so predictable in her reaction. I empathized with her feelings, but if anyone should be wary it should be me.

"Autumn, must it always be athletes? I understand the appeal, honey, but can't you for once go for a boy with more brains than brawn?"

"Mom, you're painting Blake as a stereotypical jock without knowing him at all…"

"Autumn, you should know better. After what those boys did to you at school. They were bred to believe they are gods, above reproach, and that every woman is their own personal plaything." My mother glared at the wall behind me. "And they don't change when they become men. I mean Thomas Bridges was a decorated football coach and he thought it was perfectly fine to be attracted to a seventeen-year-old girl."

My stomach seized up and I blinked away tears. I had to stand my ground when it came to Blake and not show weakness. "He's not Mr. Bridges or Hunter or Talon. Blake is good to me and I'd be a hypocrite to think less of him because he plays football."

My mother walked over and cupped my cheeks gently in her palms. "I trust your judgment and I want you happy. You're smart and beautiful and you deserve a man who will cherish you. I have a hard time letting go and I have so much guilt over what happened. I feel like I should've seen the signs and if I was a better parent, I could've shielded you."

"Mom, don't blame yourself. And honestly, I'm sick of blaming myself. I want to move on and Blake is helping me do that."

She stroked my cheek with her thumb before releasing a long breath through her teeth. "You're right. Of course, you're right. I'm sure he's wonderful and as long as he treats you well, I'll keep the pitchforks in the shed."

"Thanks, Mom."

While giving me another overpowering hug, she relieved the tension by giving me a noogie. I giggled and beamed at her. My parents had been my safe haven for so long, it would be just as hard for them to let go. But I was ready to take risks again. I wouldn't be foolish with my choices, but putting myself out there and not letting my neuroses hold me back could be the best thing for me. My heart could be broken in the process, but it wasn't the only possible ending.

Chapter Fifteen

I flipped onto my belly as I tried unsuccessfully to find something to watch on TV. Since I had no hometown friends, it made spring break a very uneventful week. I had exchanged text messages with Casey and Lexi, but they were busy reconnecting with their high school friends. My parents and I spent a lot of time together, but by eight o'clock, they were unwinding for the night by watching television and getting ready for bed. Blake's nightly phone calls were the one thing I looked forward to after the sun went down.

I shut off the television and took a minute to study my old bedroom. The reason I left my side of the dorm room bare was because I was trying to define college Autumn. I felt zero connection to the girl who had decorated my bedroom. There were cheerleading trophies and plaques next to pom-poms and sparkling hair ribbons. All of the furniture was the color of bone and accented with girlish touches like my pink frilly bedspread and a bedazzled lamp. The room was tacky and overdone and I decided it was time to redecorate. I supposed I never cared enough to bother changing anything after I quit cheerleading, but if I was going to spend breaks at my parents', I should have a room that didn't give me the urge to vomit.

My phone rang and my heart fluttered as I answered, "Hi, Blake."

"Hey, what are you doing?"

"Thinking I may have decorated my bedroom using every teen girl cliché as inspiration. It's giving me a headache just looking at the walls. No wonder I left my dorm room plain for so long."

At the dorm, after hanging up Blake's print on my wall, I had picked up a few more posters at the bookstore. I picked simple and feminine art prints, relaxing images I could get lost in before I fell asleep at night. The Georgia O'Keefe print evoked the most emotion because I could attach it to the memory of my trip with Blake to the museum. I was trying to locate the print of the painting he had chosen for his term paper, thinking it would be nice if we both had a physical manifestation of the turning point in our relationship.

"What are you doing tonight?"

"Probably read for a couple of hours before bed." I shrugged although he couldn't see me. I had thought of making up an exciting itinerary of what I had planned at home, but decided to drop the pretense immediately. I wouldn't pretend with Blake and be embarrassed over who I was.

"Why don't we go out? I'll come pick you up."

I sat up in bed. "Blake, it's an hour and a half drive."

"So what? I want to see you and of course you want to see my sexiness." I laughed and he continued, "Come on, say yes and I'll hop in my car right now."

"Yes, of course." There was no reason to hesitate. Although I would see him again in a few days, I wanted the instant gratification of being near him right away. "I'll just let my parents know and get changed. I'll text you my address."

After we hung up, I took a quick ten-minute shower and tried to decide what to wear. We hadn't discussed where we would go, but I figured it would be casual. I put on a black tank with a sweetheart neckline and a pair of black leggings. To break up the black, I added a gray open-knit cardigan. Instead of pulling my hair back like usual, I left it down and spritzed it to soften the waves. After applying a raspberry-colored stain to my lips and swiping my lashes with mascara, I felt ready to go.

I padded downstairs and found my parents watching game shows in the family room. My mom's eyebrows lifted, as she noticed I had changed out of my yoga pants and T-shirt. "Are you going out?"

"Yes, Blake wants to take me out. Is that okay?"

My father nodded while my mother's smile was strained. "Wonderful, we can't wait to meet him."

"Wait, what? You want to meet him?"

My mother stared at me as if I had grown a second head. "Of course. What did you expect? For us to be fine with some man honking his horn and you taking off without us at least getting a good physical description and a peek at his license plate?"

"Really, Mom? You went there?"

"I get that you're in college and don't have to answer to us while living there. But you told me Blake treated you with respect. I don't think it's very respectful to come to your home and not at least say hello to your parents."

My dad put down his newspaper on the coffee table in front of him. "Your mom has a point."

It was unavoidable—Blake would have to pass Vivian and Carl Dorey's inspection before I left the house. Blake meeting my parents was awkward on several levels. For one, I didn't know how serious we were about one another. Meeting the parents seemed like an event reserved for couples dating for months. Also, my mom could end up embarrassing me by trying to prove Blake unworthy of my affections. I imagined her quizzing him on art and literature to get her point across that there wasn't much depth beneath his handsome exterior.

I wanted to avoid meeting Blake's mother as long as possible. From what he told me, she sounded awful and would probably consider me a distraction in his pursuit for NFL glory.

He was close to his sister, but I wouldn't expect an introduction after only dating a couple of weeks.

When Blake arrived an hour later, my thumbnail was chewed to the quick. I had texted him to give him advance warning about coming inside before we went out, but he hadn't returned my text. I assumed he was driving and didn't have a chance to reply. I jumped out of the armchair when I heard the doorbell ring.

Before my mother could get to the door, I hurried over. Blake smiled as we locked eyes, but I could sense his disquiet. "Hi," he said softly.

"Hi," I parroted back. "We can head out in a sec."

His movements were stiff as he walked by me into the house. His size was overwhelming and everything in the house dwarfed in comparison. My mother was waiting for him in the foyer, straining her neck to study his face. She held out her hand. "Vivian Dorey. I'm Autumn's mother."

"I'm Blake Preston. It's nice to meet you." His gaze moved over to the direction of my father, who remained on the couch.

My dad rose and took long strides to reach Blake. My dad pumped Blake's hand vigorously as he said, "I'm Autumn's dad, Carl. It's always nice to meet a friend of Autumn's."

"Blake, do you mind taking off your sneakers? We have a no shoe policy around here," my mother said, gesturing to her own bare feet. Blake looked surprised by the request and looked to me for guidance. I assumed he hoped, as I did, we would be in and out of the house in record time.

My mother was being antagonizing, but she only gave me an innocent look.

"It's not necessary, Mom. We're leaving in a minute."

"What's the rush? Blake may want to stretch his legs after the long drive," she countered.

"It's not a problem, I'll take off my shoes," Blake said and sat down on the bench my mother had in place to implement her rule. As Blake focused on untying his sneakers, I tightened my jaw and glared in my mom's direction.

My mother ignored me and turned her attention back on Blake. "So, Blake, where are you from? Do your parents live nearby the school?"

"I have an apartment a couple of miles from campus that I live in year-round, but I grew up in Clark."

My mother's lip downturned and the lines on her forehead became more pronounced. She seemed displeased by his answer and I tried to puzzle out the reason. I guessed it was because he had an apartment and she had concerns about my virtue being compromised. I could've reassured her that if anyone had untoward thoughts in our relationship, it was me.

My mother temporarily distracted me, but I took a second to indulge in how gorgeous Blake looked for our date. He had rolled up the sleeves of his plaid button-down to his elbows and I noticed his skin had already taken on a deeper golden hue from his regular outdoor workouts. His jeans were distressed with a relaxed fit, hugging his muscular thighs before tapering off. His caramel brown hair was damp with the ends curling around his ears. With a small nick on the corner of his chin, I guessed he shaved before arriving to take me out.

Everyone was staring at me and my cheeks flamed as I realized I must've spaced out. My mother's voice was strained as she said, "Blake asked where you would like to go, Autumn."

"Oh, I don't know. Maybe Valley Amusements? They have a pizza place, bowling alley, and arcade."

"Sounds great," Blake said and I was comforted when I saw the stiff set of his shoulders had relaxed.

"So, you play ball for Cook? How did the team do this year?"

I grinned at my dad's question. I appreciated him trying to make Blake feel comfortable, especially after my mother's likely upcoming inquisition.

"Good, sir. We were nine and four during the season and

second place in the conference."

"Blake was MVP," I offered. "He had almost two thousand rushing yards and made eighteen touchdowns."

Blake gave me a quizzical smile. "How do you know that?"

"I read a couple of articles about you in the campus newspaper. You told me you were good, but I didn't know you were crazy good."

My mom interrupted. "Do you want to borrow my black heels, Autumn? They would look nice with your pants."

"Sure."

"Okay, take a walk with me upstairs to grab them." My mother volleyed her head between my father and Blake before she said, "We'll be just a sec."

Blake nodded while my father began asking him more questions about Cook's football team. My father had no problem finding common ground with anyone and I was glad he wasn't peppering Blake with uncomfortable questions about his intentions toward me.

Following my mother upstairs, I understood she was looking for an opportunity to talk in private. As we entered the master bedroom, she gently closed the door behind her. "Autumn, *you can't be serious.*"

"What? You talked to him for five seconds and you've already decided you don't like him?"

"Blake seems fine. It's you that I'm concerned about. You've turned into an automaton since he arrived."

I didn't conceal the hostility in my voice. "Thanks, Mom."

"I'm sorry, but it's the truth. *He had almost two thousand rushing yards and eighteen touchdowns.*" She mimicked my tone in an unflattering way.

"So what? I can't be proud of him? I used to follow football and those numbers are impressive."

My mother's brown eyes were sad as she studied me. "Why does this happen to you? Why are you so easily dazzled?"

I stumbled backward as if her words had reached out and shoved me. "I'm not seventeen. It's different…"

"But it feels the same. The scene downstairs was all too familiar to me. Every basket Hunter made, I heard about. Every championship game Coach Bridges led the team to, I heard about. When will I get to hear what you've accomplished?"

I closed my eyes. "I am accomplishing things, Mom, every single day, but they're not the normal things you talk about in polite company. I felt nothing for so long—like I was empty inside and all I could hear around me was white noise. I'm learning to deal with my emotions and not let them kill me slowly from the inside out. I'm learning to make friends and go on dates without counting the seconds until the other shoe will drop. I've discovered I want to help people and be a social worker. I'm smart and compassionate enough that it will be the perfect fit for me."

My mother's eyes filled and her voice quavered. "I'm sorry I jumped to the wrong conclusions. You sound stronger and I'm so proud of how you've found your own identity."

"It has been something I struggled with and the reason I latched onto Faye and Hunter. But I'm not like that any longer. I'm supportive of Blake because that's how he is with me. He's interested in what I have to say and he's just as impressed with me as I am with him."

My self-confidence was shaky and Blake's encouragement meant a lot. When I was worried about my midterms or uncertain about our relationship, he didn't let me wallow. Isolation was how I dealt with things before, but it didn't work. Hearing Blake tell me I could do anything I wanted and to stop hiding from the world had transformed me.

"I won't hold up your date, but as long as you promise you're being careful, I'll trust you implicitly."

"I promise."

Chapter Sixteen

Blake leaned me against the passenger door and teased my lips with his thumb. When his lips met mine, it was hard to recall the promise I made to my mother about being careful. His tongue slipped inside the warm recesses of my mouth and I shivered from anticipation. He traced a line with his forefinger down from my chin to my collarbone as we kissed and my skin protested when his touch disappeared. I squeezed his shoulders before rhythmically stroking my hands up and down his biceps.

When Blake pulled away, he playfully bit my lower lip before nuzzling his face into my neck. My spine tingled as I heard his choked whisper against my ear, "I've been waiting all week for that."

Minutes before, we arrived at Valley Amusements and by the look of the steamed up windshields in the parking lot we weren't the only ones making out. After I returned downstairs with my mom's heels in tow, she shuffled us out the door. I figured she was too rattled by our conversation and decided to stop questioning Blake prematurely. Blake seemed to pick up on something being off, but didn't ask me about it. Instead, he said my parents were nice and it was sweet how overprotective they were.

Shivering, I slipped my hands beneath his shirt. I massaged small circles around the hard planes of his stomach before walking my fingers lower, just above the hem of his jeans. Blake reached for me again and his kiss felt urgent. His hands were always controlled when we kissed, but his movements had turned reckless. Clumsily, he knocked the cardigan from my shoulders as his palms ran alongside my silhouette. He cupped my ass and yanked me to his body. Our breathing was labored as we broke the kiss. He grunted, "I missed you. I know you're back on campus in three days, but I had to see you tonight."

"I missed you too."

"We better go inside before I keep you out here the entire night." He kissed the tip of my nose before releasing me. When he took my hand in his, I liked the way he intertwined our fingers instead of limply grasping my palm.

I paused slightly at the entrance, but took a fortifying breath before pushing through the glass double doors. Although Valley Amusements was popular in Newpine, I hadn't spent a lot of time there. My feelings were neutral about the hangout and it was the reason I suggested it for our date. My high school friends had preferred house parties where they could raid their parents' bars and medicine cabinets. We had also gone to the mall outside of town often and it was the reason I steered clear of there on breaks.

"It smells good. Do you like the pizza here?"

"No, it's awful." I giggled at Blake's expression, still giddy from our kiss. "But you'll eat anything so I figured it was fine."

"You act like I'm a caveman." He lowered his already deep voice and growled, "Blake play football. Blake eat food."

"I like your caveman side, especially when it comes out when we kiss."

He looked placated. "That was hot outside. My mind has been in the gutter since I came to pick you up and saw you wearing something tight and black again." He gripped my hand tighter. "You have no idea what you do to me."

"You weren't the only one, I might've had a naughty thought or two..."

"Really? You're going to have to tell me all about these dirty thoughts later. Preferably in long and explicit detail." Blake's tone was joking, but his gaze burned as he stared down at me.

"I think you're corrupting me, Mr. Preston."

"Funny, because I think it's the other way around, Miss Dorey."

I silenced my retort when we reached the food counter. After we debated for a couple of minutes, we settled on a pie, wings, and a pitcher of soda. The tables were mostly filled, but we were able to snag a booth once a family got up to leave.

While we waited for our food, Blake twisted around to survey the bowling alley. Valley Amusements had a retro feel with yellow plastic chairs at the square tables, disco lights hanging from the ceilings, and linoleum flooring with decades' worth of scuff marks. Leaning back in his chair, he said, "Is this where you hung out growing up?"

I shrugged. "Sometimes. More so when I was younger. My mother was big on setting up playdates since I was an only child and when the weather was bad, this would be where we'd go."

His eyes widened. "Is that laser tag over there?"

I spun to look in the direction of Blake's stare. "Yup. Probably the only upgrade done here besides a few new arcade games."

"We're playing. I haven't played laser tag in years and I was outstanding back then."

"Well, I'm good at it too. So prepare to get your male pride wounded when I beat you."

His smile lit up his entire face. "And here I was planning to let you win…"

I groaned. "You were not! You're only saying that now because when I win, you can pretend to have thrown the game."

"Okay, I'll bring it when we play."

"Good," I said, appeased. I pulled at the hem of my cardigan. "Sorry to spring the whole meet the parents thing on you. They insisted once I said we were going out."

"It was fine, your parents were cool."

"Are you sure? Because you seemed a little off when you came in."

He wet his lips, triggering my need to memorize every indentation on them. His mouth was perfect and felt perfect when crushed against my own. His lower lip was swollen, a slightly bit fuller than his upper lip, leaving a permanent sexy pout expression on Blake's face.

Finally, he admitted, "I never met anyone's parents before. I wasn't sure how to act."

I sensed his sincerity by the embarrassment I heard in his voice. Confident and sexy Blake was brought to his knees by the thought of winning over my parents. It was adorable.

We hadn't gotten to the point of exchanging romantic histories, but I assumed he had left behind a trail of girlfriends nursing broken hearts. Blake knew about Hunter in the vaguest of terms. His understanding was I dated a dick who spread rumors about me. It was a half-truth, but close enough to understand why I'd been reluctant to get close to another man after Hunter deserted me.

"Were you ever in a serious relationship?" I colored as I realized how leading my question must sound. "Not to label us that way. I only mean meeting the parents is a normal step when you've been dating someone for a while."

"No. The longest I've ever dated someone was about a month."

I eyed him carefully. "But I assumed you were burned by someone. The way we met…"

"It was a bad night for me and I was caught by surprise when I saw you. I hope you haven't thought this entire time I liked you because you looked like an ex."

Blake was only twenty-one, but I wondered how his lack of committed relationships boded for us. I didn't want to be another woman in a long line. I liked him a lot and it hurt to think of his interest waning after only a few more weeks.

He reached across the table and took my hand. I watched his thumb trace careless circles around my knuckles. "Autumn, I've kept things casual because I've never wanted anything more from someone. You make me want more. And if I hold back from you, it's only because I'm afraid of you seeing every mistake I've made in my life and finding out you no longer want to be with me."

"You're so hard on yourself. You keep telling me what a bad guy you are, but I feel like the only one who believes that is you." I lowered my voice. "You've never been disrespectful to me and it gives me an idea about how you treat the women in your life. I left myself completely vulnerable with you when we shared a bed, but you never took advantage of that. Your mom and sister obviously drive you crazy, but you put up with their antics because you're a good guy. The whole school worships you—and believe me it's not only because of football. It's because you're down to earth and don't believe you're better than us peons who can't catch a football."

"I do actually believe that," he deadpanned.

"And your self-depreciating sense of humor is appealing."

"Well, if I never need to have my ego stroked, I'm calling you." He looked over at the counter and said, "I think our food's going to be ready in a sec. I'm going to use the bathroom and then I'll pick it up. I'm starved." He stood up and pecked my cheek. "Try not to miss me."

"It will be hard, but I'll manage."

He left and jogged across the linoleum to head to the men's room on the other side of the building. Relaxing into my chair, I smiled as I recalled our conversation. He had admitted wanting more from me and I was willing to give it to him. He made me laugh and the best thing he did was make me forget. With Blake, I was able to look forward to the future. Blake wasn't a diversion—he was opening up my eyes to the possibility of not letting one person define my future.

"Autumn?"

One word, one voice, and I was vaporized on the spot. My chest ached from how hard my heart started pounding. Although I didn't want to acknowledge the voice, my head swiveled toward the sound. Hunter was standing before me and had the decency to look shocked to his core over my reappearance in Newpine. The last time I'd seen him was on my final day of high school. The next day, my mom had pulled me out after I told her about the boys grabbing me in the stairwell. I hadn't resisted her decision but regretted it later on. It was giving Hunter, Faye, and the football players another win—because they were powerful enough to run me out of school for good.

Hunter's shock and awe lifted from his expression as two of his friends banged into his shoulders from behind. I recognized the men as former teammates of Hunter—Sam and Daniel Nichols, who were cousins. They were Hunter's lackeys and were partially responsible for spreading the lies about my promiscuity. At first, Hunter resisted believing what everyone said about me. Eventually, he came to embrace the lies and started adding his own to the mix. The rumors were his way of salvaging his pride. He had to put distance between us. If he turned me into a slut, it somehow granted him immunity to my actions. He could say our relationship was meaningless and he was in it for sex alone. If only the student body had known how far-fetched Hunter's claims truly had been.

Hunter hadn't changed a bit in the year and a half since I last laid eyes on him. No scars marred his perfect face despite the ugliness living inside of him. His flaxen hair fell in front of his forehead and he pushed it out of the way as he gaped in my direction. He had always been thin and tall, but his arms looked more defined since I last saw him. His friends were carbon copies of Hunter, all dressed in athletic T-shirts and baggy jeans.

Sam's brown eyes were wary while Daniel sneered at me with open hostility.

"Oh shit, Whorey Dorey is back in town," Daniel chuckled.

The boys were idiots and I had wasted way too much time mourning the loss of people like them in my life. Why had it mattered so much what the popular kids of Newpine High School thought about me? They were completely insignificant. If I could go back to high school as a freshman, I would have a do-over. I'd never aspire to be one of the elite. Because I would know that to be at the top of the high school food chain, you had to devour everyone below you.

"Fuck off, Daniel."

Daniel found my remark unnaturally funny and clutched his sides as he let loose a loud and obnoxious laugh. "Damn, babe, if I knew you were back in town, you could've gotten me off. My dick hasn't been the same since you left."

Hunter's eyes narrowed, but he didn't come to my defense. Not that it was expected. Hunter was weak and selfish. When my world was coming apart at the seams, he didn't bother to put himself in my position for a split second. Hunter only wanted what he felt was rightfully his. He demanded sex because he didn't want to be considered the cuckolded boyfriend.

"Let's go. Isn't this shit getting old?" Sam demanded of his cousin. It gave me hope that at least one of the apes had evolved.

"What's going on?"

I hadn't sensed Blake's approach and neither had the three men. I could see each of them sizing him up, wondering if they could take him on. Blake gave me a concerned look, pulling his eyebrows together, likely picking up the tension emanating from me. I felt as if I had landed in a surreal dream where my life at college was colliding with my high school existence.

Daniel slithered over to Blake before patting him heartily on the back. Blake looked at him with disdain as Daniel spoke.

"Is Autumn your girl? No judgment here, dude. We've all been there, *done that*."

Blake pushed Dan's arm away roughly, making him stumble backwards. "I'd watch what you say next. Because unless I hear an apology to Autumn, your teeth will end up on the floor."

Finally, Hunter snapped out of his stupor and rose up to face Blake. They were almost the same height, but Blake was constructed from solid muscle. Hunter would never win in a one on one fight with Blake, but Hunter had his ass clown friends as backup.

"I'm not sure what you know about Autumn, but I've known her for a long time. I was her boyfriend and the bitch fucked around on me the entire time we were together…"

Blake poked the center of Hunter's chest with his pointer finger. "If you're her ex, then you definitely deserve at least a punch in the face."

After grabbing my purse, I jumped out of the chair. I addressed Blake while turning my back to Hunter and his friends. "I want to go. They're looking for a fight and I don't want to give it to them."

Hunter barked out a humorless laugh. "That's funny coming from you, Autumn. Like you're better than us." I spun to face him and was chilled by the hardness in his eyes. There was a brief pause, a second when I was able to recognize that Hunter wasn't a fool. He still could find my weaknesses and I knew he was about to exploit them. "You're the one who was fucking a teacher."

He shocked me into silent submission. I should've expected the blow, but hearing it voiced aloud again stole away the confidence I built up since leaving for college. I had showed him my hand and Hunter would keep playing until he had won it all.

He looked over my head at Blake and demanded, "Did she tell you about her teacher, our school's football coach? She was letting him fuck her six ways from Sunday." Hunter snarled in my direction, "And the cunt did it all to get a better math grade."

Hunter's fury returned me to the night he had accosted me. He had demanded the truth, wanting to know if I hadn't only fooled around with other guys, but if I had slept with Mr. Bridges. I had told him no, told him I never wanted anybody but him to touch me. But it wasn't good enough. He wanted to take what wasn't his because he had the warped idea I owed it to him. In reality, even if any of the lies were truth, he had no right to demand I spread my legs for him. Instead of spreading my legs, I kicked him in the balls and told him to stay the hell away from me. I had hoped he would've manned up, but his reaction only cemented my resolve to cut him out of my life.

Daniel was gleeful over Hunter's verbal smackdown. Daniel was vicious and we had never gotten along, even back when I was Hunter's girlfriend. When I was accused of sleeping with Mr. Bridges, he had been triumphant. "Fucked him and then she got the poor schmuck sent to jail over it," Dan added.

Blake quickly moved me out of the line of fire by putting his hands on my hips and setting me down behind him. Before the men could react, his fist went flying toward Hunter. Hunter didn't have time to block the blow and Blake's knuckles bashed into Hunter's cheek. Hunter's head snapped to the side and he didn't react immediately. I gasped as I watched Sam and Daniel dive toward Blake in order to protect their friend.

The employees and other patrons starting yelling at them to break it up, but by the cold rage on Blake's face I knew he was too far gone to walk away. He shoved at Sam and Daniel, knocking them both into an unoccupied table. The restaurant area was emptying out as people scrambled to get away from the fight.

Hunter barreled toward Blake and was able to get in a gut punch. Blake hunched over and Hunter took advantage of the split second when his guard was down to connect his fist with

Blake's mouth. His lower lip split open, blood gushing out and dribbling down his neck.

"Blake! Stop it!"

Blake ignored my pleas and retaliated by throwing out a series of wild punches. He had no control as his fists went after Hunter, Sam, and Daniel. He was outnumbered, but his unpredictable movements were making the men unsure how to defend themselves. He was pummeling their faces and chests one at a time. While one of the men recovered from the hits, he moved on to the next. Daniel was able to land one more punishing hit over Blake's eye, but it still didn't stop his recourse.

Several men rushed over trying to break up the fight, but Blake was an unstoppable force. A few of the men tried to hold him back, but he carelessly tossed them aside as he lunged for Hunter.

"We called the cops!" a female employee yelled from behind the restaurant counter. Hunter and Blake ignored the warnings, but the mention of police seemed to spook Daniel and Sam. They tried to pull Hunter away from the fight, but he refused. He was too occupied with pushing men out of the way to continue exchanging blows with Blake. Daniel and Sam gave up and took off running out of the bowling alley.

Blake parted the sea of people before him and reached Hunter again. I cringed as I watched his fist pull back and collide with Hunter's nose. Hunter lost his balance and landed on the floor. I could see the blood flowing freely as he cradled his nose between his fingers.

I could see it at that moment—the beast inside that Blake kept caged. He was savage in the way he pounded the three men, as if they were nothing more than an inconvenience to him. There was a fierce intensity as he fought and his body jerked as his breathing grew ragged. I wasn't scared of him, but scared for him. How could he pull back and be able to walk away without killing Hunter?

I sprinted over to Blake and his body jerked when I grabbed him. "We need to go now!" He ignored me as he glared down at Hunter. I dug my fingernails into his forearm. "The cops are on their way. We need to leave before you get arrested."

"You broke my nose!" Hunter grunted. His eyes narrowed as he examined me. "Always quick to play the victim card, Autumn. He'll see it one day, he'll find out you're a liar and a whore."

"Don't you look at her," Blake growled at Hunter. "Never even say her name again, unless you want another ass kicking."

Forcefully, I yanked Blake in the direction of the door. I heard sirens in the distance and took off in a run toward Blake's car. I pushed him toward the passenger door and held out my hands. "Give me your keys," I commanded. He handed them over and I ran to the driver's side. As soon as we were both inside, I started the car and peeled out of the parking lot. As I drove away from the bowling alley, I noticed two police cars approaching from the other side of the road. I let up on the gas in hopes of not drawing their attention.

My palms stung as I kept a death grip on the steering wheel. I didn't loosen my hold until we were at least a mile away and it didn't look like the police or anyone else was tailing us. Daring a glance in Blake's direction, I noticed he was searching through the glove compartment. He found a pile of fast food restaurant napkins and began to use them to mop up the blood on his face. The interior of the car was cast in shadows and it was difficult to tell how bad the damage was to his face.

"What the hell were you thinking?"

"What?"

"Why would you pick a fight with three guys? You're lucky they didn't beat you to death."

Blake scoffed. "Like that was going to happen."

"Blake, they were trying to rile you up. It's the kind of thing Hunter and his friends get off on."

Blake pulled the napkins away from his lips. A small white cotton square remained stuck to the top corner of his mouth. "What did you expect me to do? Sit there while he calls you a slut? Maybe shake his hand and say nice to meet you?"

"No, but Hunter is a head case and some things that happened to his family was what helped shape him into the misogynistic asshole you saw today."

"Please tell me you're not defending them. Most people have shitty parents. It doesn't mean he gets a free pass to be a dick because of it." He placed another napkin into the building pile of saturated tissues in his lap.

I breathed in and noticed the tinge of iron in the air. "I'm going to drive you to the hospital. You probably need stitches."

"I'm fine," he insisted. "Head wounds just bleed like crazy."

"Just what you need, another head injury. Like you don't get knocked around enough on the field." I noticed a convenience store ahead and pulled in. "If you won't go to the emergency room, I'm going to at least grab some ice to put on your face. I'd take you to my house, but my parents would freak."

He nodded and I put the car in park before heading inside the store. As I roamed the aisles, I tried to concentrate on taking care of Blake's injuries. I didn't want to think about Hunter's words or what they may mean to Blake. Because Hunter was forcing me to have a conversation with Blake I planned to put off for a long time. I couldn't have Hunter's words echoing around in Blake's head. He may decide to look more into my past and I needed to give him my side of the story before that happened.

I found a small first aid kit among the shelves and also purchased several frozen packages of vegetables. Frowning, I reentered the car and scanned Blake's injured face. He had wiped away a lot of the blood, and I could see the swelling on the left side of his face. The gash wasn't as large as I suspected and I hoped it wouldn't leave a scar. My hand reached over to him and removed the pieces of tissue from his mouth. I handed him the frozen vegetables and he held them over his left eye. I began collecting the tissues and placed them in the plastic bag that had held the items I bought.

"I'm sorry if you're pissed. But I'm not sorry for hitting them." His nostrils flared. "If that's the kind of stuff they pulled to make you leave school, then they got off easy."

Removing the tissues, he stared at me, likely trying to gauge my feelings. His eyes were luminous and my temper cooled as time passed. He was only trying to defend me and hadn't realized what an exercise in futility it was. Hunter and his friends were a perfect example of herd mentality and would never have an original thought. If the consensus was I'd slept with Mr. Bridges for a better math grade then nothing could change their minds.

I covered my hand with his and guided the frozen package back to his eye. "I'm not pissed at you. I'm pissed at them for ruining our date and messing up your perfect face."

The corners of his lips upturned in the faintest of smiles. "They'll look a lot worse tomorrow."

I rolled my eyes. "Okay, tough guy. I'm going to clean your cut now. I don't think we can do much for your busted lip, but once you take the veggies off your eye, put them over the lip." I tore open the alcohol wipe and he winced as I glided it over the cut next to his eye. "It doesn't look deep. They must have grazed you with a watch or something."

"What did you ever see in that guy?"

"Well…" I shifted in the seat awkwardly. "Hunter isn't the same guy and I'm not the same girl. We had a lot more in common when I was in high school."

"What could you possibly have in common with him?"

"I don't know. At one time, my priorities were cheering, being popular, and dating a hot guy. Once high school was done, I wanted to leave Newpine for good and do something incredible with my life. It wasn't until I lost it all that I was able to get my head out of my ass and see how freaking shallow I'd become."

"You're hard on yourself about high school. You shouldn't be. And any mistakes you made have been done with for a long time. Hunter needs to move on." He touched the ends of my hair and twirled it between his fingers. "You were the best thing to happen to him and he probably hates himself for losing you." He paused and added, "I know I would."

I smiled wistfully at his compliment. "Hunter is convinced I betrayed him. It's the reason he hates me so much." I looked down at my lap as I said, "What he said about my teacher…"

Blake's voice was strangled. "Autumn, please don't feel like you have to explain anything to me. Anything those idiots had to say carries no weight in my mind."

I looked at him from under my lashes. Blake was good to me and I was glad he wasn't the type of man to demand answers after Hunter's accusations. He accepted whatever I was willing to give him.

I think about running for a split second—bolting out the door and finding my own way home. It seemed less terrifying than having to hit Blake over the head with the tale of my own sordid personal tragedy. But for the first time in forever, wanting Blake outweighed hiding away my pain.

"I didn't sleep with a teacher. Mr. Bridges was my math teacher and I spent a lot of time with him because I struggled in pre-calculus." I dug my fingernails into my palm as I continued. "Mr. Bridges had a reputation. He was one of the school's football coaches and the rumor was he favored students who cheered. My friends thought if I flirted a little, it would help my grade out. I never thought…"

Blake looked like he was about to get violently ill. He didn't meet my eyes. Instead, he vacantly stared through the windshield and I could see his mind whirring, trying to make sense of my words. He seemed to be holding back, wanting to push me to tell him more, but scared at the same time of what I'd say.

I tried not to focus on my humiliation and relay the story as if I was an outside observer. "Anyway, Mr. Bridges must've picked up on my lame attempts at flirting and he offered to tutor me. He made promises, told me he could help me get into a school in New York and would work with me to win a lot of scholarship money in order to afford it. "

Blake swung back toward me and I could see the growing sadness in his eyes. He swallowed hard and took my hand in his. His intentions were clear. He wanted to be supportive, but hearing a story of someone he cared about getting hurt was painful. I had planned to give him an abridged version of the story, but if I was going to reveal my past, I wouldn't hold anything back.

Chapter Seventeen

"I wish Mr. Bridges taught my math class. I would totally be slutting it up like you," Faye teased as she leaned her back into the locker next to mine.

I slapped her shoulder playfully. "I'm not slutting it up for Mr. Bridges." I swung my head back and forth to check the hallway. The halls had emptied out since school ended an hour earlier, but Hunter had mentioned going to the weight room after classes. I could imagine him materializing at the other end of the hall as Faye accused me of trying to seduce my teacher. "Besides, don't let Hunter hear you say that, he'll go crazy."

Faye blew out an exaggerated breath. "Why do you bother with Hunter? He's like a jealous freak when it comes to you."

I frowned. "Give him a break. He's going through a lot right now. I would probably be a little touchy too if I had to deal with his mom."

"We're going to be seniors in a couple of months. We need to free ourselves of these high school boys. Hunter may be a popular basketball player at Newpine, but once he goes to a college with a population of more than four hundred, he'll be a nobody again."

I pulled my math textbook out of the locker and slammed it firmly. "Be nice, Faye. He's my boyfriend."

"I know. I think I'm just feeling bitchy because I still don't

have a date for the prom. Talon asked me, but I told him I
wanted to see if I could do better first..."

I smirked. "Faye, you didn't! But you probably have a
point. He's nice to look at, but a cocky jerk most of the time.
Brings his attractiveness down a few notches."

"I need someone to take back to the hotel afterwards and it
looks like Talon may be the lucky guy. You and I'll both get laid
and then we can commiserate over breakfast the next morning
about how small Hunter and Talon's junk is."

"You're crazy. I want a romantic first time with Hunter..."

"And you're delusional if you think your first time sleeping
with Hunter will be romantic. You're both going to be lost over
what to do. I recommend lots of porn before prom night."
Faye's brown eyes glittered. "Or you could just practice with
Mr. Bridges. He's not bad looking for an old guy and at least
you know he's experienced."

"I'm leaving now," I said and spun on my heel away from
her. My black sandals clicked against the floor as I rushed down
the hall.

"You know you want it, you sexy bitch," Faye called
teasingly down the hall. I tried to take confident steps, but Faye
had flustered me. Her sexual innuendoes were conveniently
timed since she knew I was off to my after-school tutoring
session with Mr. Bridges. I shook off her words and plastered on
a bright smile. Mr. Bridges held the keys to the things I wanted
in life and I'd play the game to get them. I smoothed down my
red skirt and knocked on his classroom door before entering.

He was bent over paperwork, but looked up and beamed as
I came into the room. "Hi, Autumn. Sorry for making you stop in
later than usual, but I had a staff meeting I couldn't miss."

"No problem. Faye stayed behind with me."

Depositing myself in a desk at the front of the classroom, I
crossed my bare legs in front of me. His blue eyes gazed down
until moving to rest on my white top. The fabric clung to my skin
and the neckline dipped to just above my cleavage. My palms

began to sweat under his inspection and I wondered if I should make an excuse to leave. Faye's words had bothered me and I needed some time to consider my intentions. How far was I willing to take the flirting game with Mr. Bridges? He promised to help me and I knew he had taken liberties with my grades. Laughing at his jokes and flipping my hair was one thing, but allowing him to gape at me like he was a starving man who had finally stumbled upon a five-course meal was another. It was the first time since tutoring started that he made me feel cheap.

"So, let's go over Friday's quiz. Do you have the practice tests I gave you?"

His smile was affable and I shook off the early feelings of unease. Even if he had been checking me out, I reasoned it didn't mean anything. I was young and pretty and he liked what he saw. He may have enjoyed the view, but he would never try to take it any farther.

Mr. Bridges was the most well-liked and admired teacher at Newpine. He taught sophomore and junior math classes while also coaching the football team in the fall. He was easygoing and had a relaxed way of teaching and coaching. The players liked him because he had a quiet passion that he used to inspire them in lieu of hurling insult after insult their way. The whole town loved him for putting Newpine's championship football team on the map.

When he had offered to tutor me a month earlier I hadn't passed on the opportunity. I liked how he talked when we were alone. He made me feel like I was something special and not just another follower of Faye's. He would tell me about his family and how he got into teaching and football. He had a teacher who helped him get into college on a football scholarship and he felt like he was paying it forward by working with me to improve my grades.

The material for the quiz was hard to grasp and Mr. Bridges patiently explained the concepts. My brain had a mental block when it came to anything math-related. Although I was struggling, he never made me feel stupid. He would wait until the light bulb went off and sit back and admire his handiwork.

"See, isn't pre-calc fun?" he quipped.

"Loads," I giggled. "Thank you for this. If I can get a B in your class, I think my parents will die from shock." I looked outside and frowned at the darkening sky. "I didn't realize how late it was." I had turned my phone off and realized I likely missed dinner.

"Me either. My wife will probably lace my supper with arsenic if I don't get home soon." He stood up and motioned to the door. "It's getting dark, so let me walk you to your car."

"Thanks," I said and slipped my canvas bag over my shoulder. I felt bad for making him walk me to the student parking lot, a hike compared to the faculty lot, but I would feel safer if he saw me off.

The student lot was behind the football field and adjacent to the main building of the high school. It was a tiny lot with an unpaved surface and a few lampposts. The lot had completely emptied out and my Toyota was the last remaining car. Sports practices had ended about a half hour earlier and there must have been no other events scheduled for the night.

Mr. Bridges chattered as we made our way to my car. He spoke about his kids and wife often and he was telling me a story about how his daughter had asked him to teach her how to play football. She wanted to start her own co-ed team at her school. The way he spoke about his family was sweet and I reasoned I shouldn't have been so weirded out before when he looked me up and down. I had dressed with intent and I shouldn't have been so shocked when I was able to produce a reaction from him.

I arrived at my Honda and unlocked the passenger side door. I tossed in my bag before turning to thank Mr. Bridges. I was taken off guard by his nearness as I swung around. My elbow bumped into his chest as I moved to face him. With Mr. Bridges in my personal space, I noted how much larger he was than me. He was a head taller with a husky build and slight paunch.

"Do you have a boyfriend, Autumn?"

"Yes, Hunter Cirillo," I answered automatically. I realized a second too late how inappropriate it was for my teacher to ask if I had a boyfriend.

"Oh yes, Mr. Cirillo. He was in my geometry class last year. Not the brightest student if I recall. It took two weeks of having him cut out shapes for him to grasp the idea of an isosceles triangle." Mr. Bridges leaned in closer. I automatically pressed my back into the car's doorframe. "Is he good to you? Does he make you feel good about yourself?"

My head felt dazed from his words and my eyes darted from side to side. If anyone else was around, he would back off and I could get into my car and drive away. "Yes," I whispered. I began to fidget, trying to make it crystal clear how much I wasn't liking how little space stood between us. "You're making me very uncomfortable right now."

"I'm sorry. I just thought you were feeling the same thing I was. There's something here. I'm not imagining it, right?" His voice was laced with desire and he stayed planted in front of me.

My eyesight blurred as tears stung my eyes. "No, you're my teacher..."

"What about how familiar you've been around me? And how provocative you've been dressing since tutoring began?" His voice was mocking and I was flooded with shame and remorse. He had assumed the flirtatiousness was an invitation. To him, he saw my clothes as a representation of a pretty little bow I tied over my body.

I pushed down my embarrassment and allowed righteous indignation to sneak into my expression. "You have the wrong idea and you're freaking me out. Just walk away and we'll forget this ever happened."

"Don't be embarrassed. I saw your flushed cheeks when I looked at you before. You liked it, right? Liked the idea I was peeking up your skirt and thinking about your pussy?"

His words defiled me and I was too shocked to speak. It was an out-of-body experience, a waking nightmare where my teacher tried to seduce me. Sweat formed under my arms. "No. That's not true and please stop saying these things to me."

I was naïve because I thought my words would be enough. I never thought he'd act on his feelings. I was still under the misguided impression Mr. Bridges was a good man who had just been a victim of crossed signals. When his hands gripped my waist, the panic finally set in.

"Autumn, don't be scared. No one has to know about us. And I'll stand by my word, I'll help you out any way I can."

He was bearing down and it felt as though the force of his stare would cause me to incinerate on the spot. I had tempted a wild animal and he pounced at the first sign of weakness. I had to figure out a way to talk myself out of the situation or make a run for it. I was unmatched physically and my only hope was to take him by surprise.

I tried to dart around him, but he tightened his hold and threw me back inside of the car. My legs were splayed across the passenger seat with my feet still sticking out of the car. Quickly, he shoved the passenger seat to a reclining position before moving inside of the car. He covered his body with mine and I attempted to push him off of me. He was unmovable. "Please stop…"

When he didn't change position, I opened my mouth to scream. Rubbery lips pushed against mine and I was silenced. When my teeth clamped down, preventing his tongue from finding it way inside, he stopped and used his palm to cover my mouth. I choked back a sob as the smell of chalk assaulted my nostrils. "Shh," he commanded. "You made it clear what you were offering. And you took what I gave you. If you weren't interested, you should've never accepted the better grades."

My whole body jerked as he took his free hand and ran it up the length of my thigh. He reached the hem of my underwear and tugged at it. I was stuck under him, but I tossed side to side, trying to escape. My elbow grazed the horn, but the sharp beep didn't distract him from his single-mindedness. He kept me pinned on top of the cloth seats with the shifter digging into my spine. The awkward position made it difficult for him to pull down my underwear. I was horrified when I heard the sound of cotton tearing, exposing me completely.

Time sped up and later I would only be able to recall the events as if I was viewing a collection of snapshots. My thighs refused to stay glued together as he roughly dug his nails into my knees. My skirt had lifted in the struggle and the hemline was bunched around my waist. He had stripped me bare, demanding my nakedness without my consent. He looked me over with undisguised lust on his face. Tears spilled out of the corners of my eyes as I continued to fight him off. But it was becoming so hard. It would be easier to just disassociate, to separate my brain from my body, and to not feel the agony.

He positioned his frame between my legs, preventing me from closing them. He reached under my blouse and fondled my breasts. His hands were rough and greedy, squeezing and pinching at my nipples. I yelled out, my muffled screams begging for him to make it stop. He licked his lips, taking pleasure from my cries and from being able to completely own my body.

"You like it, don't you, baby?" Spittle fell on top of my face as he spoke.

He removed his hand from under my shirt and rested it on top of my mound. Please stop, I begged him with my eyes. I wanted him to see me, view me as a person, as the girl who he had in his class second period. Because if he saw Autumn again and not a sexual object then maybe he would let me go.

"So fucking hot," he mumbled.

My body shook with shock and pain as he shoved his fingers inside of me. I wanted to hide in the farthest recesses of my brain and only emerge once he finished. Because I couldn't stand to feel the sensation of being touched against my will. It was the worst kind of vulnerability, a defenselessness where my body was the pawn in a game a twisted man had forced me to take part in. And it didn't stop—endless amounts of time marched on as he violated me over and over again.

Mr. Bridges rose off of my body, his face hovering above me. He no longer looked me in the eyes, his gaze trained only on what he was doing to my body. He slid his fingers out of me and brought his hand back to his body. The sound of his pants being unzipped crushed the silence and had the effect of forcing me out of my self-imposed stupor.

I had held onto my virginity, wanting to share my first time with Hunter. I had heard the stories of my friends' firsts. There were tales of regret intermingled with stories of first love. I craved the latter and it was about to be stolen from me. My first time would be a forced sexual encounter with my teacher, a man more than twice my age who up until minutes ago had been a trusted advisor. There would be no romance and flowers, only a potent combination of blood and tears.

A black and powerful rage forced its way through my hopelessness. He wouldn't hurt me a moment longer. He had stolen my trust and my faith, but he wouldn't walk away from the night with my virginity as another one of his spoils.

His hold relaxed as he fumbled with his pants. With his body no longer pressed into me, my hands were free to attack him with as much force as possible. I curled my hands into fists and launched a punch against his chest. My knuckles stung as I pulled away. He had been crouching over me as he undid his pants and the hit was enough to cause him to stumble farther back. I pulled my leg out from under him while he remained stunned, and I concentrated on pushing through his heavy body. I drove the heel of my sandals into his gut. He tried to grab onto my leg to keep from falling out of the car, but he was unsuccessful. He tumbled onto the gravel and landed on his backside. Instantly, he sprung up and tried to reenter the car. I grabbed the door handle and tried to close it before he could *make his way inside again. I was remorseless as I slammed the door into his spine and I swore if he wouldn't get out of the way, I would crush his bones until he was no longer a threat. He clambered to his feet and at the last second he jumped out of the way as I pulled the door shut. My palm slammed down on the lock at the same time he reached the door handle. My panic eased as the door didn't budge. I hopped over to the driver's seat and hit the automatic locks to keep him from entering the car from the driver's side.*

His palms smacked on the passenger window and I could hear his rage-filled screams as I tried to search through my bag for the car keys. I tuned him out, allowing his hateful words to fly over my head. I found the keys nestled on the bottom of my canvas bag but my relief was short-lived, as I dropped them onto the floor. I scrambled to grab them, cursing as my trembling fingers tried to retain their hold on them. The car shook with the force of the blows Mr. Bridges was delivering to the windows and doors and I wondered how much longer I had until he ripped a hole in my car and dragged me out by my hair.

My survival instincts kicked in and I steadied my hand enough to grip the keys and shove them into the ignition. My foot pressed down on the gas pedal and the car roared away from the scene of my attack. I refused to look behind me to see if Mr. Bridges had dared tried to chase down the car.

The violation could've lasted minutes or hours. I lost track of time as I sped away from the school. I drove on autopilot, no idea where I was headed. I thought about pulling over until I calmed down, but I was irrational, fearing Mr. Bridges would somehow catch up to me and finish what he started. I kept seeing the raw hunger in his eyes and I knew he would be furious being left unsated. I wasn't sure where I was heading until I arrived in front of my house.

I didn't leave the safety of the car at first. I continued to grip the steering wheel, my fingers bloodless. Finally, I let go, my hands flying to my mouth, trying to stifle my screams. I wanted to be inside with my parents, but I had to find the nerve to unlock the car door and step out into the open. The sky had darkened and it was a moonless night. The interior lights gave the house a warm glow and I wanted to run inside and never come out again.

I left my belongings in the car and sprinted up the porch stairs. I barreled through the front door, sliding the deadbolt in place once the door slammed behind me. As I turned around, I saw my parents had rushed out of the kitchen into the foyer to investigate the commotion.

My mother took a tentative step in my direction. "Autumn?" Her arms reached out as she closed the distance between us.

I crashed against the door to prevent her from reaching me. "Don't touch me," I hissed.

"Autumn, what's going on?" My dad tried to fill his voice with authority but I heard the crack in it. I closed my eyes, feeling my shame bleeding out of my pores. I imagined my parents could see what had happened—I visualized imprints left on every part of my body Mr. Bridges touched. I tried to find my voice and explain, but I didn't want to say it out loud. I wanted another second to hold onto the belief it was all a horrible and surreal nightmare I would soon awake from.

"Autumn, you need to tell us what happened, so we can help you," my mother said softly. It was a lie—she couldn't help me. The only thing that would help was if I could scrub the last hour out of my memory forever.

"I need a shower." I shoved past her and the shock of the violent outburst made her let me go. I took the steps two at a time and ignored my parents' pleas to come back and talk to them. I had no idea what they were thinking, but maybe it wouldn't be too far off from the truth. I would give them a reprieve before I forced them to share my pain.

I shut the bathroom door and locked it. Turning on the overhead light, I squinted from the brightness. I caught my reflection in the mirror hung over the sink and gaped at what I saw. My tawny hair was in complete disarray, tangled in messy bunches on top of my head. My tears caused my mascara to blacken the skin under my eyes and create messy trails traveling the length of my face. My natural glow was gone completely and had been replaced by a sickly gray pallor.

I stripped down and flinched as I saw the fingernail scratches on the inside of my thighs. Blood was seeping down my legs and I couldn't move my eyes to the source. I knew there was more blood and bruises leftover from the night, but a physical inspection was the last thing I wanted to do. I walked over to the shower and turned the knob of the hot water as far as it would go.

Stepping under the spray, I welcomed the sting of the hot water. The droplets burned as they fell against my delicate skin. I grabbed a scrub brush and moved it rhythmically over every part of my body. My skin protested, becoming enflamed as I refused to stop trying to scour away what had been done to me. It was a fool's errand because no amount of scrubbing would make me feel clean again.

Chapter Eighteen

I didn't cry when I told Blake about what happened two years earlier. I could feel the dam building behind my eyes, but I wanted to get through the story without falling apart. Surprisingly enough, by the end, the need to cry had passed. I felt lighter, as if I had needed to share my secrets with him in order to ease my own burden.

I brushed over a few details, one being the fact I was a virgin. It was irrelevant—even if I had a laundry list of sexual partners, it wouldn't negate what Mr. Bridges had done to me. I had also not gone into explicit detail over how Mr. Bridges violated my body. I would never be spared the visual, but at least I could do that for Blake.

"My parents were able to coerce the story out of me and we filed charges."

The aftermath was another circle of hell to get through. Going to the hospital and having my mother stand next to me as I explained to the doctors and nurses how I'd been violated was humiliating. My clothes and ripped underwear were sealed in a bag and I was put in a hospital gown. I sobbed when the nurses asked for me to spread my legs. Swabs and combs were used as part of the collection and I again used my ability to fade into a state of nothingness to cope. I wasn't supposed to shower, but no one blamed me.

At first, I wouldn't say who assaulted me. But then I thought about the possibility of him doing it again or worse yet, Mr. Bridges having assaulted a girl before me and never getting caught.

"An investigation was launched and it became his word against mine. He may have gotten off, but he said it was consensual." Bile coated my throat over the thought. "He said I had set off to seduce him and that it was a mistake, but he had fallen into temptation."

"But the police didn't believe him," Blake stated.

I shook my head. "It looked bad for him, the fact he would even consider sleeping with a seventeen-year-old student. There was also evidence, my ripped underwear and the marks on my skin. Although he said it wasn't an act of violence, that I liked it rough, he knew his defense was flimsy. He took a plea deal and has been in jail since."

"You didn't want to go through a trial?"

"No, I couldn't. The press kept my name mostly out of the whole thing once they got word a teacher assaulted one of his students. But Hunter and my best friend Faye leaked my identity and for some reason decided to make my life a living hell." I bit the inside of my cheek before continuing. "Everyone believed Mr. Bridges' version of what happened. Faye corroborated I flirted with him to help out my math grade and shared a lot of unflattering pictures of me on Facebook. They were mostly taken at her house while we were partying and every sin was publicly displayed. And Hunter may have believed me, but I don't think he cared. I had been sullied in his eyes. I think whether or not it was consensual was a moot point. We broke up when I wouldn't sleep with him…"

"Motherfucker," Blake muttered.

"He and his friends started rumors about me. Made up all kinds of stories and everyone believed them. Mr. Bridges was a revered football legend at our school and his arrest made me a target. Our school had a bad case of hero worship when it came to him and it was easier to accept I was a Lolita than that Mr. Bridges was a predator. Two guys grabbed me in the stairwell when I went back to school in the fall and I was done with Newpine High School for good."

Blake's eyes iced over as I spoke and his expression turned menacing. It was the second time his temper got the better of him, his dormant bloodthirsty nature pushing forth. The frostiness melted when he saw me watching him. "I wish I could do something. I wish I could go back and protect you from all of it."

I reached for his hand and squeezed it. "You are doing something. You're here for me now. I haven't been able to talk about what happened with anyone besides my parents. I have trust issues and I've been afraid if I open up to anyone else, they'll desert me like Hunter and Faye."

He was silent as I studied him. He was feral looking with his bloodied face and wild green eyes. But I trusted him. My feelings about Blake were turning serious and I wouldn't pretend to be someone I wasn't. I didn't like talking about Mr. Bridges, but despite my wish that he was a nonentity, he had altered the course of my life. Blake couldn't return my feelings if he only knew the parts of me I selectively chose to show him.

"Hunter and Faye weren't worthy of you." His expression turned sad. "I'm probably not either, but I'm trying to be."

"I was afraid to tell you, scared of what you might think of me…"

Blake looked appalled. "What would I think?"

"You would think I was stupid to flirt with my teacher. I invited him into my life by tossing my hair and giggling when he spoke, letting him open up to me about his personal life…"

His hands settled on my elbows and I stopped talking. "Did you tell him no? Did you tell him to stop?" The tears forced their way out and I nodded as I stifled a small sniffle. "Then none of the other stuff matters. It was his responsibility to draw the line. Your actions didn't warrant what was done to you." Brushing away my tears, he leaned in closer. Blake's anguish for me was in his eyes. "I can't imagine what it's been like for you and I'm so sorry. But I'm here now and nothing is going to happen to you again."

"I don't need a protector..."

He pressed his lips to my forehead. "I don't only want to be your protector, Autumn. I want to be everything you'll ever need—because that's exactly how you make me feel when I'm with you. Like you give me everything I'll ever want and need."

Chapter Nineteen

"Autumn, I hate to tell you, but you're terrible at poker." Finn laughed as he pulled the pile of chips toward him.

"Not true, I always beat Blake when we play," I protested.

"Then he must be letting you win. It seems like your losing streak started the minute he left the room."

I let out an annoyed breath and looked toward Blake's closed bedroom door. He had invited Finn, Lexi, and Casey to come to his apartment for the night. I appreciated the gesture. After arriving back on campus three weeks ago, I felt like I was neglecting my friendships because of the amount of time I spent with Blake. After the fight with Hunter and my confession, our relationship solidified. I no longer felt like a secret was stuck in my throat and everything I said to him about my feelings were half-truths.

Blake's talk also encouraged me to open up to Lexi. Faye and I had had a superficial friendship and it was the reason she betrayed me after the scandal. Lexi and I had only known each other for six months and we had ten times the friendship I had with Faye. Although my panic attacks had been better, I wanted her to understand the root of them. Remembering the feeling of being trapped and the sensation of Mr. Bridges' unwanted touch on my bare skin were what triggered the panicky feeling. It was worse in the months following the attack, but with distance between me and Newpine and starting my new life at Cook, the anxiety was lessening.

Blake was my champion in all ways. He gave and gave and never asked for anything in return. He wanted me to need him and although I insisted he was giving me more than enough, it never satisfied him. He wanted to strip me of my pain and it was hard to explain to him that what he wanted was impossible. I wanted him to accept what I had learned to—the hurt would lessen, but it had become a part of my chemical make-up.

We had been playing poker for the past hour, but Blake left the table twenty minutes earlier to take a phone call. Since I was out of chips, I left Casey, Finn, and Lexi to finish the game. I joined Darien in the kitchen, helping him clear away the empty beer and soda cans from the counter. "Sorry you're stuck playing host. Should I go get Blake?" I asked, tilting my head in the direction of his room. I was looking for an excuse to interrupt because as much as I'd become an open book, Blake had secrets. Secrets I needed to unravel before my heart surrendered and I handed him all of me on a silver platter.

"Don't bother. He's talking to his mom and if he doesn't answer the phone, she'll keep calling until he picks up."

My shoulders hunched with relief. Blake's mother was overbearing and I witnessed it firsthand when he tried to send her calls to voicemail instead of answering his cell. Relentlessly, she called until she reached him. She had a hold on him and I didn't entirely understand it.

"What's up with that?" I asked and leaned my elbows on the counter. "He's twenty-one, shouldn't she be letting go a little bit?"

Darien snorted. "Because she's a gold digger and it's her son's money she's after."

"What money?"

"She invests in Blake because she wants him to go pro and take care of her. She's already milked him of most of the family money willed on his dad's side."

Darien looked guilty and turned away from me. I circled the counter and stood next to him. "I'm not going to tell him what you said. I'm just curious why he seems to shut down when I bring up his family."

Darien glanced over my shoulder to recheck Blake's door. "You know Blake's dad died, right?" I nodded. "Well, his dad's parents tried to be involved in his life, but his mother wasn't interested. They felt bad about it and set up a huge college fund for him that he'd get access to when he turned eighteen. When he went to college, Blake left enough money in the account to pay for his tuition, but gave the rest of the money to his mom."

"Is she the reason he doesn't work? He mentioned getting a part-time job, but said his mother was dead-set against it."

Darien nodded solemnly. "Because while he's at school, she doesn't want anything interfering with his 'training,'" he said, emphasizing his point with air quotes. "Blake works construction during the summer to manage while he's at school. But I'm sure she still takes a big cut of what he makes."

"But why? Why does he feel so obligated?"

"I think it mostly has to do with his little sister. He doesn't want her to go without anything so he tries to be the man of the house and provide for her and his mom." Blake didn't talk much about what life had been like after his dad's death. The impression I got was men tended to float in and out of his mother's life, including the man who fathered Blake's half sister.

I had a dozen more questions, but was cut short by the sound of Blake's door opening. He came up behind me and enclosed me in his powerful arms. I leaned back against him as he kissed the top of my head. "Sorry about that. My mom was in lecture mode and I couldn't get her off the phone."

"It's fine," I said and turned around to grin at him. "Although I did lose all of my money to my friends as soon as you left. They figured out you were letting me win the entire time."

He clutched his hand to his heart. "Me? I'd never do that. You were owning it in that game."

"Not likely," I grumbled.

He tucked a piece of hair behind my left ear and bent down to whisper into my ear. "You do own me."

My entire body buzzed as his warm breath tickled my earlobe. In an instant, my concerns over his complex relationship with his mom vanished. Things were crazy good between us and although I still had a tendency to overthink things, I was allowing myself a chance to enjoy the ride. Blake was a total departure from the callous playboy I imagined he would be from our first meeting. He was respectful of our relationship, totally understanding of my past. Our relationship had become more physical in the past few weeks, but he never pushed for more.

"Will the two of you stop looking like a freaking cheesy telenovela and play poker?" Casey chided from the kitchen table.

Blake smiled and took my hand as we rejoined the group. Casey shot both couples at the table a disgusted look before addressing Darien. "What's with them? We're in college, most people in college are allergic to monogamy."

"Not Blake and Autumn. I feel like I'm stuck in a tampon commercial crossed with an erectile dysfunction ad when the two of them are around," Darien teased.

"Why don't you go out with Will like I told you?" I asked.

Casey pulled a face. "Because he's so *nice*. It gives me the creeps. I imagine a serial killer lurking behind those pearly white teeth and khaki pants."

"He dropped off a half of a pizza for her the other night," Lexi offered. "It was cute."

"Yeah. I was completely swept off my feet to receive his discarded food."

"Will's a good guy, you should give him a shot," Blake piped in.

He was silenced by Casey's glare. "You're the campus mayor, of course he's nice to you. He's not going to reveal his serial killer tendencies to a football player who can crush him with his inhuman strength."

Blake turned to me. "I have inhuman strength now. Can I add that to a résumé?"

"I'm sure you have other talents you can include," I said and patted his knee.

"Yeah, have you heard Blake sing? We went to karaoke a couple weeks ago and he left all the girls fanning their hoohas."

I lifted my eyebrows. "No freaking way! You can sing and you've deprived me of the pleasure of hearing you all these months?"

Blake's cheeks colored and it was likely the first time I witnessed a blush from him. "Darien's exaggerating. His memory is all screwed up because he was doing shots of Sambuca that night."

"Bullshit, dude. I live with you. I get a free concert every morning when I hear you in the shower."

"Finn is a good singer too," Lexi said while Finn shot her daggers. It was the first time I'd seen his brown eyes look at Lexi with anything less than adoration.

"We should do karaoke now," I said although the men looked less than thrilled with the idea. "Come on, Finn is clearing us all out anyway."

"No karaoke machine here. Sorry. Guess we'll have to figure out something else to do," Blake said.

"I can download a karaoke application on my MacBook," Darien said. I laughed at Blake and Finn's shared look of utter misery.

I pouted. "What's the matter? Is it emasculating for the big strong football player to sing?"

He rose from his chair, towering over me. "I'm not worried about that. I just didn't want to show anyone up with my raw talent."

I clapped and cheered as Darien and Blake set up a makeshift area in the living room for us to do karaoke. I was an average singer, but I was hoping we would get bored before it was my turn. While he moved around the furniture, I gave Blake a once-over. He had been working out a couple of hours a day and paying close attention to what he ate. His body had been sexy before but his recent efforts made him look ridiculously attractive. His core and back muscles tensed under the strain of rotating the couch and I wanted to swallow my tongue over how cut he looked. We'd been mostly clothed during our kissing sessions and when he finally got undressed, I'd be ready to drown in him.

Once they were satisfied with the furniture placement, the men went into Darien's bedroom to tinker with his MacBook and figure out how to work the karaoke application. Casey turned toward Darien's bedroom and squinted in the direction of Blake. "Are you finished blushing and fantasizing over how hot your boyfriend is?"

"I'm not," I protested. After a beat, I whispered, "Okay, maybe a little. But we haven't applied the boyfriend and girlfriend label yet." I kept my voice low enough to not carry to Blake's ears.

"That's a technicality," Lexi said. "You're both not seeing anyone else and he's obviously into you as much as you're into him."

"He's great. I thought maybe it was a physical attraction between us, but it's a lot more than that."

Casey slipped her thumb inside of her mouth and made a popping sound as she yanked her thumb away from her lips. Lexi and I both gaped at her with confusion. She chuckled. "Sorry, I was providing the sound effects of Autumn's cherry being popped in the near future."

I swatted her arm playfully. "Maybe...I don't know," I stammered. "I haven't mentioned the virgin thing and I'm not sure when to. Do I tell him right before we're about to have sex?

Or if I say it beforehand, would it put too much pressure on both of us?"

Casey opened her mouth, but Lexi spoke up. "Just tell him. Blake's a good guy and he'll want to take care of you for your first time."

"Am I being old-fashioned about it? Should I be asking him to take me into his room and jump his bones?"

Casey laughed. "Is that what you want? I picture you as more the candlelight and rose petals kind of girl."

I was torn over what I wanted. In one sense, my sexuality had been basically latent since I was seventeen and I was relishing how Blake's touch had reawakened my urges. I was afraid of losing those feelings and it was the reason I thought over and over again about sleeping with Blake.

On the other hand, I was the victim of sexual violence, my body exploited against my will. What if the moment I lay naked before Blake, all the revulsion and fear associated with my attack returned?

But I was trying to separate sex from my assault. Because I never truly believed it before that night, but the attack had little to do with sex. It was about power and control because Mr. Bridges saw me as a conquest. I was part of a fantasy and although I showed resistance, he thought I would really enjoy what he did to me.

The men returning with Darien's computer cut our conversation short. No one wanted to sing first, but Lexi wore Finn down until he agreed. He chose "Friends in Low Places" by Garth Brooks and it was a good first choice. Finn had a solid country crooner voice and the room sang along with him during the chorus.

Casey decided to go next and sang "Umbrella." She was slightly tone deaf, but her sultry dance moves made up for her lack of singing talent. My hopes for her and Will were diminishing as I watched her and Darien track each other with their eyes. I wasn't against the two pairing—Darien was a great guy—but Will worshipped Casey and I imagined his smitten heart breaking from her rejection.

"Not sure how you're going to follow that performance," Casey said to Blake. She was breathless as she resumed her seat next to me.

Blake followed Darien to his computer and pointed out the song he wanted to sing. Darien looked skeptical over the choice. "Are you sure?"

Blake winked at me. "Yup. It'll show Autumn I'm not afraid of losing my big studly football player label."

"I think you're the only one who gave yourself that label," I volleyed back at him.

"Maybe so," he said and my toes curled when he trained a big grin in my direction. Darien handed Blake his cell phone. It was functioning as the microphone for karaoke since the guys didn't have a traditional karaoke setup. Blake held the phone up close to his mouth and waited for the song to start.

The familiar chords started and I covered my burning cheeks with my palms. "Please, Blake, no, you can't be serious."

Lexi and Casey erupted into giggles next to me as Blake bounced his head up and down in time with the music. "*Oh baby, baby. How was I supposed to know that something wasn't right here? Oh baby, baby. I shouldn't have let you go. And now you're out of sight, yeah.*"

Blake's green eyes flashed with humor as he began to shake his hips in time with the music. He smirked as he continued to sing while the rest of the room couldn't stop laughing. As silly as Blake was being, Darien was right about him having a good voice. It was deep and gravelly and he had a good vibrato as he continued with the song. He made it to the chorus and he sidled up to Darien who joined him in singing. "*My loneliness is killing me.*"

"*And I,*" Darien sang with a flourish.

"*I must confess I still believe.*"

We all sang together. "*Still believe.*"

Blake chuckled and it was a trial for him to finish out the song while attempting to keep a straight face. I was laughing too, but my heartbeat was also pounding between my ears. Because it was the moment I realized how I was falling more and more for Blake. I had been empty inside before him and it was a miserable existence. Every day I spent with Blake filled me with regret over all of the things I'd been missing by closing myself off. I wasn't sure how he had done it, but he penetrated my walls completely.

He finished the song and I applauded as he took an exaggerated bow. Lexi was up and Blake took her spot on the couch next to me. "Are you duly impressed?"

"Very," I said.

He studied my face. "What are you thinking about? Was my singing that bad you had to check out for a few minutes?"

"No. I was actually wondering if you were too good to be true." My tone was joking, but there was an underlying seriousness to my remark. Blake was perfect. Sexy as hell, generous, funny, kind—every quality I could possibly want in a boyfriend he possessed. I wanted what we had to be real so bad, but it was hard to trust my instincts when they had been wrong a million times before.

"Searching for my warts?" His smile wavered. "I have them, I just hide them well."

"I think I can handle a few warts if you ever want to share them." I took his hand and squeezed it. I acknowledged his family life was complicated and he distanced me purposely from the drama. But I bared my deepest scars and I wanted to reassure him he could do the same.

He pulsed my hand in return and I leaned my head on his shoulder to watch Lexi sing. Blake would open up when he was ready and I wouldn't push it. It had taken a lot for him to tell me about his father's death and he would divulge everything else about his family in time. Having his secrets wasn't as important to me as having him.

Chapter Twenty

The weekend after the karaoke get-together, Blake loaned me his car and I took full advantage of it. I hadn't been shopping in ages and needed a few new outfits for the warmer weather. I was also trying to move away from the utilitarian bra and underwear sets and buy something that didn't scream granny panties.

I'd been dating Blake for over a month and it felt like sex was on the horizon. He was reserved when we were alone together and it was refreshing in a way. He wanted me to set the tone, tell him what was okay and what wasn't. I wanted more, but it was smart to take it slow. It was easy to get swept away by desire and offer up my body fully to him. When we became entangled in bed and he rained feverish kisses on my face and neck, I could feel his need. My skin was set aflame when he touched me and it took a concentrated effort to not remove every piece of clothing standing between us. But it would happen; I only had to be patient.

When I arrived at the apartment to return Blake's car, Darien opened the door. He was pulling on a jacket as he gestured me inside. "I'm heading out for a while so maybe you can take over babysitting duty. Blake's in one of his moods and hasn't come out of his room for most of the day."

My stomach dropped. "Is he okay?"

"Not sure what's going on with him. He hasn't had too

many emo nights since the two of you've gotten together, but it has happened before." Darien looked apologetic and I understood he wasn't going to betray his friend's confidence by saying any more. I wondered if Darien regretted telling me about Blake's mom and their complicated relationship. I pushed, but if I had no idea the cause of his hurt, I had no means to fix it.

"Okay. Have fun and don't drive if you're drinking. I'll pick you up," I offered.

He nodded and waved as he ambled down the path to his Ford SUV. I shut the door and frowned as I looked at Blake's closed door. I walked over and tentatively knocked. When I didn't receive an answer, I opened the door a crack and whispered, "Blake?"

The room was dark and I blinked to adjust to the surroundings. Slipping inside, I closed the door behind me. I noticed the glow coming from Blake's iPhone and followed it to find my way to his bed. I reached the bed and I could make out Blake's closed eyes. His chest rose and fell steadily and I tried to slip into bed without waking him up. He started as the mattress moved under my weight, but relaxed once he stared in my direction.

He turned on the bedside lamp and as he sat up I popped one of the earbuds out. Positioning it in my own ear, I grimaced in his direction as a Radiohead song played. I noticed the empty beer bottles littering his nightstand as I handed the earbud back. "Drinking in the dark while listening to Radiohead? How very self-indulgent of you."

Blake chuckled darkly and fell back onto his pillow. "I like how you're never afraid to call me on my bullshit."

I shifted until I was flush with his body. I draped my arm across his waist. My forefinger traced the striped pattern of his T-shirt. "What's going on? Are you okay?"

"Just having a bad day. It's better now that you're here."

I flipped onto my belly and watched him for a long moment. "I think it's more than that. You can tell me the truth."

"Don't worry about me. I'll be fine," Blake insisted.

I leaned my chin on his belly. "Fine, if you won't tell me, let's play a game instead."

Blake stretched his arms over his head and the tension left his jaw. He seemed to relax over the thought of changing the subject. "What kind of game?"

"It's called two truths and a lie." Blake pulled a face. "Come on. I'll even go first."

"Okay. How do you play?"

"I'm going to tell you three things. Two of them are true and one of them is a lie. You have to figure out which one is the lie."

"Can't we play another kind of game?" Blake's voice turned husky and I pressed my body closer to him in response. His fingers took their time running through the long waves of my hair and I was hyperaware of his hand as it rested on my lower back. I almost yelped out in agreement, but pushed my physical urgency for him aside for the moment.

I had to find out his secrets because his pain terrified me. It was too reminiscent of how I used to be—trying to mend unfixable things about myself. I may have related to his yearning to keep his secrets safely tucked away, but I couldn't accept it.

"No," I said and racked my brain for the three things to tell him. At the last second, I altered my three confessions. "I've suffered from panic attacks for the past couple of years and need to take medicine sometimes to control it. I had an incurable crush on you since we met and I tried to fight it because I thought you were completely wrong for me." I fought to keep my voice neutral. "And I'm not a virgin."

I saw understanding flicker in his expression. He opened up his mouth to reply, but I leaped on top of him and placed a finger over his lips. "You don't have to say your answer out loud. I just…wanted to put it out there."

He removed my finger and lifted his head up and pressed a firm kiss on my lips. "All right," he said softly once he pulled away. It was another burden I was able to get rid of by telling him. I was nervous about sex and since I nominated Blake as my first, I wanted him to keep my virginity in the back of his mind when things went to that level. Blake would be gentle regardless, I was certain, but I wanted to be honest with him and have us share the same expectations.

"Your turn," I prompted.

"I know." He leaned up on his elbows and chewed on his lip. Finally, he stared down at me and said, "I hate football sometimes, like the enjoyment I once got out of playing the game has been zapped away. I've always put my family first, no matter what, and people have been hurt because of my blind loyalty." I held my breath as his eyes bored into mine. "And I'm not in love with you."

I stilled and stared back at him in disbelief. I opened my mouth to try and blurt out some type of response, but in a familiar gesture, he put his finger over my lips. "No fair. You can't answer if I wasn't allowed to."

My chest constricted and I released an unsteady breath. I should tell him *I love you*. But I couldn't, not yet. I wasn't sure what was harder for me—to make myself emotionally or physically vulnerable. Blake returned to the prone position on the bed and I leaned my head on his chest. I heard his heart thudding against my ear, his body alerting me of his anxiety. He had given me something special—an unforgettable moment I could reach back to when things got hard.

I snuck my hands under the edge of his T-shirt and drifted my hands over his bare flesh. I pulled at the hem and once I bunched the fabric around Blake's chest, he took the hint and removed the shirt. I took my time to study every bit of his exposed body. He was perfect, his skin unblemished with the exception of a modest-sized scar on the underside of his ribs. I gave him a questioning look as I rubbed the pink line.

"Believe it or not that didn't come from football. I had a bad fall off my bike when I was twelve."

I smiled and continued my visual inspection of him, trying to memorize every glorious inch of him. I became tied up in knots as I noticed his tan line peeking out of his low-slung jeans. I coasted the hem of his jeans with my fingertips, stroking the area liberally.

"Come here," he commanded in a deep growl. I obeyed his request by straddling my body across his waist. I laced my fingers behind his neck and my mouth instinctively found his. There was no hesitating on my part as I kissed him with feverish need. Our kisses were wild with my tongue exploring his mouth and I tasted the remnants of the cinnamon gum he frequently chewed.

His hand reached under my shirt and the feeling of his calloused hands on my bare back was intoxicating. I needed more from him and in a swift motion, I removed my yellow T-shirt and tossed it onto the floor. Blake moved from massaging my back to cupping my breasts through the blue silk fabric of my bra. He never stopped kissing me, even when I moaned into his mouth, enjoying the feel of him fondling me openly.

I stopped for a moment to catch my breath and reached behind my back. Blake put his hand over mine as my fingers reached around to my bra clasp. "Are you sure?" he asked. We were entering new territory, but I wasn't ready to stop. I nodded and undid the back of my bra. I shimmied out of it and fought the urge to cover my breasts.

His eyes became hooded and the way he wet his lips turned me on. I lay down on the opposite end of the bed, switching positions with Blake. Instead of returning his attention to my breasts, he looked me over with a ravenous expression. I held my breath as his eyes darkened with need.

His body looked strong and powerful as I stayed sandwiched between his arms. My skin tingled when he didn't rush to pull his gaze from my nakedness. "You're beautiful. I could spend hours looking at you and still wonder if I'm dreaming. It doesn't seem possible that this is real and you're here with me in bed."

I cupped his cheek, feeling the day-old beard scratch my palm. "I'm real and I'm yours."

I watched his Adam's apple bob as he took his hand to my left breast. His thumb brushed my nipple and my back arched in pleasure. He worked my right breast in a similar motion and I squirmed with pent-up sexual energy. I could feel electricity shooting through my body and making its way between my legs. He positioned his mouth over my breast and I cried out as his tongue circled around my nipple. He teased me with his tongue, flicking it over the nipple before he returned to tracing slow and seductive circles around the center of my breast. He mimicked his movements on my other breast and I got lost in the sensation. My overanalytical brain fled the premises as I became acutely aware of what his mouth was doing to me.

His attentions didn't stop with my breasts. He kissed down my belly before reaching the button on my pants. As he moved his mouth back the way he came, he used his right hand to massage the area between my legs. His movements were controlled and he found a steady rhythm that made my body hum. He stopped only when I reached out for him. He was aroused and I wanted to give him the same pleasure he'd been giving me. He crawled back to the head of the bed and gave me a strained smile.

"Not yet," he said softly. "I think I'll need a dozen ice cold showers, but I want to do this right with you. And I think that means not rushing into this."

I bit down on the inside of my cheek before answering. "And that's okay with you? Waiting?"

"Yes," he answered automatically. He reached out his arm and pulled me up once I latched onto his forearm. "Although I want nothing more than to take you right now, I can't. It wouldn't be right and I would feel like an ass if I pushed you too hard."

"But I think I'm ready…"

He interrupted me. "You sound unsure and I'm fine with that. Because when we do have sex, I want you to have zero regrets."

I didn't think I'd have regrets, but I needed a little perspective. Lying partially naked in his arms couldn't provide the reassurance I was thinking with the right body part. But I had a strong sense as soon as I left him, my body would be begging to let him finish what he started. I had it bad for Blake Preston.

"Do you know I have a favorite math theory?" he said.

I pressed my breasts against his solid chest and got comfortable in his arms. The sexual tension was still between us, but I was intrigued by Blake's sudden change of subject.

"No," I giggled. "But I think it's adorable that a big strong alpha football player has a favorite math theory."

His smile was contemplative. "It's called unsolvability. It means there are math problems that don't abide by a set of rules, you can't verify if they're true or not based on a math theory. They defy logic and can't be solved in the usual way." His voice dropped to a near whisper. "And it reminds me of us. On the outside, it seems like things can't work. There are too many variables trying to keep us apart. But despite it all, we're together and being with you is the best thing to ever happen to me."

"You're the best thing to happen to me too." I pressed my lips to his bare shoulder. "But what variables? What's trying to keep us apart?"

"Things from before that I can't tell you. I should tell you, but I don't want it to ruin everything. Because it feels like what we have is fragile and the more you get to know about me, the more likely it will all shatter."

"I can accept you as you are right now. No more questions until you're ready to give me the answers. But I do want them from you one day. Because I'm not afraid to know you and I can take it. I'm patient and I'll wait for as long as you need."

His eyes were filled with pain and I resolved to let him be. I needed to be pushed, but not everyone processed pain in the same way. Whatever was haunting Blake would be driven out when he was brave enough to face it.

Chapter Twenty-One

"Thanks for letting me practice on you," Lexi said as she braided my hair for the fourth time that evening. Finn had invited her to a family wedding and she had a complicated braiding style in mind she first wanted to try out on me.

"No problem," I said and reached for the bowl of chips we were sharing while watching a marathon of classic romance movies on cable. We'd been waiting for Casey to join our girls' night, but she was a no-show. It was a Friday night and Lexi and I guessed she bailed to go to a party.

"How do I look?" I asked as she tied the braids in place. The style involved two French braids coming together at the nape of my neck secured with several bobby pins.

Lexi sighed. "You look amazing, but I have a feeling I won't be able to pull it off and will look like a ten-year-old. My hair isn't long enough and I'm worried the extensions will be obvious."

I jumped out of my chair and checked out my reflection in the mirror across the room. "I think it will look great with the floral dress you're wearing. It will give you a cool bohemian chic vibe."

"Maybe."

A minute later, I paused the movie as Lexi and I heard persistent knocking at our door. After checking the keyhole, I let

Casey in. She barreled into the room and sank into the chair I previously occupied. Her cheeks were flushed and a sheen of sweat had broken out across her forehead.

Lexi stood up and brushed the chips off of her black pants. "What happened to you? We told you to come by two hours ago."

"It's your fault I'm late." Casey settled her accusing stare on me. "I ran into Will and somehow I ended up back in his room..."

"I thought you smelled like Chinese food," Lexi squealed.

"It's all Autumn's fault I hooked up with him. She and Blake were so sickly sweet with their you complete me nonsense I was feeling lonely and vulnerable."

"I would never be cheesy enough to tell Blake he completes me." By Lexi and Casey's matching disbelieving expressions, I guessed they didn't believe it.

I held up my hands in surrender. "What? We're talking about Casey here."

"Anyway, I was doing laundry before I came here and I ran into him in the laundry room. He had this big dopey smile on when he saw me and I couldn't resist. I figured I'd kiss him and see if there was any chemistry there."

"You hooked up with him in the laundry room?" Lexi asked.

"No, we went back to his room."

"He mustn't have been too bad of a kisser considering you're hours late."

Casey fluffed her hair. "Well, we do have chemistry. I'm not ready for another boyfriend, but it would be convenient to have a boy toy who lived on our floor."

The phone rang, interrupting our laughter. I checked the call screen before setting my cell back down beside me. Lexi frowned in my direction. "You can't avoid your mom forever."

"Probably not. But I could probably go at least another week until she decides to drop in."

"Why? What's up with you and your mom?" Casey asked, leaning forward.

"We're fine, but she's nervous about my relationship with Blake. A friend of my dad's saw Blake and Hunter fighting at the bowling alley and told him about it. I explained it to my mom, but she's concerned I'm dating another violent sociopath. I guess having Hunter as my only ex makes her skeptical about my ability to pick quality men."

"But she met Blake?" Casey asked. After I nodded, she asked, "And she wasn't swept away by his dreaminess?"

I grinned. "Hard to believe, but she hasn't become a major Blake fan yet. My dad liked him, but my mom is the one he'll have to work the hardest to convince. She's worried I'll completely sacrifice my identity for our relationship and forget my own goals."

"It will be fine once she gets to know him better. Any plans to meet his parents soon?" Lexi asked.

"There's only his mom and he has a younger sister. His mom sounds a little intense, so I'm not going to push a meeting unless he suggests it. From what he tells me, he really only goes home to spend time with his sister." Blake was overprotective of his sister and their closeness made me anxious to meet her. He was guarded when he spoke about her and I got the impression he wasn't quite ready for us to meet. I grinned at Casey. "What about you? Any plans to meet Will's parents?"

Leaping out of the chair, she picked up a throw pillow off of Lexi's bed and launched it at me. The pillow knocked into my arm before falling to the ground. "No!" she sneered. "I'm not going to hook up with him again for at least another two weeks. Can't be having him get too attached."

"Will is cute and a sweetheart. He'll treat you like a princess if you give him a chance," Lexi said, pausing as she twirled her hair into a messy bun.

"I'm not taking dating advice from you, Lex, no offense. You're the one who set up Autumn with Josh." Lexi scowled at her, but Casey was undeterred. "At least she was smart enough and took my advice to go for the highly fuckable player."

"Football player," I muttered with a mouthful of chips.

"Josh is nice," Lexi insisted. "And what was the harm? They're still friends."

Josh and I were still friends, but I think the failed date put a strain on our friendship. I also knew he didn't like Blake—Josh declined any time I tried to invite him anywhere with Blake—and I was uncertain if it was simply a personality clash or jealousy. I still met Josh for lunch from time to time, but he pointedly changed the subject if I brought up Blake.

"These adjectives you use to describe men, Lexi, make me want to throw up in my mouth. *Nice. Sweetheart. Cute.* All I hear is boring, boring, boring." Casey caught my gaze. "What about Darien? Is he single?"

"Yes, but I'm afraid he's nice."

We broke out into a fit of giggles and once we quieted down Lexi resumed the movie. I kept glancing at Lexi and Casey while we watched TV, sighing contentedly. Cook University had been the new start I needed. I had good friends and our connections ran deeper than the superficial friendships I had in high school. Lexi had stayed up with me for hours on nights when I suffered from a Mr. Bridges–induced nightmare. If it had been Faye, she would've told me to stop acting like a freak and would've forced a Xanax down my throat after she stole two for herself.

I'd also found out things about myself I never knew. I'd been so entrenched in cheerleading and trying to be popular I never made room for anything else. I loved art and literature and my passion for the subjects grew at Cook. I researched more about entering the social work field and I was getting excited for my future. There was a women's shelter near the beach house my parents rented and I put in an application to volunteer there during the summer.

I blossomed because I was away from Newpine and had

escaped the looming shadow of my past. Mr. Bridges' release was a couple short months away, but I wouldn't give him the satisfaction of withering away. I had emerged from my brush with hell stronger and smarter. And I had reached the point where I was ready to let go. I had been his puppet despite miles and iron bars separating us—because I allowed him to control who I let into my life. I craved a physical connection with Blake and I'd have it. It was time to shove the ghost of Mr. Bridges into a box and forbid him from controlling me ever again.

Chapter Twenty-Two

Blake leaned his forehead against mine and I saw his inhale. It felt good to see him drink me in, being able to witness the unsettling effect I had on him. His green eyes twinkled as he looked down at me. We were lying in my bed and had been kissing for a good twenty minutes. Blake's art history textbook lay untouched on my desk—our attempt at studying together lasting a grand total of ten minutes. I had reached over to remove a piece of lint from his tan sweater and somehow landed in his lap. I had kissed him tentatively at first, but the intensity gradually increased.

I felt ready to combust as Blake continued to kiss and touch me through my sweater. The room suddenly felt sweltering and I lifted my sweater over my head. Blake's eyes danced over my exposed flesh and I was grateful I decided to go lingerie shopping. His thumb fingered the black lace on my bra.

"You look very sexy, but what about Lexi?" he asked and motioned to the door.

"She'll text me before she comes back. I do the same for her when Finn is over." I laughed. "It's the modern sock on the door handle."

Blake smiled, but I could still see the want in his eyes. "What time will she be back?"

"Not sure. Maybe not for another hour or so."

"Definitely not enough time to do everything I want to do to you," Blake murmured. My heart pounded wildly at the suggestion and it became impossible to talk, no less breathe. He bent over and kissed the underside of my bra before making a trail down the center of my belly. His lips stopped moving. "Do you know you have this lone freckle next to your belly button?"

"No, I wasn't aware of that," I managed.

His thumb slid over my bare belly and I tingled all over. "It's actually very adorable. I like it so much I think I'll name it Blake's Freckle." He grinned at me and cupped his palm over his ear. "What's that, Blake's Freckle? You want me to do dirty things to you? Well…okay."

"You're impossible."

His smile didn't leave his face as he began to tease my belly with his mouth. His tongue moved in slow circles around my belly button and he finished the move by releasing a slow, hot breath close to my skin. It felt incredible and I whimpered when he pulled away.

I arched my back and lifted my rear off of the bed. I undid the button on my jeans and began to shimmy out of them. Blake's look was hungry, but I could see other emotions warring behind his eyes. He was afraid of losing me if things went too far.

I pulled him down closer and felt every hard muscle as his body crushed against my breasts. I kissed him deeply while rubbing my arms up and down his back. I stripped his sweater off and tossed it across the room. My hands trembled as I found the button on his pants. Before he could notice my hesitation, I steadied my hands and unfastened the button. While Blake removed his pants, I had a moment to admire how strong and beautiful he was clad in only his white boxers. They were the boxer briefs style and clung to his body like a second skin. When he climbed back next to me, I felt his hardness rest against my leg.

The tremors started building and my entire being was

rocked over how much I wanted him inside of me. I was ready to explode with need for him.

Blake groaned and began to kiss my neck in a frenzy. His hands snuck beneath the bra and he squeezed both my breasts in time with the kisses. His eagerness inspired me to reach for him and I stroked him through his boxer shorts. Blake stilled and his eyes drifted shut, his face filling with raw lust. It was all the encouragement I needed and I began to pump my hand up and down in rapid succession. He moaned and I felt him grow larger under my hands. It was arousing, using my hands to give him the pleasure we both were craving.

He hooked his thumbs over the sides of my underwear and pulled them down. I waited for the alarm to set in, but it was nonexistent. The only emotion I had was heady desire as I saw Blake slip two of his fingers between my legs.

I paused with my hand still wrapped around Blake's hardness. I gasped as I felt him inside me, exploring between the folds. His movements were slow and he kept tossing glances at me as his fingers glided inside and out of me. There was no need to say I was all right since I was certain he could see the way he was making me die a slow, pleasurable death underneath him.

I cried out in protest as he moved out of my reach and centered his mouth over my left breast. "You feel so good and I love how you touch me, but let me make you come. Tell me if you need me to stop."

I nodded because I could tell he needed the go-ahead. I unhooked my bra and his mouth closed over my left nipple. He sucked gently while thrusting his fingers inside of me. A scorching heat spread everywhere and I noticed how wet I was getting as more time passed. I panted beneath him and murmured how amazing he was making me feel.

I threw my head back as Blake nipped at my breast lightly. My reaction inspired him to repeat the process on my right breast before taking my nipple in his mouth. The way his tongue trailed up and down my breast matched what his fingers were doing inside of me. "Please don't stop," I said in a small voice.

"I won't unless you tell me to." His voice was a husky growl from below.

Gazing down, I watched his lips move away from my breasts. I locked eyes with him as he stroked his tongue down the center of my pelvis and stopped with a kiss at my opening. The stimulation from his fingers didn't stop as he sucked and kissed me in my most sensitive areas. My hips lifted and he increased the pressure of his mouth. My moans deepened and I felt like the room would start spinning any second. I expected him to let up, giving me a chance to reciprocate for him, but he never stopped the erotic invasion. Soon, I found myself on the cusp of an orgasm. Blake's fingers traveled deeper inside of me and I completely lost it. The pleasure overtook me and I bucked wildly as warmth flowed from my core outward. Blake took a spot by my side and held me as I finished.

I shivered as I rose up onto my elbows. My eyes lowered to Blake's boxers and my fingers gingerly reached to remove him of the remainder of his clothing. "Blake, I'm ready."

His fingers had felt incredible inside of me and I could only imagine how good it would feel to be filled up with him. I understood the first time would likely hurt, but I was anticipating the times in the future when we would both finish with our bodies locked together.

"That was the hottest thing I've ever seen in my life," he said and took his time to run his eyes appreciatively over my body. He grabbed both of my hands and clasped them tightly. "And I imagine the second I'm inside of you, I'll be done for."

"I want you, Blake, so freaking badly."

"I want you too, but I need to tell you some things first…"

I snatched my hands away. "Tell me what? Please don't say there's someone else. Because I know we're not official or anything, but I will kill you if you're sleeping around."

He wrapped his arm around my back and drew me to his

chest. "Of course not, Autumn. And of course we're official. I thought you realized that after we talked about not seeing anyone else."

I relaxed. "So, are you my boyfriend?"

"If you'll have me."

"Absolutely," I said. I started to question him further, but the sound of my phone interrupted me. After twisting out of his arms, I swore under my breath. I turned to face him. "It's Lexi. She's coming back from the library and will be here in ten minutes."

I retrieved my discarded clothing and then tossed his shirt and pants in his direction. Instead of dressing right away, he watched me slip on my clothing. I was nervous about what he wanted to talk about, but my body was still reeling.

He stood up and rested his palms on top of my shoulders. "Darien is going home next weekend. Why don't you come stay at my place? We'll talk and…"

"And finish what we started," I interrupted. I tilted my head to the side. "I'm not bullshitting you, Blake. I'm completely ready to be with you."

"Autumn, I'm trying my best to be a good guy and show some restraint. If I fuck this up, I know I'll lose you."

"You're not going to lose me." *Because I won't lose you.* He had undone me in a way that I couldn't imagine going back to the way things were before. Our connection was electric and I sensed how rare it was to feel the way I did. I'd do anything to keep from losing him, including risking my heart despite my fears of being left vulnerable.

I frowned at the time on the clock. "But I may lose my roommate if you don't get dressed."

His eyes closed for a second before he turned away to put his clothing back on. A part of me wished we hadn't stopped, but it was for the best. I wouldn't want to rush our first time and I wouldn't be the jerky roommate asking Lexi to remain scarce so I could hand over my v-card to my boyfriend. Staying at his place for the weekend would be romantic and, most importantly, private.

There was an uneasy feeling over what Blake wanted to talk about, but there was also a hopeful anticipation. Blake was closed off about certain parts of his life, most notably his family, and maybe if we talked everything out, it would solidify what we had. If he wanted to share something about himself only to me, I was eager to find out what it was. Any piece of himself he would willingly carve out and hand over, I would hold onto and never let go.

Chapter Twenty-Three

The next week, I met up with Lexi, Finn, and Josh to study in the student lounge in our dorm. Deadlines for our final papers were coming up and exams were two short weeks away. Despite the distraction of a new relationship, I was confident with my grades for the semester. I still had to cram, but I was less stressed than my friends.

Lexi covered her head with her hands and moaned. "I will never get this material. Why the hell am I a chemistry major?"

Finn rubbed the back of her neck. "You'll get it. Don't psych yourself out."

Lexi lifted her textbook and set it against her forehead. "Maybe if I keep the book against my head long enough the words will seep into my brain."

"You need a break. Why don't we get something to eat?" Josh suggested.

"No way. I'm not leaving this room until I memorize all of the rules for assigning oxidation numbers." She gave Finn a pleading look. "But maybe you could make a food run?"

Finn tilted his head, making his shaggy blond hair fall into his eyes. "Do you mind if I go in an hour? I'm almost done with the first draft of my essay."

Lexi set her puppy dog brown eyes on me. "Could you go, Autumn? You're the only one caught up and I'm really in the mood for a pizza with mushrooms and peppers from Anthony's. Finn will lend you his car."

Finn looked nonplussed over his girlfriend offering up his car. "I don't mind, but it's up to you. I'll pick up the pizza if it's a pain."

"It's not a problem. We'll call ahead and I'll bring it back here." I stood up and stretched. "Hey, do you care if I drop off some food for Blake on my way back? He's studying at his apartment and the last time I checked his fridge he only had beer, milk, and eggs in it."

"Yeah, sure," Finn agreed and handed over his keys. Blake had declined my invitation to study together. I had to agree we made awful study buddies and ended up hooking up more than cracking a book. He told me to call him later and we could meet up later at night if I felt up to it.

Minutes later, Finn called in our pizza and sandwich order and I jogged to the student parking lot. After wandering aimlessly for several minutes, I finally found his Acura. Anthony's was less than ten minutes from campus, not far from Blake's apartment. Blake was a cheesesteak connoisseur and he'd appreciate the surprise lunch of a pizza steak and fries.

The dinner crowd at Anthony's hadn't arrived yet and I picked up our order quickly. Lexi would have my head if I returned with cold pizza, so I would have to drop off Blake's lunch with only a quick kiss to hold me over until later. Our weekend date was only two days away and every time I thought about it, butterflies took over my core.

Blake hinted at arranging something romantic for the weekend and I couldn't wait to see how he planned to surprise me. In all honesty, the thought of giving him my virginity was all the romance I needed. I had no idea what it would be like to be connected to Blake in that way and I couldn't wait to find out.

I left Finn's car running as I parked in front of Blake's apartment unit. Grabbing the bag with his sandwich inside, I headed down the pathway to his door. I straightened out my V-neck blouse as I rang the doorbell. A minute later, a girl I didn't recognize swung open the door. As she looked me over, open hostility snuck into her features. "What the hell are you doing here?"

I almost demanded the same thing back at her, but my throat seized up. In seconds, I realized I was staring at the secret Blake had to tell me. This gorgeous girl with her long and glossy blonde hair and captivating blue eyes was my worst nightmare come to life. She was a couple of inches taller than me, accentuated by her high heels. She wore a short white dress and from my quick inspection, I could see her body was flawless. The girl was thin, but had enough curves to fill out the dress perfectly. I was certain of his infidelity because why else would she be staring at me as if it was an effort not to rip my hair out.

"What's going on, Delia?" a woman's irritated tone came from behind the girl. The door swung open wider and I blinked in shock. I waited for the ground to open up and swallow me because what I was seeing couldn't be real.

Cassie Bridges stood inside of Blake's apartment for some inexplicable reason. The world stopped and I imagined my body and mind dividing. I couldn't get a handle on how one of my nightmares escaped my head and appeared in the flesh and blood before me.

Cassie had looked to Delia for answers before swinging her gaze in my direction. Instantaneously, her face flushed with anger and she knocked Delia aside to storm up to me. "What are you doing here? How dare you show your face to me?"

I backed away, priming my body to make a run for it. Because it was the only way I knew how to survive. *Running, always running, but never being truly free.*

Before I had a chance to bolt, Blake's voice pulled all of our attention away from the standoff. "Mom, what are you guys doing out here?"

"No," I choked out. Because something was infinitely wrong in the universe if Blake had just called the wife of the man who tried to rape me his mother. My brain couldn't compute what was going on and I was too shell-shocked to continue my plan to flee. A million more sensible possibilities ran through my brain, like the idea I'd died and gone to hell.

Blake moved past Delia to stand on his front stoop. Dawning horror entered his features as he saw his mother bear down on me. Cassie swung back to face me and before I could make a defensive move, she slapped me across the cheek. My skin stung and tears blurred my vision. "You don't know how good that felt to do, you little slut. Are you stalking my son now? Luckily I caught you before you cried rape and tried to throw him in jail too."

"Mom, stop it!" Blake roared. He stepped between us and his large frame blocked her from my view. "Are you okay?" he asked and tried to move my hair away to examine my cheek. I stumbled backwards and almost fell as I tried to avoid his touch. His fingers, the ones that merely days ago had me crying out in delicious ecstasy, appeared to me as swords that would leave behind mortal wounds if they touched my skin.

"What are you doing here?" Delia shouted at me. I knew Blake's sister's name, but it was the first time I'd seen her in person. She looked closer to my age than sixteen and it was the reason I assumed at first Blake had been cheating on me with her. *If only.* What a horrifying thought that Blake sleeping with another woman was a welcome alternative to the truth.

Delia's blue eyes, the same eyes as the devil, had the most unsettling effect on me. I felt dizzy, black spots erupting into my vision field, and I was certain it was only seconds before I would faint.

Blake answered as I inched toward Finn's car. "Mom and Delia, you need to go inside. I need a minute alone with Autumn."

"Are you out of your goddamn mind? Do you realize who this is? Do you remember what she did to our family? To your father?" His mother's hands curled into fists and by the fire in her hazel eyes, she was waiting for Blake to move out of the way so she could proceed to pummel me.

"Mom, she didn't know who I was..." Blake trailed off and I understood his meaning perfectly. I may not have known who he was, but there was little doubt in my mind he'd known exactly who I was.

"But she knew my husband was a married man," Cassie seethed. She bared her teeth at me. "Did you care? He had a wife and children and we depended on him. Did that thought ever cross your mind when you whored around with him?"

Cassie's take on what happened didn't come as a surprise. I heard about her stance during the days surrounding her husband's arrest. She was choosing to stand by her man and believe his side of the story: the tale where I had set out to seduce him, wanting to improve my almost failing grade, and had used any means possible. He had succumbed to my charms, but had quickly broken things off. His version featured me as a vindictive teen who reported him for sexual assault because of his hurtful rejection.

I took a step backward. Blake grabbed onto my elbow, likely guessing I was about to run off. He spoke to his mom. "You need to go inside right now. If you don't, I'm withdrawing the rest of the money from my bank account and I'm never speaking to you again."

His mother's expression skewed up in disgust. Her stature was small, but her presence was formidable. It felt like a cold blanket thrown over my body each time she scowled in my direction. "Where's your loyalty? Your father gave you *everything*. He has loved you—"

Blake broke in. "Mom, stop it. I'm serious. If you want me to keep helping out with money, you need to walk away."

Cassie crossed her arms in front of her chest. "I'll go, but this isn't over." She turned her icy gaze once again on me. "I'm calling my lawyer and I'll take out a restraining order to keep you away from my family if I have to. You've done enough damage."

Blake ushered his mother inside. Delia bit her lip and looked at her brother questioningly. "It's going to be okay, Del. I'll explain everything." Delia's eyebrows pulled together as she looked at me like a puzzle she couldn't quite figure out. I averted my eyes because the weight of her gaze was too heavy and it became even harder to breathe. I felt close to hyperventilating and the last thing I wanted was for the family of the man I hated to come to my rescue. Finally, Delia turned on her heel and disappeared inside the apartment.

During the exchange, I had backed up completely to Finn's car. I went to open the car door, relieved I had left it running. As my hand circled the door handle, Blake came up from behind me and pushed against the window to prevent me from entering. "Get the hell away from me," I hissed without turning to face him.

"Autumn, please, you have to at least hear my side of things…"

"I said get away from me." I had temporarily forgotten the takeout container I had been holding the entire time. I launched it at him and the box crashed into his chest. His lunch fell to the ground and spilled at our feet.

In minutes, I had become afraid of Blake, but my anger outweighed my fear. I slammed both of my palms against his chest. When he barely moved, I made a tight fist and pounded at his chest and stomach. I was trembling with rage, my only aim wanting to cause him a fraction of the ache I was feeling. Mr. Bridges had been my teacher and his betrayal of my trust had stung. Blake's betrayal felt as if he had cut into me a thousand times and then decided to drown me in a vat of salt.

Blake took each hit and I hoped to get some satisfaction from the anguish etched into his features. His eyes were moist, but I refused to believe he was capable of real emotion. They were crocodile tears—brought on because he had been caught in the web of lies he spun.

I didn't want to cry and I wished the numbness from before would return. But a sob escaped as I punched him one last time and my arms fell to my sides. "When did you know? When did you realize who I was?" Blake squeezed his eyes shut before looking away shamefaced. It was all the admission of guilt I needed. "You saw me at the party and recognized me. So, from the moment we met, you've failed to mention *your father* was the one who tried to rape me."

"He's not my father. I did tell you the truth about my dad dying. Thomas married my mother when I was six."

"Did he put you up to it? Was it some kind of twisted revenge scheme?"

Blake appeared horrified by the suggestion. "God no. Is that what you honestly think I'd do? I know how bad this looks, but I never set out to hurt you. I haven't talked to Thomas in a year and I've tried to move on after his arrest. I saw you at the Football House and it felt like I was seeing a ghost. The decent thing to do would've been to stay away from you. But I didn't and instead fell in love with you."

I scoffed, a fresh rage igniting that I felt down to my bones. "Fell in love with me? You're a manipulative monster and although he's not your blood, Thomas obviously raised you to follow in his footsteps." I tilted my chin and stared him down. "Now, let me leave before I scream."

Because a terrible scream was building up and I imagined the world crumbling before my eyes when I released it. I was barely holding on and I couldn't stand to see his beautiful deceptive face for another second.

Blake released his hold on the door and stepped away from the car. "I'm so sorry, Autumn. I fucked everything up and it's killing me to know how much you must hate me right now."

"Fuck you and fuck your apology."

I refused to look at him as I rushed into the driver's seat

and slammed the door as he continued to blurt out a string of bumbling apologies. Nothing he could say would change the fact he was the son of the man who tried to destroy me. Thomas Bridges was at the heart of every one of my nightmares. Blake had connived his way into my life and heart—pretending to be a man I could trust. Lie after lie had carelessly slipped from his lips and I had bought them all.

Why did I always blindly trust the wrong people? I had enough faith in Blake to give him my heart with plans to give him my body as well. I had sensed he was holding back something from me, but never came close to suspecting what type of skeletons he'd been hiding. They weren't merely skeletons—they were rotting corpses who wanted to drag me back down to hell alongside them.

I pulled to the side of the road several blocks away from Blake's apartment. I rested my head against the steering wheel and released a wail from my lungs. I let go of every pent-up emotion and my back began to shake as an endless number of sobs racked my body.

I had suffered loss before, but losing Blake felt like my heart was being shredded over and over again. I tried to tell myself I should feel nothing since loving Blake was an illusion. It wasn't love if you never truly knew who that person was. But I gained no comfort from the thought and I surrendered to the hurt. I was mourning the loss of the man I thought Blake was and trying to come to terms with my hopes for a forever with him vanishing in the span of minutes.

Chapter Twenty-Four

The sensation of having my spirit broken was oddly familiar. My limbs were heavy and my only desire was to crawl under the covers and hope to remain unnoticed as the world passed me by. To stop my automatic impulse to check out of my life once again was to tap into my rage. I had built a life away from Newpine, and Mr. Bridges and his son were trying to steal it away from me.

I returned to the student lounge in a daze. Lexi took one look at my face and rushed me back to our room. I had pulled it together enough to drive back to campus, but I was on the verge of another breakdown and didn't need an audience for it.

Lexi was appalled as I told her what had happened at Blake's and revealed his true identity. She comforted me as she voiced many of the questions I had out loud. Why did he seek me out? What did he have to gain by pretending to be my friend and then later my boyfriend? Did he still have a relationship with his stepfather since he was imprisoned?

When I couldn't answer any of her questions, she quieted down and sat next to me while I laid my head in her lap. She smoothed my hair back and made comforting noises in the back of her throat. My mom was miles away, but Lexi would be there for me as I tried to survive my devastation. I wanted to call my mother more than anything, but I was too ashamed. It was humiliating to admit what a fool I'd been. I'd been blinded by Blake's beauty and his manufactured kindness. Again, I had failed to see what truly lurked below the surface.

"What's wrong with me? How could I miss something this major?"

"You never saw what his son looked like, right?" I shook my head. "And Blake must have been careful about what he told you so you wouldn't figure it out."

I knew Mr. Bridges had a son and a daughter, but I hadn't known much about them. Mr. Bridges spoke mostly about Cassie during our tutoring sessions and only mentioned his children in passing. If he ever mentioned their names, I hadn't remembered them. They hadn't appeared in any media reports and my guess was their mother had kept them out of the spotlight when the scandal broke. Before Blake approached me at the football party, they were innocent bystanders to what their father had done.

Looking back, I could see a few scarce hints at what Blake was hiding, a breadcrumb trail to the truth. Our first meeting was awkward and he'd been standoffish about me being at the party. Belatedly, he must have realized I didn't recognize him. He had the opportunity then to walk away or to at least tell me who he was and give me the chance to avoid him. But he had tried to foster a friendship and I had no idea why.

"I don't know what to say to make this better. I honestly thought Blake was a good guy and it's so hard to believe that he did any of this to hurt you." Lexi chewed her nails as I sat up next to her. At my questioning look, she added, "It seems far-fetched to me that Blake would spend months trying to build a relationship with you if he was looking to get revenge for what happened with his stepfather."

"So, you think he honestly loves me?"

"Yes, I do." I opened my mouth to protest, but Lexi held up a hand to silence me. "I'm not saying just because he loves you makes anything he has done any less repulsive. Blake's obviously troubled and I can't even begin to dream up a good reason he lied to you."

"He kept saying he wanted to be honest about his past, but he never followed through. He said we were going to talk this weekend."

I cringed as I thought about how close I'd come to losing my virginity. At least he had enough of a conscience to not sleep with me without coming clean about who he was. Blake had always held back when we began a physical relationship and I thought it was because he respected me. The truth was he knew every filthy detail about my past before I confessed. The only question remained was whose version did he believe: his stepfather's or mine?

***

Hours later, I finally convinced Lexi to return to her studying. She would gladly set it aside if I needed her, but there was no magic remedy for what ailed me. I considered taking my medication, but panic wasn't the only emotion I couldn't get a handle on. I was angry and hurt and didn't understand what I'd done to deserve being dealt such a shitty hand. Why did I have to fall for the one person I could never have a happy ending with?

I had two miserable weeks to finish out at Cook and it seemed impossible. I was going to have to write my term papers and take my finals while my life imploded. I'd have to call my art history professor and ask about taking my exam at an alternate time since I couldn't stand the thought of being in the same room with Blake for an hour. I'd have to make up a good excuse since the truth was beyond belief.

Lexi set her book aside and looked over at me as I crumpled another tissue and tossed it in the garbage. "Do you want to go anywhere? Maybe try to take your mind off of him?"

"I don't think I would be good company right now. I'm

debating just calling my mom and dad and asking them to pick me up." I put more steel into my voice as I continued, "But then I think about it and I realize screw that. I'm so sick of being chased away. I had to leave high school because of Mr. Bridges and I refuse to leave college because of Blake."

Lexi looked relieved and a few minutes later she returned to her books. I stood up and dared a glance in the mirror. After sobbing for hours, it showed on my face. My cheeks were swollen and tear-stained. My eyes were lifeless and bloodshot; they burned from the lack of moisture. My hair was unruly and frizzy from lying in bed. I was chilled by the reflection and recognized the girl I saw—she was the seventeen-year-old version of me.

I started at the knock on the door and looked to Lexi for guidance. She shrugged as if to tell me she wasn't expecting anyone. She skirted around me to check the keyhole. A second later, she breathed out, "Shit. It's Blake."

My heart plummeted and my legs threatened to give out from under me. I gripped the edge of my desk to steady myself. Lexi gave me a reassuring smile before squaring her shoulders and turning back to the door. She opened it and before I could hear Blake say a word, she barked out, "Go away, Blake. She doesn't want to see you."

"I need to talk to her and at least explain myself—"

"Haven't you done enough? Are you some sort of masochist? You have to come here and see what kind of pain you caused her?"

"No. It's true I'm a fucking horrible person for lying, but I thought telling her the truth would only hurt her more. I'm a coward and I deserve it if she hates me. But I still need to make sure she's okay."

Lexi scoffed. "Of course she's not okay. And if you don't walk away in the next five seconds, I'm calling security to remove you from this building."

I chewed on my lower lip before making a move in the direction of the door. I sidestepped Lexi and said, "It's fine, Lex. I want to talk to him."

Lexi's eyes bulged and I could see her inwardly question my sanity. "Autumn…"

I squeezed her shoulder. "I want to know the truth about everything and he's the only one who has the answers."

I remembered what a mind fuck it was to have questions that would forever go unanswered. Almost daily, I would want to march down to the prison and glare at Mr. Bridges as I screamed, "*Why?*" Why did he choose me? Why didn't he walk away before he destroyed us both?

Lexi looked conflicted and nodded. "Should I stay?"

I hesitated. "I should probably talk to him alone." I gave Blake an uncertain glance. "He won't hurt me."

Blake flinched and I could tell it bothered him how unsure I sounded over the possibility of him hurting me. I didn't believe Blake would physically hurt me, but it was too late to undo the psychological damage done. He looked like hell—his hair was standing up straight in the back and his eyes were bloodshot— but how could I believe any emotion he showed me was sincere? The only fact I knew about him for sure was he had the ability to break me without lifting a single finger against me.

Lexi took her time gathering her things and I appreciated the time to pull myself together. I could feel Blake's eyes on me as I leaned against the desk and stared at the far wall. He stood to the left of the doorway and I could feel his uncertainty about venturing further into the room. It felt like we had fallen into an alternate universe compared to the last time we were alone in my room together. Blake shifted his gaze to my bed and I wondered if he was thinking the same thing.

Lexi stopped in front of me and handed me my cell phone. She wrapped my fingers around it and instructed, "You need anything, just call me and I'll be here."

"I will."

Satisfied with my promise, she hurried out of the room, but not before giving Blake a warning glare. I was taken aback by her fierceness and acknowledged once again how lucky I was to have her.

Once the door closed behind Lexi, the room remained quiet and still. Blake stuffed his hands in the pockets of his hooded sweatshirt and took a tentative step toward me. His voice cracked as he began, "I wanted to tell you who I was so many times, but I always backed out at the last minute. I knew the second I said I was Thomas's stepson, I would lose you forever."

"You never had me, Blake, if I never knew who you really were."

Blake's expression crumbled. "I deserve that. I was going to tell you this weekend when you stayed over. I never wanted you to find out that way. My mother…"

"I don't want to talk about Cassie Bridges and you're delusional if you thought you'd tell me Thomas was your stepfather and I would still sleep with you." I crossed my arms in front of my chest. "Why did you try to be my friend?"

Blake raked his fingers through his hair. "It took me a while to recover from seeing you at the Football House. I saw your picture a couple of years ago when you went to the police about Thomas. Delia and I looked you up online and we were able to see your Facebook profile before you took it down. Later, we got hold of one of your school's yearbooks and I saw your picture again. I needed to put a face to the name of the person who my parents accused of ruining our family."

"So your family hated me? That's no surprise. I'm guessing by how you gave me the look of death at the party, you shared their feelings?"

Blake seemed to collapse into himself at the assessment. "I should probably start from the beginning so this makes sense. My father died when I was two, so I don't remember a single thing about him. I have a few pictures and I share his last name, but that's the only connection I have to him. I was pissed off as a kid and I did get into a lot of fights, especially around the time my mom started dating Thomas. But he started spending time with me and we hit it off..."

I cut him off. "He was the boyfriend of your mom's you mentioned who got you into football."

Blake nodded. "They married and had Delia soon after the wedding. Thomas was my father in every way but name. He came to every one of my football games and shelled out the money I needed for the clinics in the spring and summer."

If it were anyone else, I'd be moved by the story. But it was all too familiar and only fueled my wrath. I had wanted to scream at every person in Newpine, *So what if he was a nice teacher and a good football coach? Why does that make what he did to me forgivable?*

I gave him a wry look. "So he obviously pulled the wool over your eyes too. It still doesn't explain your actions."

"We were totally floored when the police arrested Thomas. I was a freshman here, but I came home as soon as my mom called and told me what he was accused of doing." His green eyes became earnest. "Thomas told us he had made a stupid mistake and he would regret it for the rest of his life. He convinced us you were a sexual deviant and had begged him to bed you."

"And of course you believed it." I allowed him to hear the disappointment in my voice. He was admitting to having the same mindset as every boy who had harassed me after I filed charges. The truth wasn't setting me free as promised, it was throwing me back into confinement.

Blake looked at the floor. "I found the stuff Faye posted about you online. I saw the pictures and read the stories and I took it at face value."

"And you thought what?" I shouted. I stood up on my toes and got into his face. "You wanted to see if I was really Whorey Dorey?"

I wished he would leave because hearing what he said was akin to being flayed alive. What had Blake wanted from me—to try me on for size and see if I was worth his family's destruction? The thought led me to hold my hand over my mouth to stop whatever was left in my stomach from spewing out.

Blake's guilt-stricken face was all the confirmation I needed. "Thomas went to jail and we lost everything. Delia had to switch schools and we had to rely on the money left from my grandparents to live on. It was embedded into my brain that Autumn Dorey was responsible for every problem in our lives. But there's always been a niggle of doubt in the back of my mind. It seemed like fate when I realized you went to the same college as I did."

I sneered. "It wasn't fate, it was a coincidence. The worst kind of coincidence—the kind where the universe decided to give me the middle finger."

The vitriol I hurled in his direction shook him up, but after a grimace, he continued on. "I met you and decided I wanted to find out the real story. I tried to be your friend because if you found out I was Thomas's stepson, I would never learn your version of things."

I scowled at him as I put distance between us and resumed my perch on the desk. "So you decided to play junior detective and question me about my past? You're pathetic."

"It soon became crystal clear you were nothing like I expected and every fear I had about Thomas was confirmed."

"Okay, so you stopped thinking I was the real predator and your stepfather wasn't the hapless victim of my feminine wiles. Then why did you continue to stick around?"

"I saw how hard of a time you were having coping with what had happened. I liked you from the get-go and I hated knowing my stepfather caused someone so much misery…"

I shook my head. "I don't know what's worse—you trying to investigate me or you thinking your friendship would somehow fix what your father did to me."

"Nothing could fix it, I realize that. It was a horrible feeling, knowing how much pain someone I loved had caused. And I hated myself for not seeing sooner that there was something dark inside of him. Maybe I could've prevented you from getting hurt."

"So, instead your plan was to make me love you to ease the hurt? Blake, you had to know I was going to find out the truth eventually."

"I made so many mistakes with you and I told myself to walk away over and over again. But I did feel a connection to you and I found it impossible to break it. I'd see you at a party or at class and I could only think about holding you and kissing you. You had so much warmth about you and I found it unforgivable Thomas had hurt this beautiful girl I was falling for. I had the insane thought that despite the universe saying we didn't belong together—it could actually work." Blake ran his hands up and down the side of his face before resting them against his cheeks. His eyes widened and I could feel the desperation of his pleas coming off of him in waves. His entire being was willing me to believe in him. The intensity of his stare forced my eyes away.

"Does he know about us?" Who *he* was stayed unspoken and I hated to even think of his name. Blake was humanizing Mr. Bridges and I resented it. Mr. Bridges was a callous villain and I didn't want to think of him as a husband and Blake's surrogate father. Because how could the man who assaulted me be the same man who had helped Blake deal with the loss of his father?

"No. I haven't spoken to him in more than a year. For the first year he was in prison, I'd go see him and I would demand to know why he would have an affair with a student. He had been a teacher and coach for almost twenty years. What drove him to throw his family and career away? I couldn't understand why my mom forgave him and why she didn't hold him accountable for what happened. But my mom has no idea how to survive on her own. She may not have liked what Thomas had done, but she can't imagine a life without him."

"He's getting released next month," I said in a harsh whisper.

Blake's shoulders slumped. "I know. My mom told me and Thomas has written me several times from jail. He wants to start over when he gets out and rebuild our relationship."

"Is that what you want?" I was horrified over the prospect and I was certain the revulsion was clear on my face. Why should Thomas be allowed a fresh start? Would Blake be willing to accept him after knowing the truth about his stepfather?

"I haven't written him back and I didn't open up the last two letters he sent. I miss the person I thought he was, but I won't forgive him." Blake looked regretful. "My mother will let him know about us and I'm sorry for that. I told her how I feel about you and she's furious. She sees it as a betrayal and although I told her the truth about our meeting, she'll warp it around in her mind until she believes you targeted me. I asked her to leave today and told her I didn't want to see her again."

Everything he was telling me was too much to process at once. The Blake I had known yesterday was an entirely different person than the Blake who stood before me. He belonged to a family that included Cassie and Thomas Bridges and I had no idea where his loyalties truly lay. I'd known Blake for less than six months and he wanted me to believe he would willingly walk away from his family for me.

"What I've done is unforgivable. I've lied to you and although you opened yourself up to me, I never did the same." Blake closed his eyes as he finished. "But I'm asking you to forgive me. *I need you*, Autumn, and I'll do anything not to lose you. If there's one thing you have to believe it's that I love you. I tried to hold back because I understood how dangerous it would be for me to have these feelings—but it was impossible not to fall for you."

Blake closed the distance between us and kneeled down to press his forehead against my own. My hands itched to push him away, but my eyes closed of their own accord. I breathed him in, understanding it was the last time and feeling lost as I caught his seductive and familiar scent. I didn't want to be comforted by his nearness, but my body wasn't cooperating with my brain. I whispered, "How can I forgive you? How can I forget who you are?"

Blake didn't answer and I felt his arms wrap tentatively around my waist. Blake was a Trojan horse. He was beautiful and I felt as if he had been my prize after all I suffered through. How could I have anticipated what he concealed from the world? His lips grazed across my own and I could feel my mouth tingle when the peck ended. The electricity was still there between us, despite the fraudulence surrounding our relationship.

I moved out of his embrace and crossed the room to regain perspective. Being in his arms clouded my thoughts and made me question whether he was truly the enemy or not. "Blake, I can't be with you. I took a huge risk trusting you and I can't do it again. After my attack, I isolated myself and thought I'd never get close to anyone again. You made me feel safe and protected, but my intuition was horribly wrong."

"I can't change what I already did, but I promise you I'll never lie to you again. I waited so long to tell the truth because I wanted to steal as many moments as possible when I was just Blake and you were just Autumn."

Blake's size was imposing, but he looked very small suddenly. As if his words were breaking him down and leaving him the most vulnerable he had ever been. But what Blake was asking of me was unimaginable. I couldn't stay inside a bubble with him and pretend outside forces didn't exist.

"You should go," I sighed. I was exhausted, drained dry of all emotion. I no longer had the energy to rage at him. The emptiness inside was growing rapidly and I acknowledged I'd soon be able to escape into the nothingness.

"Will you call me? Can we talk some more?"

"There's nothing left to say, Blake." I held my head high as I strode past him and opened the door. "You said you thought before the decent thing would've been to walk away. Please, can you do it now? I need you to let me go."

He joined me at the door and I sensed the unspent energy coming off of him—his seemingly innate need to do more to convince me to give him another chance. "I love you, Autumn Dorey, and I say a big fuck you to every last person who tells me what I feel for you is wrong. I'd do anything for you and if you want me to leave you alone, I will. But I feel like although I never told you everything about my family, *you still know me.* You get me and I hope if I give you time, you'll see I want to share everything with you. I want to share every moment, not just the good ones. I can't take away your pain, but I want to be there whenever you need me."

"Goodbye, Blake," I managed and tried to stop the trembling threatening to make my legs give out. He needed to go because if he stayed I would say something I regretted. My heart wrapped around his words and I wanted to reach out and tell him never to leave. He was a beautiful fraud, but maybe if he loved me, could it somehow cancel out the bad parts of him? Could I accept him fully: the good and the bad?

He glided past me and I slammed the door closed behind his retreating back. I rested my forehead against the door and told myself it was all for the best. There was no phoenix that could rise out of the ashes left behind by his betrayal. Every moment of our relationship was fabricated and I couldn't hand my heart over to a proven liar.

Blake was the son of a monster. He may not have had a blood connection to Mr. Bridges, but he had been raised by him. I tended to lean toward the nurture side of the nature versus nurture debate and where would that leave Blake? Blake had loved someone so terrible that the very thought of him brought upon a horrible clawing feeling deep in my gut.

But Blake's words softened me, making me think of my mistakes. I may not have loved Mr. Bridges, but I had respected and admired him. The pain had seared my soul when I realized how wrong I'd been. What had Blake felt the moment it became clear the person he loved was sick and twisted up inside?

Chapter Twenty-Five

I watched the waves break on the shoreline with my mouth set in a grim line. The moonlight reflected over the ocean and I tried to immerse myself in the beauty of the setting. But like each night previous, I couldn't shut my brain off and stop the sadness from creeping into my heart. I shivered against the cool ocean breeze and blinked rapidly, trying to dispel the tears threatening to escape.

I heard my mother approach and felt the soft chenille blanket rub against my skin as she set it upon my shoulders. I leaned against her and she tucked a stray piece of my hair behind my ear. "I made popcorn and found a few good movies we could watch on TV. Why don't you come inside?"

My smile was watery as I turned in her direction. "Just give me ten more minutes and I'll be inside."

"Are you okay? Do you need to talk?"

"I'm just thinking about going back to school next month. It's going to be hard."

My mother's brow furrowed and she motioned for me to follow her to the set of Adirondack chairs centered on the deck of our beach house rental. We were in Seaside Park, New Jersey, in the second month of our summer vacation at the beach. The house had become a refuge for me after the way things ended with Blake. Although nights were hard, it had been easy to turn off my brain during the day when my mother had a full day of summer activities planned for us. We would go to the beach, shop, and visit all of the touristy destinations overrun with the summer crowds.

The final couple of weeks of the semester before I moved out of the dorms were pure torture. I was nursing a broken heart while trying to study for finals. I gave myself two days to have a good cry and then I decided to turn everything off until I left for the summer. Every time Blake popped into my head, I'd ground my teeth together and force myself to refocus on my coursework. I had worked too hard for my grades to go to hell over a boy. He may be a boy who had stolen my heart before crushing it, but still a boy nonetheless.

My art history professor had been accommodating and I took the exam during the makeup period. My palms were damp and my heart thudded loudly in my head as I walked into the classroom. The memory of the first day of the semester when I had seen Blake caused all the hurt to come flooding back. A panicked feeling scratched at my chest as I worried Blake rescheduled his exam as well and I'd be forced to see him. I collapsed into one of the desks and focused on the podium at the front of the room as I tried to regulate my breathing. *In and out. In and out.*

It wasn't until the professor handed out the exams that I was able to relax. I couldn't see Blake yet because I had no idea how to react. It would be easier simply to hate him in the same way I hated his stepfather. I nurtured the hatred of Mr. Bridges, allowing it to grow more and more each passing day. I allowed myself the luxury of thinking of elaborate ways I could hurt him. But those emotions made it impossible to move on. If I was being perfectly honest with myself, allowing myself to love again was what I needed to heal from my past.

Lexi and Casey were my support system as the semester came to a close. They never left my side and they tried to cheer me up while pointedly not mentioning Blake. I tried to rally on their behalf, but it was hard. I wanted to label Blake a liar and a master manipulator and be glad he was out of my life for good. But it wasn't that straightforward. Because a part of me did believe Blake had developed genuine feelings for the girl his family had declared enemy number one.

I decided to hold off on telling my parents about Blake until after I came home. It felt like a conversation I couldn't have with them over the phone. It was humbling to approach them and admit once again I failed to see what should've been easily discernible. Was there something irrevocably broken inside of me that I couldn't recognize those with dark intentions in their hearts?

My parents were shocked and I think my easygoing father entertained the idea of hunting Blake down and making him pay for hurting his daughter. My mother wanted to call our lawyer and see if they could file a motion to prevent Blake, and his stepfather upon his release, from making contact. But I didn't find it necessary to treat Blake in the same way as his stepfather. Blake was many things but he certainly wasn't cut from the same cloth as Thomas Bridges.

Mr. Bridges was released on the same day my mother and I left for the shore. He would've been a fool to seek me out for retribution, but my parents and I weren't taking any chances. I wanted to be out of state and as far away from Newpine as possible when he was a free man. As it was, a summer in Newpine held no appeal for me. The wounds over what happened during that fateful spring night seemed to fester the closer I was in proximity to the high school.

There was pain at the beach, but I had also found a healing spring. It had come in the form of volunteering at the women's shelter. I'd been wrong at first to think it would be too much to be around so much suffering. I pictured my pain being contagious and spreading to all those who dared to come near. But when I was at the shelter, it had the opposite effect. It was the strength I found there that was contagious and was what made me driven to snap out of it and one day be able to move on.

My mother crossed her legs after she sank back into the Adirondack chair. We enjoyed a few minutes of comfortable silence while she waited for me to speak.

"It's July and I'm going back to Cook in a month and I still feel like the breakup with Blake happened yesterday. I don't know how I'm going to run into him around campus and not fall apart on the spot."

"Have you talked to him?"

I shook my head. "I told him to leave me alone and he has. And I should be happy he respected my wishes, but after I wade through all the heartache I have over his lies, I'm left with a hollow feeling knowing he'll never be a part of my life." I curled my fingers tightly around the arms of the chair. "I mean I have to let it go, right? It could never in a million years work."

My mom lifted her legs and brought her knees to her chest. I could see her trying to process my words and wondered what she thought. Getting over Blake should've been as easy as it was to mourn my relationship with Hunter. I should be able to walk away relieved I uncovered the truth about him. But there was no relief, only a strong sense of desolation.

"Why couldn't it work?" I gave her an "are you serious?" look and waited for her to elaborate. "Well, I know the reasons I have for being against a relationship with Blake, but I'm curious over your feelings."

"Well, he's a proven liar for one. How could I ever trust him?" Before my mom could reply, I added, "I mean he never outright lied to me about who his stepfather was or wasn't, but isn't an omission of that magnitude the same thing?"

"Besides Thomas Bridges being his stepfather, do you think Blake lied to you about anything else? Like what kind of person he was? Or how he felt about you?"

I pulled the blanket tightly around me, tucking my legs underneath my behind. At first, his deception was all I could see when I pictured the time I spent with Blake. His words were infected and polluted the air and nothing he had said to me could be real. But my traitorous heart wouldn't allow the visual to stick. "No, but he only befriended me because he wanted to see if I was a slut and a liar. What kind of foundation is that for a real relationship?"

"To play devil's advocate for a minute. Let's say your father was accused of murder tomorrow. A man you have loved your whole life and that gave you all of the support you needed growing up. Would you believe it? Or would you try to find out the truth before you made your final judgment?"

I gave her a slack-jawed look. "Are you *sticking up* for Blake? You wanted us to take out a restraining order when I told you."

"I'm not defending him at all. What Blake did was misguided, but the more you tell me about the nature of your relationship, the more doubts I'm having over the maliciousness of his actions. I think he wanted to get to the truth about what happened between you and his stepfather. No one was there that night besides you and Mr. Bridges and Blake's gut reaction was to believe that the man he loved and respected would never try to rape one of his students." My mom's eyes watered and I could hear the hitch in her voice. "From the moment you walked through that door in May, I knew someone evil had hurt you. But I'm your mother and Blake didn't know you until years after it happened. It sounds like once he got to know you and saw what kind of person you are, he was able to accept the truth about his stepfather."

"But he was raised by Thomas Bridges. His mother is the woman who went to the press and painted me as the devil incarnate. How can he be a good man? I trusted Mr. Bridges and thought he was a decent human being and didn't realize my mistake until he grabbed me and forced me into the car."

My mother shuddered and was quiet again. I liked that about my mom. She was never careless with her words. She understood that once the words were out there, they were much harder to take back. "Did you really trust Thomas Bridges though?"

"Of course I did, he was my teacher."

"But you told me about his reputation with the female students and how accepting he was of your flirting. If he was someone that could've been trusted, he would've called you out on any inappropriate behavior and not encouraged it."

I cringed. "You're saying I should've known being alone with him was a mistake."

"No, I'm saying you trusted him to not cross the invisible line you created. You trusted him because he was put in that position by the school, not because he earned it. Blake had to earn your trust through his actions. So, if he behaved in a way that made you uncomfortable, you wouldn't have let him in." My mother grabbed my hand and I watched as her thumb grazed over my knuckles. "I see how sad you are, Autumn, and I'm scared of you going backwards after all you've been through. You're strong and beautiful, but I think you have a hard time accepting that side of you. Missing Blake doesn't make you weak, it only means you saw something wonderful inside of him."

"I did see something wonderful, but every second I spent with him is tainted now. I look back at our time together and now understanding who he is distorts the images."

"I don't want you to hurt again and you have to decide for yourself if Blake is deserving of you. In my personal opinion, no one will ever be good enough for you." I forced a smile in her direction before she continued. "Now that the truth is out there, I'd understand if you wanted to try and make new memories with him that don't feel contaminated. If he still isn't the person you thought he was, you'll be able to have the closure you need to move on."

It was an intriguing concept, but I wasn't sure my heart could take it. If we were both stripped bare of all our secrets and

I was able to get to know the real Blake Preston, what would he be like? Would he still be kind and funny? Would he still be respectful and gentle? The truth was I had no clue. Because although Blake had been a stranger to me when we met, his preconceptions about me had already been filled in from the second we met. I was unsure exactly how that affected the way our relationship progressed.

Restarting therapy during the summer had helped, but it still hadn't given me the answers I desperately needed. My therapist was round with a lively personality and I found myself opening up more than I thought after the first couple of sessions. Her name was Kelly and she chewed gum incessantly to try and hide her cigarette addiction. She was the polar opposite of Dr. Fabian, but I still liked her.

During one of our sessions, she had thrown a word out there: *forgiveness*. When she first uttered the word, I thought what a foreign and outrageous concept. But I was learning forgiveness didn't have to be about granting absolution for sins but being able to find freedom from pain.

I had one month of escapism left. But the bottom line was I'd be returning to Cook in the fall. I was always running and hiding, never having the strength to stand my ground. But my mother was right, I did have a strong spirit and I would always have the fight inside me that had gotten me through my darkest times. I just needed to decide if Blake Preston was worth putting up a fight for.

Chapter Twenty-Six

"What's up, bitches? Let's toast to our sophomore year!" Casey held up her beer bottle and swayed from side to side and I waited for a face-plant to ensue.

Lexi mock whispered to me, "Are you sure rooming with her was a good idea?"

Casey shot her a deadly glare. "Sorry I know how to have a good time. And to think I was going to let you and Finn borrow my single room when you needed a quickie."

Lexi made a disgusted face. "Gross, I have no idea what you do in that bed. We're not going to share it with you."

I laughed and watched fondly as my two best friends bickered. We had secured a suite in the Collins dorm on campus. The suite connected two double rooms with a shared bathroom. Casey's friend Amy was supposed to room with her but had dropped out at the last minute before the semester started. Casey had a single until the college assigned her another roommate.

We moved in that morning and spent the entire day catching up. The three of us had talked a lot over the summer but only met up once when they'd come to the shore house for a few days. My mom had been great, but I was ready to get back to college. I missed my friends and to be honest I missed taking classes. I had never gotten much out of school as a teen, but I was finding college courses stimulating in unexpected ways. I would still be taking many of my general education requirements, but I was going to start working in a few courses related to social work.

Volunteering at the woman's shelter would be something I'd continue doing for a long time. It woke me up and kept me from feeling sorry for myself. The women I met at the shelter taught me about true survival and made me grateful for the people I had in my life. I found myself able to open up about my assault without feeling ashamed. I had kept a side of myself hidden because I felt that being a victim was something I should've been embarrassed about. I unknowingly subscribed to the notion I had asked for it and deserved what had happened. I met other victims of sexual violence and realized how I wasn't alone in my feelings. There was a stigma surrounding rape victims and it was the reason a lot of cases went unreported. It was scary to think about, but I realized women might be scared to report a rape because of my experience. They may have seen how I became a victim of bullying and thought they should let it go. By going into social work, my hope was to support women as they went through the process of reporting abuse.

I was discovering so much about myself every day and it felt amazing. I felt strong and confident and it was the reason I decided it was time to see Blake. I was sure the moment I saw him I'd be gutted, but I knew it wouldn't break me. I wanted to turn the tables and investigate him and decide what kind of person he truly was. Because when it came down to it, he hadn't been honest, but it was one lie with infinite repercussions. It rested on my shoulders to decide if a single lie was reason enough to never see him again.

"How about we toast to new beginnings?" I grabbed my beer and lifted it in the air in front of me.

"I'll second that." Lexi smiled and held out her wine glass. We clinked our drinks and I took a long pull of the beer.

"Speaking of new beginnings, Autumn has decided to attend her first ever Cook football game on Saturday," Lexi addressed Casey while winking in my direction. "And we are in charge of finding her something gorgeous to wear."

"You mean I'm in charge since you would put her in a sweater set and a pair of Mary Janes," Casey said. Casey turned her attention back to me and said, "Are you sure? Because I'm all for school spirit, but if my ex-boyfriend was playing I'd go to a game but only to put Icy Hot in his jockstrap and laugh at him from the sidelines."

"No, I'm ready to see him," I said and tilted my chin. "But I would like it if you two came in case I need moral support."

They both nodded. Casey rested the mouth of her beer against her lower lip as she considered me. "Have you talked to Blake?"

"I thought about calling him, but I'd like to see him face to face. I have doubts about his honesty and I have this crazy idea that if he lies to me again I'll be able to read it in his expression."

"I don't think that's crazy," Lexi said. "Finn's tell when he lies is he'll stare at my forehead instead of looking me in the eye."

"Sometimes I wonder if it's better to forget about him." If only amnesia was a possibility. Because the fact was I couldn't stop thinking about him and not only about the ways he annihilated my heart. Too often, the sweet moments I had with him forced their way to the forefront of my brain. "I'm not sure what I'll even say when I see him. Do I ask him if he wants to try again? It's been months since we spoke. He could have a serious girlfriend for all I know."

Lexi and Casey exchanged a knowing look. I put down my beer bottle on my desk and squinted at them. "Does Blake have a girlfriend? Do you know something you haven't told me?"

Lexi stared down at her lap. "Blake called me a couple of times over the summer. He was trying to keep his distance, but he wanted to make sure you were okay. I told him he shouldn't call you and if you wanted to talk to him, you'd be in touch."

"Why didn't you tell me?"

"You were trying to heal and I thought it would be a setback hearing he was asking about you. You were in the middle of therapy, trying to work things out, and if Blake wasn't going to be part of your future, I didn't want to even bring up his name." Lexi looked over my head and her eyes rested on the wall behind me. "He sounded like shit and kept trying to tell me how sorry he was. He seemed sincere, but if he's untrustworthy..." Lexi trailed off.

Blake's deception was a complicated thing. Because like Lexi with Finn, I thought I found Blake's tell. I remembered seeing the overly bright eyes and the look of morbid curiosity as he tried to find out more about me. In hindsight, it was his determination to wade through the rumors and accusations to discover who I really was. After the night playing video games at his apartment, his eyes softened and his expression was filled with warring emotions: want and need. He wanted me, but his conscience told him he needed to keep his distance.

"When was the last time he called?"

"A couple of weeks ago. He seemed as nervous as you were about how things would be once school started up again. By the way he was talking, you were the only one on his mind, so it seems doubtful he's dating," Lexi said.

I asked Casey, "What do you think?"

"Will goes to all the football practices and is friends with a lot of the players. He hasn't heard any rumors about Blake dating anyone else," Casey said. "But if you'd rather have us do some Blake bashing, I hear he's been sucking so far. Maybe the situation with you messed with his head enough he'll ruin his football career."

Blake had told me of his mixed feelings about football and knowing Mr. Bridges had been his mentor helped me understand his conflict better. I hoped he was able to find joy in the game again and if he wanted to play professionally that it would happen.

"I feel like I'm at the point where I can trust my instincts. And my gut is telling me Blake may have some flaws, but deep down, he's a good guy. I worked over every angle and I've come to the conclusion he made a mistake. When he saw me at the party, he should've turned around and never said a word to me. But in a way, how can I hate him for that? Because if I never got to know him, I may have stayed closed off forever."

"Well, whatever you decide to do or not do with Blake Preston, you're still going to blow him away when he sees you at the game," Casey said, defiantly lifting her chin. "Because let me tell you nothing is worse than seeing an ex for the first time without wearing a push-up bra and your Spanx."

Lexi rolled her eyes as I giggled at Casey's brashness. It was going to be an interesting dynamic as we roomed together for the year. I had two days of classes before the football game on Saturday. Two days to either chicken out about going and two days to possibly run into Blake around campus. We had been dating when our fall classes were selected so I knew we weren't in any courses together. But the campus wasn't huge and there was a chance I could see him at the dining halls or in the student center. I wondered if it was better to see him before the game. But going to the game was the grand gesture I had come up with—a way to show him I didn't feel he was like every other jock who mistreated me.

I had said some things to hurt him when I found out the truth. It had taken me awhile to see Blake and his sister were additional casualties of his stepfather's actions. He had loved his stepfather since he was a young child and it was another father ripped away from him prematurely. Blake was forced into the role as the provider for his broken family, a huge responsibility he never asked for. Although his mother didn't deserve his loyalty, he had given it anyway and done everything he could to take care of her and his younger sister when they were left without his stepfather's income.

Honestly, I had never thought about Thomas Bridges'

children. They were faceless and nameless and I only concentrated on my pain and how I was going to survive. But my mother had made me think about how it must've felt for Blake. How terrible it must have felt to say the words *Thomas Bridges is my father*. I thought my pain was mine alone, but I wasn't the only person who had been suffering ever since that night.

***

My backside felt awkward against the cold steel of the bleachers. I tried to relax, but my spine stayed erect as I scooted over to make room for Casey and Lexi. It was nerve-wracking to be back inside the stadium. The last time I had been here was months ago during my impromptu training session with Blake.

My first concern was how it would feel to be at a football game once again. Would it bring back memories of Thomas Bridges running along the sidelines and coaching the players? My eyes darted over to the cheerleaders and I waited for the pang I used to feel when I realized I'd never be part of that world again.

It was progress when I discovered I was letting go of the past. I was so far removed from high school, I no longer experienced wistfulness over my losses. I wasn't sure if it was therapy or time providing me with perspective, but I was done looking behind me. The only thing causing my heart to pound furiously was the idea I'd be seeing Blake in less than ten minutes.

The players ran out of the brick athletic building and stormed onto the field in a massive line of bodies. I couldn't make out one man from the other and scanned the numbers on their blue and gold uniforms. I felt a jolt when I finally found number seventeen and saw him run into the huddle with his teammates. My eyes were glued to him and I liked the idea of being able to watch him undetected for as long as I desired.

"Sweet baby Jesus, I'm going to start fanning my vagina in a hot minute. Do you think if you make up with Blake, he can sneak us into the locker room after the game?" Casey mock whispered while she leaned over Lexi.

Lexi elbowed her in the ribs and she moved back to her seat. I didn't have an exact plan in mind on how to approach Blake. Lexi suggested we go to the party at the Football House following the game. Will had been invited and he in turn invited the three of us. I wanted to work things out with Blake face to face, but I was thinking it would be better to call him and arrange to talk somewhere in private.

I ran my hands over my black Capri pants, trying to get rid of the dampness gathering on my palms. Casey had suggested a short skirt paired with kitten heels, but I doubted it would be attractive if I broke my neck from a fall when climbing the bleachers. The Capri pants were tailored nicely and comfortable enough for the hours of sitting in the stands watching the game. My shoulders and mid-back were exposed by the black tunic I selected. Casey had an amazing jewelry collection and loaned me some fun chunky bracelets and a dangling gold necklace. She complained about my fondness for black clothing and although she said I looked good, the jewelry would stop people from thinking I was on my way to a funeral.

The game started and I leaned forward in anticipation. We were playing Rutgers University and the rumor was they were a tough team this year. Rutgers took possession first, giving me more time to watch Blake stand on the sidelines. He was turned toward the field with his back facing the stands reserved for Cook's fans. I wondered if it would be better to sneak over to the opposing team's side to get a good look at the face I missed all summer long.

And I was at the point where I felt okay about missing him. When I'd been alone in bed all summer long and longed to have him next to me, my desire would be quickly squelched by the guilt. I had never given myself permission to miss Blake because it felt like I was betraying my seventeen-year-old self. But I wasn't the same Autumn and I didn't believe he was the same Blake I met in January.

Our defense had kept Rutgers from scoring and it was time for Cook's offensive line to get on the field. My gut twisted up in knots as Blake shoved on his helmet and jogged onto the field. I was nervous for him and hated the idea he had a rough start to the season. I understood he had mixed feelings about football, but I thought if the pressure from his mother went away, he'd find the passion for the game again. Cassie wanted Blake to be her Win for Life lottery ticket and it wasn't fair to him.

Blake played okay during the first half, but I could see his head wasn't in it. When I watched videos of his games from the year before, his plays were full of poise and skill. He made a few decent catches and gained yards for the team, but his performance lacked heart. I wasn't going to assume the way he played had anything to do with me, but it made me curious over what his life was like since we last spoke. I wondered how complicated things were for him after his mom and sister found out about us. Thomas was out of prison and I assumed he was welcomed back into the family. Did Blake decide that since we were over he'd try to rebuild a relationship with him?

The thought left me cold. My eyes darted around the crowded stadium and paranoia set in. I'd been overly focused on seeing Blake, not considering the complications that came with coming to his game. Cassie and Delia were probably in the crowd somewhere. Worse yet, Thomas was a free man and could be at the game. He could be watching me at that very moment and I'd have no idea.

Unwanted flashes flickered in my mind and I recalled the hunger in his eyes as he pinned me down. Did he hate I'd gotten away? What if he saw me and a renewed determination took hold to finish what he started?

I jumped up from my seat and almost knocked over my

soda set at my feet. I turned to Lexi and Casey. "I can't be here. This was a terrible idea. I'm going to head back to the dorms." I grabbed my purse and gave them both an apologetic look. "I'm sorry and I'll explain later."

Lexi nodded and began to gather her belongings. I put my hand on her shoulder. "You guys should stay. I'll be fine."

"Do you still want to go to the party?" Casey asked.

It was late afternoon, the party hours away. It would give me time to think it over. Maybe I'd text Blake and see if he wanted to get together to talk. As much as I wanted to stay and watch Blake play, it wasn't safe to be at the stadium. Thanks to my therapist, I now knew the difference between running away as a coping mechanism and running away because it was the smart thing to do.

"I'll call you to let you know."

"Autumn, we can leave too…" Lexi started.

I grimaced. "I'm sorry for taking off like this, but tell me how the rest of the game goes. I just need some time to think."

Lexi and Casey shot each other concerned looks, but each gave me reluctant nods. I tried to smile reassuringly, but I was sure I looked unstable. My only thought was I needed to go and *I had to go now*. I pushed through the crowds as everyone began to descend on the concession stands during halftime.

I had a strong sense of self-preservation, and being anywhere Thomas could be was foolish. I had been naïve at one time to think he was harmless and I wouldn't make the same mistake twice. If Thomas were back in Blake's life, it would be a sign we were truly not meant to be. I wanted Blake, but I was also a realist. There was no chance for us if Blake needed to have both of us in his life.

The throng of people brought upon the old panicky feelings I had. But I breathed through it and used the calming techniques my therapist recommended. My heart slowed down and I was able to break free of the swarm of people without losing it. Circling the field, I headed toward the side exit. The college students who walked to the game from the dorms mostly used that entrance and exit. The main gate was next to the parking lot and used primarily by visitors to the campus.

A thundering sound exploded in front of me and I stilled, wondering if Pennsylvania ever had earthquakes. My grip on my purse and keys tightened as I looked up from the path and saw the football team heading in my direction. I jumped back several feet as the first of the players flew past me. Swinging my head back and forth, I realized the players were descending upon the locker room for halftime.

I moved farther back and positioned my body against the brick wall of the athletic department's two-story building. My gaze was fixed straight ahead—a challenge when all I wanted to do was check if number seventeen would notice me. If he did see me, he could decide to keep running, maybe deciding we were better off apart. Besides, he was in the middle of his opening game; it was far from the ideal time to hash out our problems.

I told myself I would try to be aloof if I saw him, but that all crumbled as soon as I heard his voice. "Autumn?"

I was glad the wall was there to hold me up because otherwise I would have collapsed to the ground. I had such a visceral reaction to hearing his voice again. It reminded me of how hard I had fallen for him and how much I missed him *every single day*. When I actually turned and saw him standing less than three feet away from me, I knew how being struck by lightning must feel.

I stared at his feet until my eyes made their way up the length of his body. He looked incredible in his uniform and I could see the outline of his powerful legs through his pants. His arms were larger and more muscular since I'd last seen him and I could make out the definition because of the pronounced tension in his body. Finally, my gaze rested on his face and so many buried emotions rushed to the surface. There was a trickle of perspiration dripping down the side of his face and his light brown hair was matted across his forehead. His green eyes were wide as he stared back at me, his surprise further cemented by the way his mouth hung open.

A minute, or maybe ten minutes, passed as I lost track of time. I cleared my throat. "Hi."

His laughter sounded strangled and he dropped his helmet onto the ground next to him. "Hi."

"I want us to talk, but it's probably not a good time." I tilted my head in the direction of the double doors where the rest of his team had disappeared. "You probably have to get back with your team."

He ignored my suggestion and took a deep breath. "How are you?"

It was a loaded question and my answer could last for hours. I contemplated blurting out every feeling he evoked—the good and the bad. Most of all, I wanted the courage to say I missed him desperately. "I'm fine. I had a nice summer with my mom at the beach."

He nodded and I could see him filing away the information. He gazed meaningfully at the keys in my hand. "Are you leaving the game?"

"Yes. I wanted to come, but it got to be a little overwhelming when I thought your parents might be here too."

He recoiled, the words a reminder of what had broken us apart. But I wouldn't shy away from the truth and I expected the same from him. "They're not here. Thomas will never be part of my life again."

The steely resolve in his voice renewed my faith in the possibility of an us. I wouldn't demand he say goodbye to the only father he knew, but Blake's choice would determine if I could be with him.

"Things are still not the best between my mom and me. It's complicated and I have a lot to tell you, but I don't want to talk about them right now. Especially since it's been four months since I last talked to you."

"Okay."

"So why did you come today?" There was a hopeful edge to his voice and it gave me the impression none of his feelings had faded over the summer.

"I came to see you," I admitted. "I thought after the game we could talk."

"I wish we could talk now."

"Me too," I sighed. "We can talk after the game. You better go. Don't you have to go over plays or something in the locker room?"

He shrugged. "Do you think I'll be able to concentrate on the game after knowing you want to talk to me?" He edged closer and my pulse quickened. "I wanted to call you, but I understood how badly I fucked up. I lied and got close to you without ever telling you the truth. I loved you, but I always knew what we had would be temporary. The truth would be out there and I'd lose the only girl I ever loved."

"Loved?" I heard the catch in my tone and guessed he had as well. Tears were building behind my eyes and I blinked hard to hold them back.

He leaned in until we were only a breath away and whispered, "Love. Of course I still love you."

I put my palm against his chest and my skin tingled over how good it felt to be touching him again. "Do you know what a trust fall is?"

His eyebrows lifted and I could tell my question took him off guard. "I think so," he said uncertainly.

"It's when you allow yourself to purposely fall and have to rely completely on another person to catch you." I reached over and clasped his hand in mine. His warm skin was rough from his calluses. I liked the way my hand felt small and delicate lost inside of his grip. "I want to try that with you. I want us to do a trust fall together."

Blake's grin transformed his face into a mask of sheer bliss. I found myself grinning back and for once I no longer had any nagging doubts. There was a litany of reasons Blake and I shouldn't be together, but I wanted a chance to see if the universe was wrong. Maybe every barrier could be broken down because we loved each other. And although I thought I never knew the real Blake Preston—that wasn't true. The real Blake Preston was the one who held me when I cried and tried to fix things he never broke in the first place. The real Blake told bad jokes and sang cheesy songs at the top of his lungs. He had favorite math rules and a little sister he protected and loved. The real Blake loved me wholly despite being told I was his worst enemy.

I lifted onto my toes and grazed my lips against his. It was a taste, a tease leaving me wanting more, but there would be time for that later. "Well, since you probably missed the coach's pep talk, I'll improvise. Go out there, get your head out of your ass, and score our team some points."

With a laugh, he wrapped his hands around my waist. His expression turned serious and I melted under the heat of his stare. His hold was desperate and it appeared as though he was terrified I'd bolt any second and disappear again. "You're giving me a second chance and it was something I never thought would happen. I won't disappoint you and I'll never lie to you again. My promises may not mean anything to you yet, but I'm going to change that. I'll do whatever it takes to earn back your trust."

I didn't argue with him because starting again would be a trial. But I had needed the time and distance. Because amazingly enough during our separation I was able to discover forgiveness.

"If you were inside my head, you would see how it felt to be apart and how much I hated myself for hurting you. I love you, Autumn, and I promise to do everything I can to make you as happy as you make me." Blake's chest rose and fell as he spoke and it was more physical proof he felt the same longing I had since we broke up.

"I love you, too." It was the first time I told him I loved him out loud and as I traced a line over his jaw with my finger I silently marveled over how such a beautiful love could rise out of such a dark past. But when his eager lips found mine, there was no denying what we had couldn't be easily forgotten or replicated. My heart would always belong to him and even if it took a lifetime, I would prove to him he deserved to have my love.

Chapter Twenty-Seven

Two months later…

"So I put my hands up, they're playing my song, the butterflies fly away. I'm nodding my head like yeah. Moving my hips like yeah."

I walked over to Blake's iPod dock and turned off the music while he shot me a look of disbelief. With shock coloring his tone, he asked, "Did you just stop me from singing? I thought you loved the incredible awesomeness of my voice."

"It scares me how well you know the lyrics to campy pop songs," I teased and sat next to him on his bed.

"I'm actually more of a classic rock fan, but I keep up with pop music to impress the ladies," he said and pulled me onto his lap. "Is it working?"

"Maybe a little." His mouth silenced my laugh as he started to kiss me. The kiss was long and slow and I liked the way his lips lingered against mine. "You're crazy," I said when I moved away.

"Crazy hot you mean."

I shook my head. "And so modest as well." I rested my head against his chest and listened to the sound of his racing heart. "Your heart is beating so fast."

"I have a gorgeous girl in my lap. I think something would

have to be wrong with me if my heart wasn't beating fast."

His arms came around my waist and we lay in the same position for a long time. It was a Sunday afternoon and we had settled into a routine of being lazy for most of the day. Blake usually had a game on Friday or Saturday and with our class schedule the rest of the week, it was the only day we had nothing pressing to do. Blake needed the recovery day too and it was the reason I never planned anything too taxing. Although he downplayed it, I was certain he was sore from all the hits he took on the field.

Two months had passed since the Rutgers game and it felt like we'd never been away from each other. We had taken things slow, but what I felt for him wasn't going to change with time. I loved him and I believed in us. Blake kept his pledge and had earned my trust. The secrets were what had kept me from giving myself fully to him and with them out in the open nothing was holding us back.

Not to say it had been smooth sailing. There were some problems that would likely never go away. I might as well have been a Capulet and he a Montague with the chilly reception we received from our families. My mom was understanding about how I felt and I think a lot of it had to do with how much time we talked things out at the beach. My dad wanted me to stay away from Blake, but once I made it clear how important it was to give Blake another chance, he told me to be careful and warned Blake he would need a new set of balls if he hurt me again.

Blake's family was even more complicated. Thomas had moved back with Cassie and Delia in May, but he had moved out by mid-summer. Things had fallen apart quickly when Cassie realized how dependent Thomas would be on her. Thomas was unemployable and Blake wouldn't come home as long as she lived with his stepfather. The choice had been easy and she had gone to an attorney about filing for divorce. The irony hadn't been lost on me that she hadn't left him because of his purported dalliance with a student, but had looked into divorce once it became clear that he had zero financial prospects. Blake held onto the resentment toward his mother, but it was hard to break his need to be a fixer. I thought one day he'd have a relationship with her again, but he insisted it would be on his terms and only if she'd come to understand my place in his life.

The situation with Delia was much more delicate. Blake loved Delia and his sister loved him back just as fiercely. I wouldn't and I didn't want to come between them, but it seemed unavoidable. According to Blake, she had been molded to hate me, but her brother's love made her curious too. She had been open to the idea of having a dinner where the three of us could spend time together. She made no promises, but if I were willing to give her a shot, she would offer the same courtesy.

I swerved my head until my chin was resting against Blake's chest. Blake had a faraway look on his face and I tried to remain motionless so I could watch him longer. I was fascinated by the small mannerisms I learned since we met. The space between his eyebrows crinkled and he grazed his teeth gradually over his lower lip. I could tell he was trying to work something out in his head before he voiced it aloud.

"Playing football has always been about the rush for me. There would be such a spike in my adrenaline after scoring or winning a game." His chin tilted and he faced me. "I never felt that intensity when dating. I'd hang out with a girl and usually sex would happen quickly."

I swallowed hard at his admission. Blake was open with me and although his status as the campus womanizer had been exaggerated, he had slept with his fair share of women. The number had been intimidating when he told me, but nowhere near the amount I had come up with.

He pushed my hair away from my face in a soothing gesture. "I love you and what we have is stronger than anything I felt before. We have something real and I never want to let you go. I see you smile at me when you wake up in my arms and I want that every day for the rest of our lives. I want to be the kind of man that gives someone as incredible as you a reason to smile."

I was paralyzed by his words. He had given me so much of himself and I hoped he knew he had mended every fracture inside of my damaged heart. "I'm happy because I wake up knowing I'm right where I'm supposed to be."

Gathering me up in his arms, he gently settled me on the bed as he hovered above. His mouth started at the curve of my neck before moving to my shoulder blade. He slid my shirt off of my shoulder and my nerve endings danced as his tongue tasted my bare skin. "You taste so good," he growled. "Before you come over, you must take a bath in chocolate and honey."

I moaned and pushed him away. I wiggled out of my shirt and he returned to his position over me. Blake was an untamed animal on the field, but handled me like a china doll. He took his time kissing and touching and each time was an erotic experience that left me aching for more.

He leaned in and my breath hitched as he continued his assault on my skin. He licked and kissed every square inch of my body and the leisurely way he went about it made me squirm beneath him. His fingers reached behind me and he unhooked my bra. My back arched and I could see by the look in his eyes he was pleased by the way I responded to him.

Blake removed his shirt and I could finally feel his bare skin against my own. My eyes and hands explored his toned body and there was enough heat between us I wasn't sure how we could survive it. He fondled my breasts while his mouth crushed down to kiss me passionately. Suddenly, the slow pace fell to the wayside and our kisses and caresses become frantic. Our jeans came off and I began to tug at the top of his boxers. Blake pulled back and the only sound for a long minute was our labored breathing.

"Blake, please don't stop. I want this…I want you," I

amended.

"And I want you—but only if you're ready. I need you to be sure first," he said. Blake knew what to give me. He always understood I had to be the one to decide the course of our relationship. If he pushed, I may have run and we would've both lost out.

"Yes, I've never been more sure about anything in my life."

I pushed his head down and we returned to kissing. I breathed him in and his masculine smell caused a stirring deep in his belly. His head moved lower and I watched as his fingers looped on the outside of my panties and pulled them down. "Gorgeous," he mumbled before kissing the skin below my belly button.

His fingers were running up and down my inner thigh and I felt like I could die from the anticipation. Each succession, his fingers seemed to move closer and closer and my body ached for the release I knew I would find once they were inside of me. I tried to kiss him back, but my body wasn't cooperating as I moaned and writhed against him. When he slipped one finger and then another inside of me, I cried out.

His fingers gently probed as I rocked against his hand. "So beautiful and so wet for me," he said, which of course had the effect of making me even wetter.

His hips went lower and as they rocked against my own, I gathered up the sheets in my hands and tossed my head back. My legs spread wider, opening up for him, accepting what he was offering. He was relentless—moving his fingers inside of me while using his thumb to stimulate me from the outside. Small quivers rushed through my body as pleasure took hold. I curled my toes and yelled out his name as I finished.

Although my first thought was I could lie here content for the rest of the night, I moved up onto my elbows and tugged at his boxers. He removed them and I then felt him settle between my legs. He was hard and I could feel him ready to enter me. His lashes lowered while his eyes clouded over with desire. I had finished minutes ago, but my body experienced another surge of lust.

"I want you inside of me," I said in a hushed voice. At my declaration, I heard him suck air through his clenched teeth.

"I have to feel you." His voice was gruff and I then felt him push against my entrance. He hesitated and leaned over to kiss me. He had a concerned look on his face and I melted over how loved by him I felt. "It's going to hurt at first, but I promise it won't last."

He waited for my nod before going to the nightstand to retrieve a condom. Once sheathed, he filled me up slowly and carefully. His eyes never left mine and I could tell he was holding back. He pulsed inside of me and after I urged him forward by lifting my hips, he rocked back and forth.

I wasn't prepared for how the pain seared my body. I was relieved Blake had taken care of my needs first because I hoped it took an edge off the discomfort. My body seized up and I tried to relax, but Blake's face faded from view and I could only concentrate on how badly it hurt. Blake dropped his head down and his mouth covered my breast. His warm tongue flicked over my nipple and I shuddered against him. He suckled my breast and took my nipple between his teeth ever so gently. I was shocked not only by how good he was making me feel, but that I hadn't noticed his hips rocking against me.

I become hyperaware of the feel of him thrusting inside of me. The pain started to subside and I began to enjoy the sensation. The way he bit down on his lip told me his level of self-control. I rocked my hips and I heard him groan. "Autumn…"

He continued to claim my body and when my hips lifted, he started to move faster and deeper. My hands moved to his back and I dragged my fingernails down the length of him. His expression was completely open and I could see how much pleasure he was experiencing with our bodies finally joined.

It was a soul-shattering experience to be with him in such an intimate way. He was my first love, my first lover, and my first everything. He had healed me and made me see I'd never been completely shattered in the first place. My feelings were powerful and being with him amplified every sensation.

Watching Blake as his body shuddered and his orgasm overtook him was incredibly sexy. I heard his groan before he burrowed his face in my neck with one final cry. I liked how he didn't rush to end our first time and he stayed buried inside of me for a long minute. His kisses were feather-light and tender and he rained them down on my cheeks, forehead, and nose. I felt worshipped.

The ache was still there, but it had become almost pleasurable as he finished. When he pulled out, my sex was swollen and moist and I was shocked at how something that had started out so painful ended feeling so incredible.

Blake stared at me and his eyes were sweet and earnest. I kissed him hard while still shivering from my arousal. "My body will always belong to you, Blake."

"I've wanted you for so long and there are no words for what that was like for me."

"Mind-blowing?"

Blake laughed and he drew my languid body to his side. "That's a perfect word for it."

Getting comfortable in the crook of his arm, I felt completely at ease. "I love you." I loved the way he always gave me a surprised smile at those three words—as if he couldn't quite believe he was lucky enough to have my love.

"I love you, my beautiful girl." He shot me a mischievous grin. "And give me another ten minutes and I'll show you again just how much."

I gave him a seductive smile to tell him how appealing the idea sounded. Not only did my body belong to him, but my entire being. There was something powerful between us and it was unbreakable. I never thought it was possible to love a man as much as I loved Blake Preston. Life was unpredictable and I would've never anticipated finding love where I had. But I had no control over my emotions. I could deny how I felt and try to live without him, but where did it leave me? I didn't want to live without the one person I connected with on every single level.

I planned to spend my forever with him. I wanted to hold onto him, loving him for as long as he would let me. Falling for Blake had forced me to take a leap into the unknown—and I was still soaring.

THE END

About the Author

Heather Topham Wood's obsession with novels began in childhood while growing up in a shore town in New Jersey. Writing since her teens, she recently returned to penning novels after a successful career as a freelance writer. She's the author of the paranormal romance *Second Sight* series and the standalones *Falling for Autumn* and *The Disappearing Girl*.

Heather graduated from the College of New Jersey in 2005 and holds a bachelor's degree in English. Her freelance work has appeared in publications such as *USA Today*, Livestrong.com, *Outlook by the Bay* and *Step in Style* magazine. She resides in Trenton, New Jersey with her husband and two sons. Besides writing, Heather is a pop culture fanatic and has an obsession with supernatural novels and TV shows.

Follow Heather on Facebook, Twitter and her blog to keep posted on her upcoming works:

https://twitter.com/woodtop255
http://authorheather.com
https://www.facebook.com/HeatherTophamWood

Acknowledgements

My incredible readers, you're the reason I'm able to live my dream and I can never thank you enough.

My super wonderful husband Bryan, you have always been in my corner and I appreciate it more than you'll ever realize.

Dominic and Luke, my two amazing boys who feed my creative energy every single day.

Ashley, an adored member of the family who helps out in so many ways.

My mother and father, thank you for being supportive of my writing.

My sisters, you are three of the strongest and smartest women I know.

My team of editors, formatters, proofreaders and cover artists, your expertise has helped my books become so much more.

To the rest of my friends and family, I love you all and will be eternally grateful for how much you've helped me succeed.

Made in the USA
Charleston, SC
13 December 2014